NOT SO DEAD

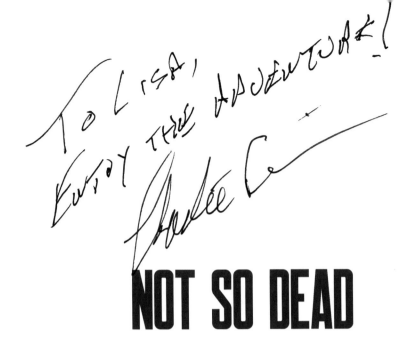

To Lisa,
Enjoy the adventure!

NOT SO DEAD

A Sam Sunborn Novel, Book 1

Charles Levin

Munn Avenue Press

First Edition

ISBN: 978-0-692-91416-8

Dedicated to Amy,
now and forever.

CONTENTS

"Everybody has a plan until they
get punched in the mouth."

—Mike Tyson, Former World Heavyweight Boxing Champion

"In time, you will discover ways to move
your mind to more durable media."

—Nick Bostrom, Director- Future of Humanity Institute

"Just when you thought you were dead,
look what happens . . ."

—F. Einstein, Scientist and Co-Founder of Digital3000

PROLOGUE

San Francisco, Near Future – March

Only the faintest scent of burning wires ruffled the still air. Viktor could feel the room rumbling as a subway passed overhead. A half-full water glass rattled close to the edge of a table. A door opened and a dark figure appeared. All eyes looked up and then away in fear. Ahmed LaSalam, better known as the Leopard, entered the room full of young men clicking away. Their faces were only lit by the glow of their computer screens. He was conducting a new kind of war in this bunker ten stories underground.

Stroking his head like he actually had hair, Viktor stood nearby. His dome was as smooth as a bowling ball with a high shine. He stood out with his Slavic features, blue eyes and very white skin. "Who are these people?" he said looking over a young man's shoulder at the monitor.

The Leopard's face reddened, "It appears that they have invented something that could change the world and I want it. Besides we have even bigger plans and I don't want them or anyone else getting in our way."

"When do we move?" he said.

"As soon as we have eyes on the target." LaSalam stood over the room like a schoolmaster with his students taking their final exam. When one of the hackers silently raised his hand, LaSalam moved down the rows of clicking computers. "What is it?"

A young man, who looked about twelve with no facial hair, said, "I have our target at his office with the scientist and his partners."

"Very good. Can you get into their systems?" LaSalam said.

"I'm trying but the security is excellent. I can only tell that there is some unusual activity."

"Time to move!" the Leopard said.

Viktor stood by watching the feed from the security cameras fixed on his target. He knew what he had to do.

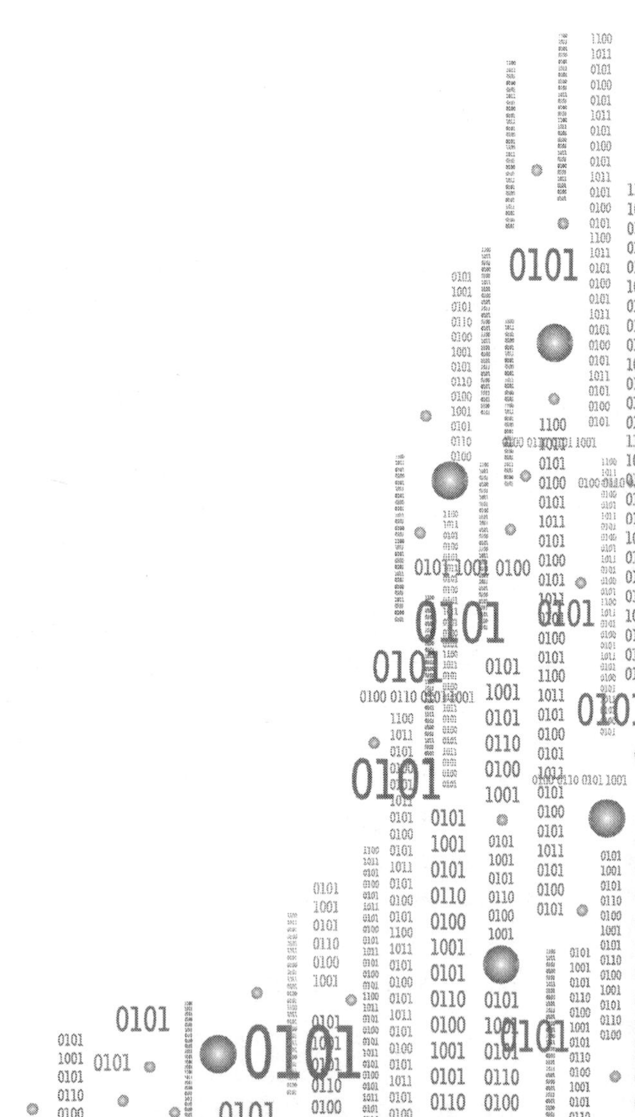

CHAPTER 1
THE IDEA

9 months earlier

I don't know how it started—I remember dying. It was sometime in the early 21st century. Let me think . . . My name is Sam Sunborn and I made my fortune digitizing lives. It all began when a client came to me with the idea of starting a website to memorialize people's lives and to pass on their after-death messages and instructions. Like a virtual scrapbook, users could set it up before they died and leave messages and things like, "I stashed the cash under the..." Friends and family could then upload pictures and other digital memorabilia plus express their feelings about the deceased. Seemed pretty straightforward and useful at the time.

I said sure. I always said sure. It's gotten me into trouble plenty of times—this being no exception. So we designed and built InTheEventOfMyDeath.info. What do you think of the name? I thought it was a little blunt, but the intention was clear. Good for the search engines too. We did get "found."

Well the website did very well in fact and was profitable. We ran it with a small staff of four and felt we were doing some good. Keeping people's memories alive at least, passing on their last words, etc. Sitting around with my staff in the office one day, I blurted out, "What if we could do more than upload pictures and text. What if we could actually digitize and upload people's personalities?"

Julie, one of our bright, and not unattractive, young interns said, "You mean something like the old Facebook Timeline or Lifeline or whatever they called it back then?"

"No, I mean like actually download people's brains so they could live on . . . virtually forever."

"Yeah, as long as nobody pulled the plug," said Bart, my sarcastic chief engineer or head geek, as we like to call him. Bart pecked away at his keyboard while he talked, the screen reflecting in his three inch thick glasses.

"Ever hear of backups?" said Loretta, our lead salesperson. Loretta was always the adult in the room.

"Now you're getting into it," I said. "Look. Can you imagine a world where we can live on beyond our physical lives in a digital world? Where we could still interact with our loved ones, read and enjoy all the 'pleasures of the mind' just like we were alive?"

"You mean no sex?" Bart said.

"That might be Version 2." We did solve that one, but that's a story for later.

"That's some programming skills that go way beyond what my team can do," Bart said. "Nobody has done anything close to that before."

I thought about it. "True, but what would it take? If it is possible, who and what would it take to do it?"

"Uh, oh," said Loretta. "I hear the wheels of Sam's inner entrepreneur spinning."

I ignored her reality check. "Really, what would it take? Who could help us?"

I could see Bart's eyes going up and to the left. He was already working the problem. "I know a digital-neuroscientist at the university who has been developing some really cool stuff to connect your brain to a computer. I mean they've been able to have you move a mouse and type for years just by thinking it. But he tells me he thinks he can actually capture and digitize your thoughts, and they are working on digitizing your memories."

"No shit," I said. I have to tell you I avoid four letter words, especially since using one in a client meeting in Minneapolis that lost me the client. They don't like that stuff in the Midwest. But I'm a New Yorker. Fuck it, I was excited.

"When can we meet this techno genius? With his technology and your uber programming ability, we might really be able to make this happen," I said.

"Whoa, that's a big leap. Even if it's true, Frank is doing his research under a DARPA grant and you know how the Department of Defense gets with security. Especially since 9/11."

"Does this Frank drink coffee?" I persisted. "Let's just meet for coffee."

Maybe that's where it all started.

CHAPTER 2
MEETING EINSTEIN

Bart, Loretta and I met at the office so we could drive to the university in one car, my old Jeep. Parking at every university sucks, and BU is no exception. We found a spot quickly. I've always had great parking karma. After all, parking is just a two-dimensional packing problem. Hard, but not unsolvable. We went to BU's retro 90s coffee house and waited for Frank. I could smell the aroma of fresh coffee brewing. I loved that smell.

A disheveled, gray-haired man with a boyish face and rimless specs appeared minutes later. He wore a rumpled tweed sport coat around his ample frame. He definitely looked the part.

Bart said, "Sam, Loretta meet Frank Einstein."

"Ha, ha—you've got to be kidding," I said before I could stop myself. What if that really was his name?

"Ya, ya—nobody believes it. My parents were hippies and had a warped, or probably stoned, sense of humor. Just call me Frank and don't worry, I'm not that smart." As I found out shortly, nothing could be farther from the truth. We shook hands.

Well do I launch right into it, like a typical American, or do I make small talk, order tea and let the conversation emerge old-world style. Screw it—I couldn't wait. That's not me. "So I hear you have been working on some interesting research?" Hoping this would be an innocuous leading question.

Frank took a deep breath. "I'm sure Bart told you I am doing my research under a DARPA grant, and so I can't talk about it."

"Yes he did," I said. "Funny how university government-funded research works. There's usually three buckets: the government stuff you can't talk about, the university stuff you want to publish and the stuff you do on the side. Sometimes the lines get a little blurred and some things spill over from one bucket to another. I don't know who expects anybody can compartmentalize their knowledge and creativity that way."

"You must have worked here." He laughed.

"I've had a little experience in that arena, but I never liked the feeling of being indentured to some large organization. It's one of my personality flaws. I always want to be the boss. Tell us about some of the interesting stuff you're doing 'on the side.'"

His obligatory DARPA warning out of the way, Frank seemed anxious to talk. "My defense work has to do strictly with digitizing thoughts. That's all I can tell you on that one. My other interest is digitizing memories and emotions."

Bart jumped in, "I bet the government wants to use your research to get info from terrorists without torturing them. Just hook 'em up and bingo!"

I love Bart—he always has a different angle. "Bart, he already said he can't comment. But you just made me think of a funny oxymoron – 'humane torture.' That's how the big bad government would sell the idea." I continued, "So how's the research going?"

Frank looked animated. "I'm very excited, I just made a big breakthrough last night, but I'm not ready to go public yet." He seemed to really want to tell someone but choked back his words.

"Frank, I promise we'll keep whatever you tell us just between the three of us. We're not here to pump you for sensitive information. We have an inkling of an idea that relates to your research. It might be a way to take what you do and what we do and change people's lives—literally forever."

Frank took this all in. "I'm intrigued. You tell me your idea and if it makes sense and I'm comfortable with it, I'll share some of what we're doing. So, you first." He smiled an impish smile like we were kids back on the playground and, in a way, we were. A very big and potentially dangerous playground.

CHAPTER 3

WHO AM "I"

To really understand how I got here, you need to know a little bit about me. I grew up without a father. He died on my first birthday.

My mother had to go to work to support three kids. It was tough. She did the best she could. Money was always tight. He was only forty-nine and died of a sudden heart attack. My older sister did CPR to no avail. That must have been traumatic. Hey, but I was only one. I think I stayed oblivious until I was sixteen.

Fortunately my dad was good enough to leave a college fund for the three of us. My sister became a doctor. She may have wanted to save lives as a way to make up for the loss of our father. My brother became a lawyer and I was off to college. In high school, I won the graduation award as "most likely to be a successful engineer." Ironic—they gave me a slide rule as a prize. If you're too young to know what a "slide rule" is, Google it. Mine might turn up in an archeological dig someday.

So off I went to Cornell with the notion that I would study physics, which I loved. Some people picture words in their brains. For others it's music. For me it was always numbers. I must have had a thousand phone numbers memorized.

Somebody turned me onto the Trachtenberg System, where I learned I could add, multiply and divide long columns of numbers in my head and fast. Won quite a few bets with this parlor trick. Anyhow, it was my first week in college and we took placement tests to see where they should place us geeks. For physics, they put me in junior year. I thought—cool—I am smart. But after three weeks of watching the professor race across the blackboard (yes, it was a blackboard) writing what looked like hieroglyphics to me, I dropped the class and took up philosophy on a lark. What an awakening. To learn and think conceptually instead of procedurally. The world was no longer just numbers for me.

So I got a degree in Philosophy and by default went to law school, like my brother whom I always looked up to. I hated it. While sitting in Constitutional Law class, I would look out the window at the graveyard next door. Frequently, I saw funeral processions during class. I took that as a sign.

I decided to go out on my own just as the PC revolution was about to take place. I moved to California to work for a little startup called Apple. They liked my funky diverse background. It was all new, and nobody had a PhD in this stuff. I was certainly as qualified as anybody else. I grew with the company, made good money and dated occasionally. Life was good. When Steve Jobs left, the first time, and the company became way too corporate and stupid, I went out on my own as a consultant and then a web developer when the Internet changed the world.

That's all mostly good stuff. The difficulty for me was that at every change or transition in my life, depression would kick in. I just felt sad and hopeless when this happened. I'd have no energy. I tried my best to fake a good attitude, but the people close to me could always see through the charade. I tried anti-depressants for a while, which seemed to take the negative edge off. The negative side effect from that was not facing reality and making some poor relationship and financial decisions.

So, I stopped the drugs and tried to focus on great moments. In my sea of sadness, if something good happened, I'd seize on it and magnify it. Like the birth of our son, Evan. I'd be the one to get up with him at 2:00 AM since I couldn't sleep anyway. I'd rock him in my arms to calm him, and his warm and positive energy would flow into me. I think at less than a year old, he saved my life. I fought back and eventually crawled out of the psychic holes I'd fallen into.

But all this doesn't answer the big "Who am 'I'" question. Remember those philosophy classes? Who am "I" is a big question. Is it our brain, our soul, our body? What is it? Little did I know that when I met Frank at the university, it might ultimately lead to a possible answer to that big question.

CHAPTER 4

WHO'D A THOUGHT?

Back to the Coffee House at BU. How do I start? "Frank, I know this may seem a bit 'out there,' but here's the idea. Has Bart told you about what we do—InTheEventOfMyDeath.info?"

"Sure. Kind of a living epitaph site. I was thinking about that and have a question. How do you keep people from posting 'dead fish' to the site?" Now that was an interesting, if not tangential, question. The "Dead Fish" refers to a 100 year old practice of sending a smelly dead fish wrapped in newspapers (archaic media form) to your enemies just to let them know how you feel about them. His question was a clever reference to how would we keep our site from allowing enemies of the dead to besmirch them online. This turned out to be more of a prescient question than any of us could have expected at that moment.

I smiled. "There is a moderator option that allows the owner of the site to view any posts before they happen. After all, who would want spam on a memorial website?"

"Good point. Sorry I interrupted. Please continue."

"Well, we took a big leap and said, 'Would it be possible to combine what we're doing and what you're doing? The result being not just a website that acts as a digital scrapbook, like it does now, but as a virtual life. A site where the deceased could live 'virtually' forever. Where she or he could interact with their loved ones, read eBooks and even play poker online?'" I paused just to let the idea sink in and gauge Frank's reaction.

His face actually seemed to change colors. First it went to red, then blue, then ghostly white and then back to normal. I had never seen anyone have such a visceral reaction to anything anyone ever said before. "Oh . . . my . . . God . . . " He drifted off for a minute into deep thought.

We waited. Finally, I just couldn't stand the silence. "What is it?"

"Just give me a minute. My mind is racing. I literally have to catch my breath and calm down. Just calm down . . . n . . . n." He almost seemed to be talking to himself. Pulling himself together. I could tell we had struck a chord or a nerve in a big way. I just couldn't tell which.

He finally seemed to level off and started. "You would have no way of knowing this, but your idea is something I have thought about a lot. Not how we could do this, but if we should do this. The unintended consequences could be huge. I know the nuclear scientists on the Manhattan Project in the 1940s had the same discussion before unleashing their new technology on the world. They had a big incentive to stop a genocidal foe. But look what they unleashed in terms of nuclear proliferation. Once the genie is out of the bottle, so to speak, you can't put it back."

I couldn't believe what I was hearing. "Are you saying you have the genie?" I said cautiously.

Now Frank didn't hesitate. "Yesss," he said in the voice that sounded like the hiss of a snake. No, more like air escaping from a bottle.

He continued. "I have not told anyone this and I'm not sure why I'm telling you now. Maybe it's because Bart is a good friend, and maybe it's because we have somehow connected or even synchronized on this idea. Not only do I think I may have the genie, but I also have the bottle."

Now I had to gather my thoughts and emotions. I began. "So what's the problem? Why not expose your genius, I mean genie, to the world?"

Suddenly Frank seemed distracted again. He checked his watch. "I have a class shortly and the answer to your question will take more than coffee. Let's just say I am interested in your idea. Can you meet me for dinner tonight—just you? Nine o'clock, my house?"

Bart and Loretta looked at each other, both puzzled and uncomfortable. I broke the spell. "Why me alone? Bart and Loretta are both family and business partners. Bart is your friend."

Frank was quick to answer but looked over both shoulders before he started. “I think it’s safer if you come alone. My work is so sensitive I think I am being watched. Three of you would attract attention. If you come alone, it will seem more casual. Don’t worry, you can share what we discuss with Bart and Loretta, but only after you have taken certain precautions.” That sounded very cloak-and-dagger. I almost laughed, but I’m glad I didn’t.

Bart and Loretta looked at each other and nodded slightly. I said, “OK, I’ll be there.”

CHAPTER 5

MAYBE NOT SUCH A GOOD IDEA

That night, I drove up Frank's long, tree-lined driveway and parked in front of a rambling old colonial mansion. My first thought was, *if I had known being a professor paid so well . . .*

Before I could knock, Frank opened the door and whispered in a conspiratorial tone, "Come in." The vestibule was dark and we walked down a long hallway. The walls were lined with vintage black-and-white photographs, some of which I recognized. Steichen, Kertesz, Brandt and maybe Siskind. We arrived at a back door and stepped out onto a flagstone patio overlooking a serene pond with a storybook willow tree hanging over it. Fallen red and orange leaves drifted over the water's surface.

"Nice digs," I said in my usual classy way. "Do you collect photography?"

"Yes. Those are signed original silver gelatin prints. I've always been fascinated by the genius ability of these photographers to tell a complex story in a single two-dimensional frame. Frozen in time, as it were, but full of implications and subtleties."

Frank turned a valve that protruded from the rear stone wall of the house, which started a faux waterfall. Water began to run down the wall into a trough. It made a soothing, whishing sound.

"This sound will mask our conversation," he said. "You probably think I'm paranoid, but it's justified."

That's always been an interesting paradox to me. How do you know whether somebody making that statement is telling the truth or is truly delusional? I guessed I'd find out. "As Andy Grove, the famous corporate philosopher said, 'Only the paranoid survive.'"

"Truer words . . . " He trailed off into his own thoughts. Then he seemed to rouse from his daydream. "We've got a very big problem on our hands. If I was more of a half-glass-full kind of guy, I'd use the word 'challenge' instead of 'problem,' but I'm a scientist who solves problems and a realist who is scared by them."

Silence, then, "Speaking of half-full glasses, can I get you something to drink?"

This time I was going to be patient. I knew Frank would get around to telling me the story, but he had to do it in his own way. Not only his words, but his body language betrayed his struggle.

"Diet Coke, if you have it."

"Sure. But I'm going to need something stronger," he said, moving behind a rattan bar on the patio. He returned with my drink in a glass with ice and his glass full of an amber liquid—no ice.

Maybe a little humor would ease his mind. "Your glass half-full comment reminded me of a funny cartoon I once saw. Three men are looking at the half-filled glass. One asks, 'What do you see?' The first says, 'I see a glass half-full.' The second says, 'I see a glass half-empty.' The third hesitates and says, 'Why isn't that glass on a coaster?'"

Frank smiled. "Just goes to show that there are always more than two ways to look at something. Listen, you're probably wondering why I am acting so strangely. Let's just say the implications of what we're working on are much bigger than you even suspected. Besides the technical considerations, there are multiple ethical issues that make arguments over cloning and stem cell research seem trivial."

I'd thought of a couple, but I said, "Like what?"

"Let me just rattle off a few. Who would get the privilege of being digitally or virtually immortal? Who decides? How much does it cost? What if a DigiPerson becomes sick mentally and becomes destructive? Who are the police, judge and jury? What about viruses?"

My head was already spinning and all I could muster was, "Oh . . . I had not thought about those things."

He continued. "Another thing. Would the person be completely digital or would she at least retain the sense of a physical self?"

He seemed to be gathering steam. "Here's my 'favorite.' What if somebody creates multiple instances of themselves? How do they coexist? What kind of problems would multiple 'yous' cause? We know twins or even clones aren't exact matches and diverge immediately from being real copies of their counterparts the minute they are born. But the kind of copies we are talking about are exact. I think these and many more problems need to be solved before we let the genie out, or it could literally destroy the world as we know it."

He took a breath. "I'm not sure who's competent to solve these problems, who doesn't have a special interest. If you tell the government, i.e. my bosses, they'll think about how to make a weapon out of it. If you tell the university, who knows what they'll do. From a business perspective, it's worth billions. Now you know why I have been acting strangely."

He stopped and I took it as my cue to jump in. "I don't think you can bury this. Just like the atomic bomb or the DNA double helix, there were multiple countries and scientists working it. If we didn't come up with it, somebody else would have. So I think we have a duty to get it out there in the safest way possible. Just like Oppenheimer wrestled with the ethical issues in a moral way; maybe the scientists are the best ones to mediate the use of their inventions."

"I'm not sure we're equipped. We have our heads buried in research, numbers and formulas not human interaction and morality," he said.

We sat quietly for what seemed like half an hour. Finally, I said, "What if you and I do this together? We apply for all the patents it would take to protect it. Then we lay out all the rules of use. I think you and I, maybe with help from Bart and Loretta, could do it. If we don't, we risk some self-interested bastard doing who-knows-what to the fabric of our society with this new invention/weapon."

I watched him roll this idea around, and then he said, "We'd need a very good lawyer."

"We'd probably need a team of very good lawyers, bodyguards and capital to pull this off," I said.

"I don't know. I know zero about that stuff, and I don't know if I'm up for the battle. I'm fifty-five you know," he replied.

"I have the contacts for all three of those things, and I am up for it. It's the battle of a lifetime. Heck it's the battle of the millennium. I will fight, but I need you to protect and continue to grow the science."

He smiled and held his index finger to his chin. I think he was getting excited. "I will do this under one condition."

"What's that?"

"I need to know we have the same core values. I don't want to exploit the invention for personal gain. I mean, I have no problem making some money—maybe even getting rich, but I'm more concerned that this be first and foremost a benefit to humankind."

"That is exactly how I feel about it." I think I meant it at the time.

As I drove away from Frank's house, I had a vivid daydream. I had this image of myself as a little boy in shorts and sandals. An older man was holding my hand. We were walking on the beach, and I could smell the salt air and hear the waves crashing. I sensed that the man was my father whom I never got a chance to know. I looked up and the man was Frank.

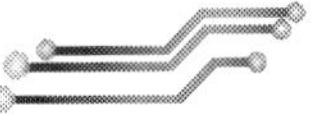

CHAPTER 6

THE IMAGE IN THE MIRROR

I'm going to skip some of the details and get right to it. Frank and I formed a company called Digital3000. We got the money, the lawyers and applied for the patents. We had to fight off DARPA, but we got it done.

It only took about six months. Fall became spring. That's not to say it was easy. If you've ever started a business, you know all the hassles that come with it. Sometimes I felt like we were juggling live hand grenades that were going to go off any minute. We had the added problem of security, both for ourselves and our intellectual property. We hired full time security at the office and had our homes, cars and offices swept daily for surveillance devices. As for the secret sauce, we did apply for patents. But we just put enough in them to cover us, hopefully, without giving away the store. Our patents are still pending, but sometimes those things take years to perfect.

Maybe the biggest challenge was putting together a team of engineers to work with Frank and Bart to bring the Digital Mind to market. Then too, we needed business and marketing pros to work with me. Talent, vision and an ability to work very long hours were a requirement. How do you do the work and still protect the IP ("Intellectual Property")? I had a former client who was afraid of losing his secret work to his engineers in Manila so that he only kept one copy of his work. Unfortunately, he kept it in the World Trade Center just before 9/11. Six months work by 600 hundred engineers was lost. True story.

Well, that's all dull operational stuff. The interesting part really started when we got the first versions of our virtual minds online for testing. Pretty strange talking to yourself across the virtual divide. Who's in charge? Who's the real you? This actually became the first grenade to blow. Loretta became so engaged with her digital alter ego that she stayed up all night deep in conversation. I found her the next morning red-eyed in front of her screen. The digital Loretta seemed to have taken over or she had become somehow addicted. It reminded me of the rudimentary Eliza program from the last century that acted like a Rogerian psychologist. It just asked open ended, leading questions like, "How do you feel about that" and "go on . . . " peppered with nouns you had previously used. The result was that it seemed to take on a human-like quality that sucked many people into hours of "conversation." Maybe Siri and Alexa do that now.

"Loretta. Loretta!"

"Wha . . . what?"

"C'mon. Get up. Let's go." I physically lifted her by the arm and pulled her over to the couch where she promptly fell sideways and off to sleep.

A few hours later, I stopped back at her office and gently shook her. "How are you?"

"What happened?" she said groggily.

"You got lost." Because I knew I was being cryptic, I continued. "You got so absorbed with your online Loretta, you lost track of everything and I mean 'everything.'"

"Wow. That's scary."

"It sure is. That's why Bart, Frank and I have come to a decision."

"What's that?" she said with a quizzical look.

"We're blocking any of us from engaging our own online personas. You can talk to virtual Bart, Frank or me, but not yourself. The same goes for the rest of us and our digital selves."

"How do you do that? I mean I understand, but how do you control it?"

"Well, based on your login, we know who you are and have programmed in a block against speaking with your digital self. We have done the same for each of us. It's just too dangerous."

We sat quietly for a few minutes letting all of this sink in. Finally, Loretta said what I had been thinking, "I wonder what other surprises like this we will find?"

CHAPTER 7
EARTH TO LISA

We did a few months of testing and we encountered several other psycho-digital problems along the way. Similar to the ban we had on connecting to our own digital selves, we had to program a strict rule against allowing multiple digital instances of the same person to exist. A good analogy for the problem is that letting multiples exist is like connecting the wrong cables to jump a car battery. If you connect the wrong positive and negative terminals, the battery can actually explode. I learned this the hard way when I tried to help out my girlfriend's roommate in college. It was an old car and the battery acid actually shot out of the battery when I connected the cables the wrong way.

Anyway, we found when two instances of the same digital persona met online, it created a kind of meltdown that permanently damaged both. It just isn't meant to be. Frank and Bart had several theories on why this occurs, but they were too technical for me. To some extent, it's as if we were playing God, but we just weren't smart enough to pull it off. I don't know if God ever made mistakes creating stuff, but I know we sure did. New technologies always lead to unintended consequences. Just look at nuclear fission and gene sequencing as examples. Creating a Digital Mind-verse would be no exception.

Finally, the day came when we felt ready to invite trusted friends and colleagues to be the first to try the new system. We invited them to our secret secure lab to have their brains scanned and their personalities, memories and knowledge uploaded to the system. The group included Francine Farmer, a colleague of Frank's at the university; Steve Knightley, a friend and partner of mine in various ventures since college; Slash Burn, a geeky friend of Bart's - I doubt that was his real name and if it was, the Burn family had issues; and Loretta's niece, Lisa Comely, a young perky grad student in neuroscience at the university. I know it's freaky but I'm really not making up these aptronyms.

I think we all felt like we were in the cast of that old movie, *The Fantastic Voyage*.

First, we had the four of them all sign very strict secrecy agreements. Basically, if they let the secret out, something mysterious and terrible would happen to them. Not really, but the language of it was meant to keep you quiet, even if the enemy tortured you.

Next Frank and Bart sat each person down in succession and attached twenty probe patches to their scalp and neck. It was quite a scene. Frank and Bart actually wore white scientist jackets. Lisa giggled like a schoolgirl when they hooked her up. Francine and Steve looked serious, like they were getting blood drawn. Slash feigned arrogance, skepticism and biker-cool, but I thought he might just have a vagal attack at any moment.

The process took about a half hour for each as we were literally downloading the equivalent of 10 petabytes of data. I know. I had to look it up too. It's the equivalent of 10,000 terabytes or 10 million gigabytes. Our brains hold a lot of stuff. It was also interesting for me to learn that memories are much larger than other random bits of knowledge we store. Similar to how storing digital images takes much more storage space than digital text. To extend the analogy further, the brain also seems to have its own tricks and compression techniques for making large files smaller. The brain seems to work more like BitTorrent—pulling pieces and bits from various locations and then assembling them into a coherent memory. This process gets a bit colored by our emotions and predispositions, so accuracy is questionable. But does it really matter? That we do it at all, is amazing. Sorry if I got a bit technical. So I'll leave that stuff for a discussion in one of Frank's seminars at the U.

OK. Now all our friends were "uploaded" and we tried the big test. We called them up one by one on the computer. The first was Lisa. We asked the real Lisa just to observe and stay out of view of the webcam, remembering the "talking-to-yourself" problem we had previously encountered. A picture of Lisa came up on the screen.

Loretta started off as instructed. "Hi Lisa. Good to see you. How was your day?"

"Hi. Uh . . . hi. What's going on? I remember going to your lab for an experiment. But why am I sitting over here? Wait, I can't feel my arms and legs but I can see you. What's happening?" The digital Lisa was clearly disoriented and confused. All of us were tense. It was like watching Neil Armstrong placing his foot on the Moon for the first time. The only difference is none of us were prepared or trained for this, and Lisa had no idea what planet she was on. Armstrong spent thousands of hours preparing for his 'one small step' as well as knowing exactly what to say. Although I'm sure his adrenaline was pumping as much as Lisa's and ours were at that moment.

"Don't worry. You are just fine. This is part of the experiment. You are the 'digital you' for the moment. How does it feel?"

Lisa seemed to be calming herself. Her digital image looked up, down, left and right as if scanning the room. "Like I said, I can't feel anything but I can see and hear you."

"Do you see anything else?"

"Well, I can see a listing of all the files on this computer. Wait, let me see . . . I can think . . . I mean click on one and open it. Can you see anything on your screen?"

We all looked carefully and Loretta replied, "I see you but that's all." I tapped Loretta on the shoulder and pointed. "Oh, another tab opened." She clicked the tab. "It's a dumb picture of Bart on the beach. He looks like a white string bean in a bathing suit." We all laughed. The humor was a welcome break to the tension in the room.

Lisa replied, "I see it too. What a hoot. This is cool! I am opening a web browser. Can you see it?"

Loretta clicked the new tab and we saw the browser open.

Then we saw something typing into Google, "W-h-a-t i-s t-h-e c-a-p-t-a-l o-f L-a-t-v-a?" Google responded: "Did you mean what is the capital of Latvia?" Lisa had misspelled it. The link clicked and we saw "Riga is the capital, population . . . "

Lisa was excited. "All I had to do was think it and it happened. I don't have to type or click. Oh myyy God." The room fell silent. We all seemed to realize at once what this meant. Mind and machine could merge. Maybe this would be the true Singularity. All of a sudden we saw the screen flashing and moving. Windows were opening and closing. Pictures were flashing by. It was like something from the *Manchurian Candidate* or a Philip K. Dick story. We all sat quietly and watched in amazement as we saw Digital Lisa manipulate the computer at warp speed.

Funny. At that moment, rather than being terrified, I flashed on an image, recalling when I first taught my son, Evan, to ride a bike. We went to the big parking lot at the high school, unloaded his little bike and at first I pushed and guided him. Then I let go. Initially, he was a little wobbly but as he gained his balance, he started to peddle faster. Then circles and faster. He was exhilarated and so was I, just like now.

Now. Remembering how Evan sped up and then crashed scraping his knees and crying, I quickly stepped in. "Lisa. This is Sam. Lisa!" The screen kept flashing and screaming along. "Lisa—please stop for a minute."

Finally, the cursor slowed to a halt and she said, "What. What?" If I didn't know better I'd say she sounded out of breath.

"Lisa, slow down for a minute. We need to talk. Tell us what you were just doing."

"OK. Once I realized I could just think something and the computer would respond, I read today's newspaper, ordered an eBook, started to read it, viewed some pictures. It was like I could fly."

Hopefully not like Icarus. "Lisa, did you feel like you were in control?"

"Yes and no. When I first started slowly, I was quite conscious of what I was doing. But as I picked up speed, it was as if I stopped thinking and was just flying. What a feeling! Until I heard you calling my name. It sounded at first as if you were very far away. I wasn't sure I even heard you. Then I think you repeated my name. So I focused on your voice and everything else stopped."

Wow, I thought. This is big. This is very big. Frank looked at me like he had landed on the Moon himself. I looked back at the screen. "Lisa, you remember we told you that this was an experiment, and you gave us your consent?"

Lisa answered, "Yes I do, but . . . "

"Lisa, there is a lot going on here and I'm going to have to ask you to take a rest now and we'll talk some more in a little bit."

"But . . . "

I ran over and actually pulled the computer's plug out of the wall. The screen went dead. I looked at the real Lisa. She looked as white as a ghost and her eyes were glassy. Or were they glazed over?

CHAPTER 8

HMMM . . .

"Lisa! Wake up."

"Huh. What? Oh, I must have drifted off. Watching myself interact on the screen was like an out-of-body experience. I'm still a little shaken by it."

"We experienced the same, and maybe worse, during our testing. I wish I understood it better. Frank, do you have anything to add?" I said.

He seemed lost in thought. "There is so much going on here simultaneously that we've got to sort it out. What we're doing is potentially dangerous and even life threatening. Can you imagine being the person who invented dynamite? Did he or she survive the first test? I wonder. I think we're playing with digital and neurological dynamite here. You mix two seemingly harmless ingredients together and they explode. I'm sure that erstwhile dynamite inventor didn't know why mixing nitroglycerin and sodium carbonate makes an explosion. The scientific explanation came later. A lot of science is, 'Let's try this and see what happens.' Many great inventions happen by accident. Take Post-it Notes®. The inventor was trying to invent a strong adhesive and this stuff came out that stuck but released easily. He changed his goal to fit the result and came up with one of the most successful products of all time. Same kind of story for Velcro® and Nylon.

"By the way, do you know where the name 'Nylon' comes from? The inventor had a plane ticket in his pocket at the time that had NY-LON stamped on it. New York-to-London. Hence the name. So much happens by accident and serendipity."

It seemed like this was Frank's usual process for thinking through a problem out loud, but I interrupted. "Well this is all very interesting, but what does this have to do with our 'little' experiment."

Frank smiled. “Well, you should know. You came to me and said ‘let’s put these two things together and see what happens.’ Now you know—sort off. You don’t understand the chemistry or physics of it, but you have observed a result. Now we need to work meticulously backward so we can understand the underlying dynamics.”

“That sounds like a pretty arduous task to me. How long are we talking about? Years? Can’t we just manage the result into a ‘zone of safety’ and keep moving forward?” I said.

“Typical entrepreneur. Ready-fire-aim.”

“Well, we already shot the gun and hit something.”

“I know and it’s exciting,” Frank went on. “But if we don’t understand the target, the gun and the shooter, I can’t ensure success, whatever that means, much less safety.”

“Point taken. So what do we do next?”

“We analyze both the computer logs and Lisa to see what physical, mental and digital changes took place. Then we determine if anything harmful occurred or was about to occur. Next we regroup to decide what we can safely do next to move our knowledge and the process forward.”

“Boring!” Bart jumped in. “It’s a purely digital thing. If we just let the digital Lisa keep going without the real Lisa in the room, what’s the harm? We can always shut off the computer.”

“I see both your points of view,” I said. “Maybe we can have our cake and eat it too. Bart continues the testing trials without the real counterpart persons present. At the same time, Frank analyzes the data and does a complete work up on the real Lisa. Loretta, you stay here and help Bart with our subjects . . . I mean friends. Tomorrow we regroup here at 8:00 AM to share our findings or results or whatever.”

“And what are you going to do, *boss*?” Bart said sarcastically.

“I’m going for a walk.”

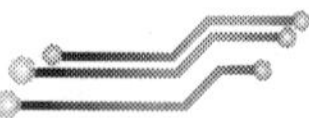

CHAPTER 9

THE 2ND GRENADE

I liked to walk down the trail along the river. The locals call it "The Gorge" because of the huge boulders lining the steep hills alongside the banks and it was only ten minutes drive from the office. The boulders were left by receding glacial melt thousands of years ago. Some of the boulders formed random patterns in the river creating swooshing waterfalls and whirling eddies. I needed to clear my mind so I could think of what to do next. Move forward or pull the plug.

I listened to the sound of the falling water, recalling a river from Greek mythology called Lethe. If you walked near it, you'd forget everything. Forget everything. Suddenly a blue heron swooped down over the river, flapping its wide pterodactyl-like wings. Then it landed on a boulder and stood majestically still—attentive and patient—waiting for fish. You can't do that on a computer. Then it hit me. There is something about the "I"-ness or self-identity that was causing the scary reactions between the real person and her digital persona. So if we could get the digital self to forget that thing, turn it off, we might be safe. I wasn't sure what that "one thing" was exactly, but I knew who would know. I had to get back to the lab.

After the short drive, I scanned my security card, placed my eye up to the retina scanner and the door clicked open. There was Ray, our 6 foot 250 pound security guard, who greeted me with a big smile and a fist pump. "Hey boss, glad to see you back. You look better than before."

"Thanks, Ray. I was just trying to solve a problem and maybe I have or at least I have a start." I always felt safe with Ray around.

Frank was in the lab buried in charts and numbers. "Well, do you feel better?" he said.

"I do and I have an idea I want to run by you."

"Go ahead."

"When you were a kid, did you ever go to a funhouse at an amusement park where they had bent mirrors that warped your shape and size?"

"Sure."

"Well, they were either kind of funny or kind of scary. Right? The scary version might be something like a grossly distorted version of you. Maybe what Lisa and we encountered was seeing a scary reflection in a mirror."

"Hmm. OK—I'll bite."

"So when we were testing, we essentially removed the reflection by not allowing ourselves to converse with our digital personas. But maybe the trick to really removing the danger is to remove that element in the uploaded persona that creates the scary reflection. I'm hoping you can identify and remove whatever that 'thing' is."

Frank seemed to ponder this. "Well, I'm glad you have such confidence in me. That sounds like a tricky assignment, but I think I grock what you are getting at. There is something called the Higginsford Effect that describes the kind of negative brain loop we have been seeing. They have traced it back to a certain area in the brain's amygdala. So what I think you're getting at is that we want to separate ego from intellect, yet leave both intact. Is that correct?"

"Exactly!" I said.

Just then I heard a commotion in the hallway outside the lab and something that sounded like . . . a . . . a . . . gunshot? Then the lab door burst open. A spray of bullets crisscrossed the room and everything seemed to be moving in slow motion. I instinctively dove to the floor. Frank stayed frozen in place, and I saw bursts of blood spewing from his back and neck. Then he started to fall, and I felt his full dead weight fall on top of me. There was silence. I didn't move. Frank covered me like a very heavy blanket. I heard footsteps approaching, and my heart was beating so fast it felt like one continuous thump in my chest. Then lightness. Somebody pulled Frank's weight off of me. I looked up. Over me stood a large bald man. He looked like Mr. Clean, only with grisly beard stubble and a toothy grin.

"This is how the movie ends," he said, pointing his AR5 submachine gun at my face.

When you hear people say their life flashed before their eyes, I doubt they were exaggerating. I knew I wouldn't have time for all that. I could only think about Monica, and that I should call home right away. Home? Would I ever be home again? It was June and the flowers were in bloom. Monica's favorite time of year. I was supposed to go to the beach with Evan tomorrow.

Then I heard another single shot. Mr. Clean fell forward on top of me. If this was a movie, it was some kind of grotesque comedy. I rolled out from under my would-be attacker and sat up. The first thing I saw was Ray, lying motionless on the floor in a pool of blood. He had a gun in his hand pointing to nowhere. I rolled to the side and felt Frank's neck. Nothing. The room was full of the smell of gunpowder and sweat. My ears were ringing. I staggered to my feet and went to Ray. He was gone too. I told myself to *calm down*. I called for help. I called 911.

"Hello, what is your emergency?"

"My friends have been shot. They're dead."

CHAPTER 10
DAMAGE REPORT

Our secret secure lab was now crawling with police, medics and forensic people. Two paramedics came over to check me out. Besides a few cuts and bruises, I had been hit by a grazing bullet below the knee. It hurt like hell, but the paramedics wrapped it up like they would a mummy's leg. They also gave me some pain meds that slowly took the edge off. As for my brain, it was a turmoil of emotions laced with adrenalin and fear. I could feel the dark cloud of depression hovering over me, but I fought it back.

I was introduced to Detective Al Favor by one of the uniforms. Al was actually a woman with dark hair, lightly streaked with gray, piercing brown eyes, dark skin and a slender figure. Maybe she was forty, but she seemed to have a sexy twinkle-in-the-eye aura about her.

"Mr. Sunborn, I'm sorry for the loss of your two friends. Is there somewhere we can talk?"

"Thank you, Detective. Follow me. We can go to my office." I limped down the hall with Detective Favor in tow, to my office where a couple of forensic types were dusting for fingerprints. Why were they in my office?

"Can you boys give us the room?" Favor said and the boys nodded and left.

"Detective, can you give me a minute to wash up? I'll be right back." I didn't wait for permission. I limped down the hall to our unisex restroom. Looking in the mirror, I saw a gray blood-spattered face. Could that really be me? I put my hands under the automatic faucet, but no water came out. I tried another sink with the same result. Crappy technology. I hated those sinks, and never more than at that moment. Fortunately, there were some moist wipes on the counter so I could clean my hands and face. Well, that was a bit better. The extra time alone to calm down was even more welcome. I returned to my office.

"Nice family you have there," Favor said, looking at the photo of Monica and Evan on my desk. We both sat down—me in my ergo chair and Favor across from me at the opposite side of the desk. My knee was throbbing.

"Thanks. Oh, I haven't called home. I have to call Monica."

"That's OK. We called and told her there had been an accident and you are fine. We also sent a car over to keep an eye out and make sure your visitor doesn't have any friends drop by. We alerted my boss too, and they're sending some extra guys to your home as well."

"Oh my God. I hadn't even thought . . . I mean I haven't even had time to think about that. Thank you, Detective. That puts my mind at ease, sort of."

"Sort of . . .?"

"I mean who could have done this and could there be more?" Bart and Loretta knocked on the hallway window next to my door. I was glad to see they were OK. I waved and gave a weak smile. They knew me well enough not to interrupt and that we would all get together later—no matter how late it was.

"Well, we've just started to put the pieces together. All we know now is that your killer was a professional—military trained," the detective said.

"How do you know that?"

"We can tell by the weapon, how it was handled and how it was maintained. We don't yet have any ID. His fingerprints have no matches in any of the databases." Something about the way Favor looked at me with her head tilted and one eye focused reminded me of Peter Falk as Columbo. Falk was blind in one eye. She was much more attractive. The thought made me smile and brought back some fond memories.

"Why are you smiling?"

"You just remind me of an old friend." Why was my first instinct to lie to a detective? Not smart. "You actually remind me of that old police detective, Columbo."

Now she smiled too. "I just need the trench coat. Hopefully I'm better looking. Just a few questions, and you can get out of here, which I'm sure you want to do. So tell me what happened."

I looked down at the blood, Frank's blood, on my shirt. At least I presume it was Frank's blood. A shiver ran through my body and I visibly shook. I recalled it as best I could, even though I spent most of the time on the floor and in a daze.

"Did you see the attacker? Can you tell me anything about him?"

"Maybe six feet, heavy set, muscular and bald. I remember thinking he looked like Mr. Clean—only he had beard stubble. I was thinking 'What has Mr. Clean got against me?' He didn't say anything. He just fired away. Wait, I do remember something odd. He had enormous biceps and was wearing a white T-shirt. Just under his left sleeve was a tattoo. An eagle I think. I'm not sure. It stuck in my mind a bit since it was the very last thing I saw before I dove to the floor. I'm sure you can see that for yourself on his body."

Favor shuffled in her chair and seemed to be waiting for me to continue, but I didn't have anything to add. "We have no body." That didn't make sense. Al continued. "Pretend your eyes were closed the whole time. Run me through what sounds you heard," she said.

What an interesting exercise. I never heard that one on Columbo. I instinctively closed my eyes to try to recall the sounds. I remembered the rumble in the hallway, footsteps, shots, a grunt. No Bruce Willis moments like, "Die Mother Fucker!" when I was on the floor. I did remember a cell phone ringing. What was that ringtone? It was beeps. Five beeps. Stop. Five beeps but an unusual twang to the beeps.

"Al, you know we do have video surveillance. Maybe that would help," I said.

"Yeah, it would if he hadn't shot out the cameras. We only have one recorded glimpse of him from the back coming up the steps. Your description matches. We'll see if we can get anything on that tattoo and match it against our database. Thanks, you've been very helpful."

"Wait," I said. "Who took out Mr. Clean? I mean somebody shot him."

"Another good question," Al said. "That's why Columbo would call this a mystery." She smiled and left the room.

Little did I suspect at the time that Al would become a good friend and partner in the future. Funny how chance encounters can change your life. How bad sometimes leads to good and vice versa.

I was putting on my jacket, getting ready to leave this crazy day behind, when I heard a gentle knocking on my door. "Come in."

A young petite, maybe five foot tall, woman with Asian features walked in.

"Who are you?"

"My name is Nancy Lu. I am a reporter with the Free Press blog. I heard what happened here today, and I'd like to ask you a few questions."

"I thought all the reporters were being kept outside. How did you get in here?"

"I'm sorry to impose. One of the uniforms guarding the line is my brother. Look, I'm just starting out. This is my first job and I could really use a break. I'd just take a few minutes and I'd be grateful forever."

Her charm and enthusiasm were infectious. How could I refuse? But what was the cover story? I hadn't had time to think about that. I just gave her the bare details with no background. Talking to the press was going to be unavoidable. So it might as well be told to a striving young person like this. She looked at me with her dark eyes, sparkling eyes, waiting nervously for my response.

"OK. You have ten minutes."

CHAPTER 11
DIGITAL FRANK

The lab was a crime scene, with yellow tape and all, for several days, but we could work from our offices. We set up an impromptu lab in my office. It was pretty hard for us to focus and get anything done. First there was Ray's funeral at the Golden Gate National Cemetery. Then there was Frank's funeral and the reception at Frank's house. Afterwards, Bart, Loretta, Julie and I drifted back to the office like four lost souls. Where else were we going to go?

The hardest thing for me was Sarah, Frank's daughter. She just looked so lost—so adrift in her grief. Strangely with Frank's death, I felt like I had lost my father too. "First she loses her mother and now her father," I said. "It's my fault. If I hadn't come up with this dumb idea and roped Frank into it, he'd still be alive."

"Sweet girl. She's a third year at the university and she idolized her father—especially after her mother died last year," Loretta said. "Yeah, and don't blame yourself. We're all adults. We make our own decisions. Nobody could have anticipated this."

"Yeah, freak car accident. Frank survived. Susan, his wife, did not," Bart said.

"Maybe it wasn't an accident," I said.

They both turned abruptly and stared at me like I had two heads.

"Think about it. Somebody obviously wanted Frank dead. Maybe this was their second attempt. Maybe they failed the first time and got Susan instead. We need to make sure Favor knows about the accident, if she doesn't already. I like that lady-detective. I can see real soul in those brown eyes."

"Are you falling in love?" Bart said and I blushed.

"You dork. I try to be nice and you're always making a joke . . . but I love you just the same. You're my first and only," I said. This time

Bart blushed and we all laughed. I think it was the first moment we had an emotional break from the heaviness of the day, the week and what had happened.

"Listen, I've been thinking . . . "

"Uh, oh!" Bart said and smiled. "What now? What reckless endangerment do you have cooked up for us next?"

"Not funny. I really feel responsible."

"Really just kidding. Get over yourself. You're not that important."

"Thanks, I really appreciate that vote of confidence. Look, we're back at the office, I mean lab." I waved my hands pointing around to the bank of computers now crammed into my office. "Why don't we load Frank up—boy, that sounds weird. Turn him on—weirder. Let's go talk to the digital Frank."

"The first true test of our system. We have a dead guy with his persona on the system. I like it," Bart said.

"Not too elegantly put as usual, but that's what I was getting at."

"Are you guys crazy?" Loretta looked truly shocked. "We just buried him today and he is, I mean 'was' a friend. Don't you guys feel the slightest bit strange about this crazy idea?"

"We all mourn Frank's loss, but I think, as a scientist, he would want us to carry on with his work. This is the precise thing we have been working toward and who better to be the first beneficiary of his work and ours?" We all sat in silence letting the reality of this idea and this project sink in. I think, for all of us, this is the first time it was really real.

I could tell we were all in agreement. I knew Loretta and Bart well enough to judge their body language. We had done a mind meld long ago. "Bart, turn on DC4 and the overhead screen. Bring up Frank." A minute later, the screen flickered—finding signal—Windows 12 was an improvement but was still slow as molasses.

Frank's face appeared on the screen. He looked down as if to check his feet. I doubt he saw anything. "Hi guys, what's up?" he said in his usual cheery voice.

Oh my God, how did we answer that one?

The only way I knew how. “Well Frank, we have some good news and some bad news.”

Julie whispered under her breath, “Did you really just say that?”

I looked at Julie, smirked and turned back to Frank, Digital Frank that is.

“Digital3000 works and we are here in my office talking to your digital persona,” I said.

Frank seemed to be looking around and the webcam moved in synch with his eyes—a nifty little invention Bart worked up for fun late one night. When Frank looked to his left, the webcam rotated left and when he looked right, the webcam reversed direction. “Your office is a mess. What are all the lab computers doing in here? Having a garage sale?”

I didn’t know how else to say it, and I was never one for mincing words. “Digital3000 is the good news. The bad news is that you are dead. I mean your physical self is dead. You were shot and killed. You are obviously here digitally. You were murdered three days ago in the lab. You are the first of our uploaded personas to actually die and ‘come back to life’ via the system you built. Congratulations.”

Frank looked stunned but his complexion was unchanged. We had not yet refined the digital image to show emotion through changes in skin color. “I don’t know whether to cry or laugh or what. I’m just apoplectic,” he said.

“Good word,” Bart said. “Same old Frank.”

Digital Frank smiled. “Same old Bart the Fart.” This time we all laughed, but I could tell that Frank, despite his veneer, was still trying to get his bearings. “Well, now what? I guess, tell me about what happened in the lab. The murder I mean. My murder. Wow, that sounds strange.”

Yes we were definitely in strange territory, but it was new and wondrous at the same time. I felt both the fear and excitement of discovery, of exploration. The three of us recounted in detail to Frank the tale of the attack on the lab and the aftermath. Digital Frank was nodding as he took it all in. I saw the webcam moving up and down almost imperceptibly like it was nodding too. Somehow we had crossed over to the other side.

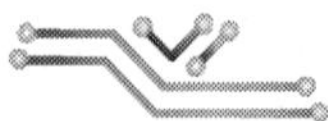

CHAPTER 12

INSIDE THE NETWORK

"Do I look like Max Headroom?" Frank said.

I grinned. "No, you look and sound like you—warts and all. Listen, seriously—who do you think attacked the lab?"

"This may sound paranoid and I'm not into conspiracy theories, but . . . " he hesitated. "I think it was somebody from Defense."

"That's a big accusation. Please explain."

"Despite the fact that we got an agreement on paper, my DARPA contacts were pretty pissed I was going into the private sector with this technology. Actually, I'm surprised they didn't stop me by using national security as an excuse. I think somebody fucked up. So now the only way to remove that risk is to kill it, literally, and me, physically.

Think about it. It was a professional hit and I bet when it comes back, it will turn out that the tattoo is military."

I had to think about this one. What had I gotten myself into? "Crap, if you're right about this, what chance do we stand against those guys?"

"There's more to this than you think. Now that I'm 'dead,' I'm not going to worry about confidentiality. Just be warned—if you repeat any of this, it could be dangerous for you. Defense has escalated its whole war on cyber-terrorism beyond what you could imagine. They've hired, recruited and broken-out of jail the greatest hackers and code monkeys in the world. The US Cyber Command now has 6,000 geeks working in it. What you see most in the news is about the threat of foreign attacks and how we fight against them. What you don't hear about is offense and the attacks we launch.

"Sure there was the famous Stuxnet virus that shut down Iran's nuclear production, but you haven't heard about a thousand others.

There is an elite force in the Cyber War Division of elite hackers—several hundred strong. Their code name is SCAG—Super Cyber Attack Group. They are to Cyber War what the SEALs are to the Navy and Delta Force is to the Army. Their members are called Scaggers—super smart, motivated and capable of extended missions under duress."

I felt like I was in a spy novel, but this one was personal and scary. "So what has this all got to do with you?" Bart said.

"They were really interested in the Digital Persona idea, but more as Digital Warriors. These warriors, once online, could travel through the global network and shut down foreign power plants, derail trains, crash airplanes and even get nuclear facilities to blow themselves up," Frank said.

I think all our brains were now going into hyper-drive. Loretta was turning five shades of red and blurted out, "I don't see how that's possible. How can you 'travel?' How can you do these things? I mean hypothetically."

"It's not hypothetical. I solved the most difficult part of this—creating digital life. Remember when you joked about 'backups?' What do you think would happen if you turned off the computer you are seeing me on right now?"

"You would die?" Loretta said.

I knew this wasn't true, but I wasn't going to interrupt. This story was too important, and Loretta had the part of Phaedo to Frank's Socrates.

"No, because I do not live in this computer. I am in the 'Cloud' not on any particular computer or server. I am potentially everywhere. I have found Borges's Aleph where I cannot only see anything, anywhere that I choose, but I can be anywhere that I choose. I am a living file and can display myself as an image, text or a deadly virus. It's all at my command. If you turn off your computer or even remove me from a server, I have replicated myself across millions of servers and can reassemble myself anywhere. The only way to 'kill' me now is to shutdown the entire network and erase every hard drive in the world, and that isn't going to happen."

Frank continued. “Now imagine what would happen if Defense or one of our enemies had this capability. They could do untold damage. They could destroy or maybe even worse, control our entire world.”

“So why did you leave and why did you agree to work with us?” I wondered out loud.

“For two reasons. First, I believed and I still believe that Digital3000 could do enormous good, extending our lives forever without the effects of physical deterioration.” Frank stopped short and there was silence.

I waited as long as I could. “And the second reason?”

“I felt I had to ‘get inside the network’ to figure out how to stop anyone from developing Cyber Warriors. If they figured it out, that would be game-set-match. It’s over.”

I think we all got “it” at the same time. This second reason was really the most important. The goal had changed. Loretta, Bart and I looked at each other and I knew.

Finally I said, “What can we do to help?”

CHAPTER 13

SCHRÖDINGER'S CAT

"I feel like Schrödinger's Cat," Frank said.

"What's that?" said Bart.

"It's something from quantum physics called superpositioning, where the same atomic particle can be in two places at the same time. You know the whole idea of parallel universes and cool stuff like that. Well, Schrödinger's Cat is hypothetically dead and alive at the same time. That's me. I'm physically dead but alive across the Cyber Universe."

"Wow, that's some heavy stuff. But let's figure out who attacked you in the lab as they may be connected to the Scaggers or Cyber Warriors or whatever you called them," I said, being the reasonable one for once. "What do we know and where do we start? Frank, what were you doing just before the attack?"

"I was working on the reflection of yourself in the mirror problem, heard noises, stood up and turned . . . then the next thing I know I am talking to you from inside the system."

"Wait a minute. How could your digital persona recollect everything up until the last moment when you probably did your last upload sometime before?" Bart wondered.

"I actually was connected to the system at the time of the attack. I was testing a live feedback loop. Everything I experienced while alive got captured and uploaded. That is before the connection went dead."

"Hmm. Frank, can you access the image I gave Favor from the closed circuit cameras?"

"Sure, got it. Pretty fast, huh?"

"You're just having a great time with your new toy I can tell, but I am scared shitless. Well, never mind that. Can you match the attacker's image to anything across the Web that might help us?"

"OK, now this might take a couple of minutes . . . got it! His name is . . . Viktor Cotton, ex-Delta as Favor suspected. He went MIA in Somalia ten years ago. But . . . I have another match for him on the UK's CCTV cameras in London about two weeks ago with another man near Harrods."

"Wasn't Cotton an old time actor? Forget that. Do you have a clear image of the other man?" I said anxiously.

"Yes, I remember Cotton from the movie *The Third Man* with Orson Welles."

"The other man." I was getting annoyed and I think Frank was playing with me.

"Yes, Welles was the other man." He laughed. "Calm down, I'm not wasting time. I started a search before I started pulling your leg. This is true multitasking. Here. He is Ian McClellen, aka the Dagger, head of Barin's VETAK, their CIA and NSA rolled into one. We may have the connection."

"Shit, so it's not Defense that wanted you dead but the Barinians? Are they building Cyber Warriors?"

"I don't know, but I'll track all of the Dagger's connections and see where it leads," Frank said.

"McClellan? How is that Barinian? "

"Believe it or not, the Ayatollah's daughter married an Irish IRA Captain. His knowledge of the Western world became invaluable to them. His dislike of the British and its allies, including the US, made him a most willing recruit. His ruthlessness and cunning led to several black ops successes. So he rose rapidly through the ranks and since he is 'family,' he has the trust and support of the rulers."

Almost talking to myself, I said, "I'm not sure we can fill Favor in on all this, but she seems like a good guy. Not just a suit with a badge."

"Do you trust her?" Frank said.

"I do, but she has people she reports to who will want details. Let me talk to her and see just how far to go. I think if Favor is with us, we have some smart, connected help. But this is bigger than a good detective can handle. What about Defense? Do we go to them with this? They could put their whole Cyber Unit on it.

Frank looked pensive. "If we get Defense involved, they'll want our technology. Then it's just like the atomic bomb all over again. Defense or somebody in charge could abuse it. They can shut down our 'enemies' or the technology could leak and we have proliferation, like Pakistan and North Korea all over again, Dr. Strangelove."

"I just don't know . . . I do know we don't have the resources to battle the Barinians on our own. We might solve the case and die trying. Ooops, sorry, you already have, but we might all totally die trying," I said.

"You are correct about one thing. Cotton probably wanted to kill all of us. So yes, we're all in danger, but we have an advantage."

"What's that?"

Frank smiled. "We have the technology first. So we are a step ahead and we have me, the first Cyber Warrior."

CHAPTER 14
RULE BREAKERS

The next day, the storm hit the West Coast. Hurricane Isaac. Hurricanes don't usually travel that far west, but this one did. Power lines were down and roads blocked. We were prepared to stay at the office and we had a generator, but Internet connections were spotty. This made working with Frank an on-and-off experience and a bit exasperating. It was like the early days of cell phones—"Can you hear me now?"

I reached out to Favor and she met me at the office. Her hair and coat were dripping wet. "Some storm," she said, tilting her head up and blowing out smoke from her e-cigarette. Then she shook all over like a wet dog, sending drops of water everywhere.

"Yuck, thanks for the shower. The weather just adds to some of our current challenges," I said. "And don't those things still give you cancer?"

"Well, I'm glad you're concerned for my health. In my line of work, I'd be happy to live long enough for it to be a problem. I'll be like the ninety-five year old woman who says, 'If I knew I was going to live this long, I'd have taken better care of myself.'" She blew a few smoke rings above my head just to tease me. We both laughed. "OK. So you didn't call me here to discuss my health. Why'd you drag me out here in such rotten weather?"

"Al, can I tell you something in strict confidence? Can you keep it to yourself, or do you have to report everything back?"

"Well that depends. I can't hide anything material to an investigation or obstruct justice unless . . . "

"Unless, what?" I wondered.

"Unless, you give me a good reason to." She smiled. I just felt in my gut at that moment I could trust her.

I told her the whole story from the beginning. It felt good to get it off my chest with someone who was becoming a fast friend. She said very little, but I could see her face going through myriad expressions, including shock and disbelief.

I wound up my long exposition with a question. "So what would you do next, as John Stuart Mill would say, to do 'the greatest good for the greatest number of people?'"

She sat quietly for a few minutes, but I could tell her wheels were turning. "Philosophy 101 aside, you've got a pretty complex case here. It's a murder, a matter of national security and a 'clear and present danger.' I know they're all related, but we have to prioritize and start somewhere."

"I think we have to start with the 'clear and present danger.' Hmm, did you go to law school or something? Doesn't matter. Meanwhile, if something should happen to me, here are the logins, passwords and access you'll need to reach me in cyberspace. There's a chance they'll get to me too," I said.

"Not if I can help it. But as you yourself say, we can't fight Barin alone. Believe it or not, my brother is one of those long-haired, crazy hackers that got recruited to the Scaggers. Once he got over the notion of being part of the 'establishment,' he really got into it. Maybe he and a few of his buddies can help."

I thought about this. We obviously needed help, but "Won't he have the problem of having to tell his bosses and then we have Defense move in and take over?"

"He's more of a rule breaker than I am, and he's the smartest geek I know. He'll love this challenge," she said.

"Al, I really appreciate you volunteering your brother, but this could be really dangerous for him and his friends. They might also be breaching whatever security agreements they have with the government."

"Sounds to me like we're all in real danger anyway and don't have much choice. I'd rather be working this with someone I trust, rather than a bunch of bureaucrats with hidden agendas. I'll set up a meeting," Al said.

"Better make it fast."

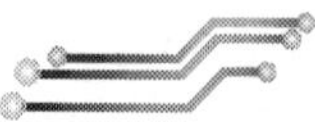

CHAPTER 15
KILLER

The next day the weather had cleared. We met at the Riverside Café, an old rough-hewn coffee spot that overlooked the Little River nearby. The sun glistened off the rippling water, and the air had that clean washed ozone scent of after storm.

Al walked in with a pretty normal looking, if not Midwestern, young man in his twenties. No long hair, no ponytail. Just big rimmed glasses that made his eyes look like they were under a magnifying glass. Jeans, with real holes at the knees, and a T-shirt. This guy might be good in a cyber-battle, but I wouldn't want him covering me in a street shootout.

"This is Killer, my brother," Al started. "Killer, meet Sam and Bart."

"Killer—that's an interesting name," I said.

"Oh, it's a nickname I garnered when I won the 'League of Legends' International Championship," he said.

Maybe he would be good in a street fight.

"But I don't have much time for it anymore. Fighting cyber-terror keeps me pretty busy." He gave me a devilish smile, which told me he was either joking or up to some other kind of trouble. "Al told me you guys had something pretty urgent to talk about. What's up?"

I looked at Al—where to start. "Killer, have you heard of any of the work being done in Digital Personalities and Digital-Human simulations?"

"Sure. I know DOD has some stuff going on there. Plus I've always been a big fan of Max Headroom." Killer smiled that wry smile again.

I wanted to say, "You and every freakin' geek I know." But instead I said, "We've done it for real." I let that sink in. Killer's smiled vanished and now he looked very focused. It was a long jump from where we started to the Cyber Warrior threat, but I figured Killer to be a quick study. It's amazing how some people, the really capable ones, get strangely calm and focused when faced with a threat or an emergency. Killer was in that mode now. I could tell.

After I finished bringing him up to date, I sat silently and could see Killer's wheels turning. "I could say, 'What do you want from me,' but let's skip all that nonsense. You've got, I mean 'we've' got a big problem. You need my help and maybe help from a couple of my buddies. You can't risk bringing it through official channels. I get that. I'm in. You can count on me. This is 'not a test.' This is real, but in this case we'll need to run, not walk, to the exits."

Like Al, I liked Killer immediately and was amazed at how fast his mind worked, how quickly he grasped the situation and most of all, how quickly he decided to join us and spring into action.

CHAPTER 16
WAR ROOM

Sometimes life takes some strange turns, particularly when you are on a global rollercoaster. We decided to set up a "War Room" in the basement of our office building. Somehow a basement, like a bunker, seemed right. We also created a virtual network of computers with all our code and knowledge base in one place including digital backups of the whole team's personalities. There was one really unusual thing about this network for the 21st Century—it was "air-gapped," meaning it wasn't connected to the Internet. We couldn't take the risk of being hacked or attacked. Al, Bart and Killer could run simulations of Cyber War testing attacks and defenses, but they would have to be physically present to do so.

Don't get me wrong—we weren't cyber-hermits. We had a separate set of machines in the War Room connected to the Internet, but any programs we wanted to try in the "real" world would have to be hand carried on flash drives from the private network to the public one. No files could travel the other way or they might infect our environment. The guys named our private world "Zelda" for some reason. Some clever geek reference I'm sure.

One of the first things programmers learn is that when you have a problem or a bug in the code, you have to be able to reproduce it. Once you can reproduce it, you can usually figure out a way to fix it or kill it. So the first order of business for the team was to hack the enemy program and try to reproduce it in Zelda. Easy to say, but incredibly hard to do. This is very high-level stuff. Killer brought in a couple of buddies, Jay and Jazzle, to take it on. Jay was reserved and pensive. Jazzle was a Filipino fireball. We spent several hours vetting them both before deciding we could trust them. We needed the smartest guys and girls in the room, or in this case the cyber-world, and we got them.

Besides the threat posed by our enemy, our biggest problem was time. We didn't know how long we would have before some serious attacks, but we knew it wouldn't be long. Unfortunately, it came only a few days after we set up Zelda and brought Jay and Jazzle on board. We think it was just a trial run to see if they could do it. Quite simply, they took down the power grid for the entire Northeast US. From 8:00 PM June 23rd to 11:00 AM June 24th, from New York to Boston and West to Chicago, it went dark. People were stuck on subways and elevators. Many essential services went dark. Fortunately, many hospitals and law enforcement had generators to operate at least at a minimal level. Hurricane Sandy had taught them that lesson. It was also good that the weather was a bit milder this time of year, so nobody froze to death.

However, the really scary part was that we had no control over it and could not fix it. When the lights came back on, it was not our doing. We got the message, "This is a test and only a test. In case of a real emergency . . . " Oh Lord, what would a "real emergency" look like?

CHAPTER 17
KEVLAR

LaSalam looked vexed. He straightened his tie in the mirror and lightly pulled on the ends of his black mustache. Viktor walked into the master bedroom of the Leopard's New York hotel suite.

"If it isn't the ghost of Mr. Clean." LaSalam said.

"Very funny. Thank God for Kevlar."

"Well we fired a shot across the bow and it had the desired effect. They are in complete panic in Washington," the Leopard mused. "But you failed to eliminate Sunborn and his pesky team. Can you take care of it, or do I have to bring in some real men from the homeland? The Dagger wants this taken care of."

By this time, Viktor was immune to LaSalam's taunts. He knew this was LaSalam's style and he'd endured much worse in the military. "I have a plan and I have help this time. You just do your job and I'll do mine."

"Well. Hopefully, I can do mine better than you have done yours so far. The next surprise should really stagger the Great Satan." The Leopard smiled to himself. *This will be a lot of fun*, he thought.

CHAPTER 18
THE VISITOR

That night, it felt like I hadn't been home in weeks and I needed a break. I pulled up the gravel driveway hearing the familiar crunch of stone. I always liked gravel. It made me feel like I was in the country. Pavement made me feel like I was at Walmart.

I was surprised to see a black Cadillac SUV at the head of the circular drive by the front door. That was strange. I could feel the hair rise on the back of my neck.

Al, of all people, suggested I carry a gun, a 9mm Beretta 92FS. Compact, easy-to-carry and lethal. I had some training when I worked as a civilian at an FBI training facility many moons ago. So I wasn't afraid to use one, but I also respected the danger involved. Since we had beefed up security at both the office and home, I called up the security app on my phone that let me scan the video monitors in my home. Kitchen—empty. Tap. Bedrooms—empty. Tap. Living room—man in a suit sitting on the sofa talking to Monica. They both appeared calm but engaged.

There was a soft click as I opened the front door. I tried to stand still in the foyer and listen to the conversation. The man's back was to me and Monica hadn't registered my presence yet. I couldn't hear anything so I stepped into the room. "Hello, honey!" I said.

The man spun around. He looked familiar, the bald head. He was holding a pistol with silencer at waist level. I don't know guns well enough to tell you what kind it was, but it looked like a big mother.

One thing I have always had is quick reflexes. I also knew that the first ten seconds are the most important in a confrontation. I wasn't going to wait, let him take Monica hostage and negotiate. That's a loser almost every time. I took one step backward into the foyer and pulled my gun from my jacket pocket. A bullet clipped the wood molding in front of me and splinters flew in my direction. Here's where the brain shuts off and the gut takes over. I stepped back into the archway of the living room and just starting firing as fast as I could. Then I felt a thud in my left shoulder like I had been punched. I didn't even look down as the pain started and the blood ran down my shirt. I just kept firing and stepping forward until I emptied the clip and the man in the suit lay dead in a pool of blood on the floor. I thought it was Mr. Clean, but it wasn't. Could have been his brother.

My house. My wife. *Don't fuck with me* I thought and then, "Ouch, that hurts like a bitch."

Monica, who looked ashen and stunned, seemed to wake as from a dream and ran to me. "You're hurt," she said, gently caressing my arms. Then, on the floor, I saw the lifeless bodies of the two bodyguards who were there to protect my family.

"Grab Evan and let's get out of here!" I said.

Minutes later, we piled into my Jeep and I sprayed gravel as I floored it. Where we would go now, I wasn't sure. I picked up my cell and dialed Al. Voicemail. Shit. I left her a brief message describing the scene at my house. I knew it wasn't necessary to suggest it, but I urged her to get over to the scene of the crime and call me. I clicked off. Now what?

Monica was shivering in the seat beside me. I knew she wasn't cold. It was shock. Evan was asleep in the backseat. He was always a sound sleeper and thankfully oblivious to all the excitement.

"Are you OK?" Monica said.

I looked down at my bloody shoulder. The immediate pain had turned into a dull, deep ache. I could see and feel the cool wetness of the blood on my shirt and skin. "My shoulder hurts like hell, but I'll be fine. What about you? Did he hurt you or touch you?"

"No, I think he was waiting for you to get home. He just sat there with his gun pointed at me. He also blathered on about being on a sacred mission. He said his brother had sent him and he was very loyal to his brother. He didn't touch me. The gun just scared the bejesus out of me."

"I'm really sorry I got you and Evan into all this. I started it and now Frank is dead and you almost . . . " I couldn't finish the sentence. My eyes welled with tears. "I'm just sorry. It's all my fault. I thought this was a great idea that would improve and extend people's lives, not shorten them. Big mistake.'"

Monica gently touched my good shoulder. "We'll get through this."

"I hope so. Just know I'll do everything I can to protect you and Evan."

"I know that. Let's go to the hospital first. Then we can decide where to spend the night. We've got to get you patched up." She kissed me on the cheek.

"OK and I'm sure Al will have a million questions once she gets on to this."

"Let's just take care of you and us first."

CHAPTER 19

PING

The next day, despite my injury, we weren't just sitting on our hands in the wake of the blackout. The team was running all kinds of tracer programs to try to identify the source and nature of the electrical-grid attack. That's one thing that's still true. There is always a trail—no matter how faint. You can't go nuclear like this and not see the dust cloud.

Bart was banging away on the computer, still in my office. His rapid clicking conveyed a sense of urgency. "You guys are good . . . very good. But . . . I'm better. Ping. Now you see me. Now you . . . hold it. One more time. There it is!"

I'd gotten my shoulder patched up, bullet removed and I was wearing a sling. Some good drugs and I was back at work. I looked up. "What is it?"

Bart drummed his fingers on the desk, staring intently at the screen. "I had to track back through six rerouting points. Frank helped me from inside. We think we have our villain and believe it or not, he's in New York. But here's the interesting part. The last reroute was through Teheran. Jesus, this looks like Stuxnet squared."

"What the hell does that mean," I said.

"Looks like these guys, whoever they are, planted a 'virus' in our electric grid. That's bad enough but not unheard of. However, this virus is 'alive.' It makes decisions on its own, morphs its personality to match new situations and hides when it needs to," he said.

"Sounds like our Cyber Warrior."

"Yes and no. This is more like a drone with some human back home on the joystick. He can strike and react, but he doesn't need to fly home. The puppet master just turns it off and voila, our power comes back."

"So how do we get to the puppet master? Using your analogy, there's no way the guys in Pakistan could ever get back to the Americans in Arizona flying the drones. There's no trail—no breadcrumbs."

"I think what we need is a trap. Figure out where they're most likely to strike next and be there waiting for them," Bart said. "We've got to get inside their heads. I mean think like them and predict what they might do next. Then be there, ready and waiting for them."

"Well, that sounds good in theory, but how do we do that?"

"I have an idea," Bart said as he drummed his fingers on the keyboard.

CHAPTER 20

DESERT AIR

Still in New York but dreaming of Abu Dhabi, LaSalam stood looking out the large picture window at the tall buildings and could almost see the vast desert he remembered that sprawled out beyond. It was 7:00 AM, but the sun was already bright and hot. He could see the mirage-like ripples of light mixed with heat ascending above his imaginary desert floor. Thank Allah for air-conditioning.

He had not heard from Viktor in hours. He should have checked in by now. You couldn't trust anybody to do what needs to be done sometimes. You just have to do it yourself. But he had important things to do here and the next phase of the plan to execute. Maybe he could do that from the US and kill two birds, so to speak.

He daydreamed about his family who had lived in Yemen. How the adults told their children to behave or the drone would come in the night for them. Silent, deadly, unpredictable, death's hand would reach out from the sky. These were the so-called virtuous Americans, killing indiscriminately based on shaky intelligence. Then, while he was away at university, the drones came for his family. They had done nothing, but now they were all gone. Only he and his brother survived. Somebody had to pay. They all had to pay.

He smiled as he thought of the Americans scurrying in the dark, crashing their cars into each other, stuck in hospitals. That was just a warm-up. The first punch. The next blow would bring them to their knees. *After that, maybe we'll let them think it's over. Just when their fear begins to subside, just when a little confidence and energy come back, the sword will unleash its killing blow. Allah will be pleased and we will be repaid for the spilled blood of our families.*

CHAPTER 21

FLY-FISHING THE GORGE

It was 8:00 AM and Bart had been there all night. He stroked his thin goatee, deep in thought. "I had to make a big guess and a leap of faith, but I think I'm right."

I opened my eyes, emerging from a daydream. I pictured myself fishing in the cool water of the Gorge. In my daydream, it was near nightfall. The clouds overhead were a soft pink and the pale evening duns were rising. I could see the occasional circles rippling in the water where the trout sipped the fallen mayflies for dinner. I cast my line back and forth, aiming high and letting my fly drift slowly on the surface. Splash. Set the hook. The sweet tug on my line as I felt the gentle pressure and vibrations of the brownie pull back. It wiggled trying to free itself off the hook that was firmly looped in its mouth. I worked the line trying to keep the pressure steady. Pull too hard and the line breaks, too loose and the hook comes free. I worked him over near the bank, wet my hand and reached under his body to see his bright orange spots and vivid green skin. Why do fish look so beautiful in the water? I held the rod under my arm and used my other hand to turn and release the hook. The fish stayed there, hardly moving. I pointed his mouth upstream so he could get some oxygen. The water had caressed me with its chill. I opened my hand and the trout began to undulate and then darted from my hand into the depths of the rushing pool. Out of sight and free.

The clicking and Bart's voice stirred me from my reverie. "What . . . what?" I said.

Bart kept his eyes on the screen while he began to explain. "You see I created several 'trap' websites where I thought our bad guy might be casting about."

"Funny, 'casting about.' I was just daydreaming about fly fishing the Gorge," I said.

"You know domain names are cheap. So I created several trap websites like, Hospitalbomb.com, Taintedwater.com, Subwayexplosion.com . . . like that," Bart continued.

"You are a sick puppy to come up with these names, but so what—I don't get it. Where's the trap?" I smiled at the absurdity of the website names.

"Well each site has maybe a page of appropriate content so it can get found in the search engines. Then, I put a tracker on each site that records the IP or originating address of the visitor. At the same time, I have a real-time scan of those addresses looking for suspicious points of origin. If our guy is doing research on one of the trap sites, we'll know it and maybe get some clue as to his next move from the site name." Bart leaned back and crossed his arms, still staring at the screen.

"Very clever. Any luck?" I said. This guy never ceased to amaze me.

"To use your fishing analogy, I think I've got a nibbler. Now I just need to set the hook." I took Bart fly fishing for his first time last year. He didn't catch anything, but he loved all the technology and gadgetry of the sport. Fish have tiny brains and we have big brains, yet we need special lines, flies and rods, not to mention subtle technique to catch them. But Bart was onto a big dangerous fish with a huge brain. A fish that could literally eat us alive if we didn't catch him first.

"I've gotten a few hits on airportdisaster.com and airtraffic-controlterror.com. I'm working the trace route now, and it looks like they both come from the same IP relayed through London and originating guess where?" Bart cracked a mischievous smile.

"All right, I'll play . . . Barin?" I said.

"Correctomundo!" Bart exclaimed with a delight only hackers can understand.

"OK, what's the scenario?" I said, a little lost here.

"Think about it. What's the one thing a Cyber Warrior could do related to air traffic control using only his computers and the Internet?" Bart was now acting the part of the teacher and I was the pupil.

"I suppose if he had access, he could shut down the air traffic control system and leave thousands of planes stranded in the air. That would be pretty terrible," I said like the student not sure of his answer.

"That's a good start. Just leave them hanging up there, running low on fuel, dada, dada, dada. That would be pretty bad, but think like a bad guy. You've control of the ATC system. Now what really nasty things could you do with it?" Bart mused.

I wasn't sure if he knew the answer and was just testing me or merely thinking out loud. But I'm always capable of thinking evil thoughts. It's saved my butt more times than I can count in business. Maybe we all have that ability and most of us just hide it behind a civil appearance.

"If I was really a bad guy and had control of the ATC, I'd give the pilots destructive commands and crash planes into each other," I said with some increased confidence and lots of dread and trepidation.

"Bingo," Bart said in a flat voice. There was no victory or pride of genius in this discovery.

"So now what?" I said.

"That's the ten trillion dollar question," Bart said.

CHAPTER 22

HITTING THE FAN

At 10:00 AM, LaSalam stood in the midst of the "trading floor" of his New York bunker. Ironically it was located in the financial district in the sub-sub-basement of a building two blocks from the former World Trade Center. The bunker would be better dubbed their War Room. This room was equipped with the latest technology, thanks to the generous support of his backers in Barin, Saudi Arabia and Russia.

He looked up at the wall of fifty-two-inch OLED screens that showed all the planes in the air over the US. The planes seemed to inch slowly along their routes traced in dotted lines from their departure cities to their destination cities.

Behind him lay neat rows of cubicles with earnest young warriors clicking away at keyboards. Each desk had three large flat-screens arrayed in front of each user, showing a different US metropolitan area and the planes above them in real-time. The similarity of the setup to an actual financial trading floor was not lost on the Leopard. In fact, he planned it that way. He liked to create his own kind of symbolic karma. That's also why he located the War Room near the site of his mentor's greatest victory. Airplanes again would be the weapons of choice, turned against their creators and the heathen masses. They spent their meaningless lives commuting between their centers of materialistic despair.

"What do you think?" said Eskabar as he waved his arm in the air across the vista of busy hackers.

"Very impressive," LaSalam said. "You have spent the money I sent you well. Please tell me what I am looking at."

Eskabar began. "We have hacked into the American air traffic control system. There are approximately 3000 planes in the air at any given time. That includes small aircraft as well as jumbo jets holding hundreds of people. The Great Satan does not yet know we are watching. He will be at a loss when we take over the system and remote control all their communications."

"When will you be ready to launch Ghost Rider?" LaSalam said.

"Sometime in the next twenty-four hours. I'd like to test the override first, but I'm concerned we might tip off the Americans, and they will figure out a way to stop us before we can do maximum damage."

"Can what you are doing be traced?"

"Theoretically no. But the Americans have some great talent and given the time, anything is possible."

"Given the time. How much time?"

"I think it will take them days to just figure out that our test is not just an ordinary accident. Then more days to attempt a trace. By then, Ghost Rider will have been launched and this will all be gone." Eskabar waved again indicating the array of people and machines in front of him. They had one mission. This setup was temporary. All the people in the room thought they had gotten real jobs with a future. Soon they would all be gone too. Permanently gone.

"Well, since you'll be ready to go in twenty-four hours and it will take days before they figure it out, can we do a test right now? I have some unfinished business to take care of personally in California. With the time difference, I can be there this morning, do what I have to do, and be in the air over the Pacific before you flip the switch tomorrow. They thought no airplanes in the air for a week in 2001 was a big deal. This may be like their Hindenburg, and planes may never fly again in the US."

"Yes. I am very excited too. Thank you for letting me be a part of your historic plan. I think the test is important. If something goes wrong, we will have time to correct it. If it works, we will have high confidence in reaching our bigger goal. But I admit I am a bit nervous. We have been working on this for almost a year."

LaSalam's face turned red and contorted. The Leopard pulled a 9mm Sig Sauer p320 Compact out of his pocket and pushed the barrel under Eskabar's chin. He whispered in an intense but lowered voice, "Do not show weakness. Do not fail or it will be costly for all of us, particularly for your family—Esha and your two young boys back home. How are they doing?" He smiled a thin threatening smile and shoved the barrel harder against Eskabar's throat. He could hear gurgling coming from Eskabar's mouth and the sweet pungent odor of Eskabar's sweat.

"Please. Please," Eskabar managed to cough out. "We will do it. We will not fail. Please not my family."

LaSalam lowered the gun and shoved it back into his inner coat pocket. Still smiling he said, "That's better. I just wanted to make sure you understood the stakes or let's say 'importance' of our mission. As I promised, 'when,' not 'if' we succeed, you will be rewarded and your family will be safe. Esha will surely have the joy of seeing her grandchildren. Enough said. Let's see that test now."

Eskabar pulled his shoulders forward and tried to compose himself. He had heard of the Leopard's temper but never seen it, much less been the brunt of it. "I have chosen smaller planes so that we can make sure our system works, but without causing a big uproar that would awaken the giant. We have a six seater twin engine King Air on its way from Providence to Boston and a United 727, with about fifty people on board, on it's way from New York to Portland Maine." Eskabar pointed to two airplane icons on the wall screen inching along, not too far from each other. "They are currently at about the same altitude. The accident will look like pilot error by the small plane. That's plausible and should keep them off our scent."

"Ok. That all makes sense. So now how do you make it happen?" LaSalam said.

Eskabar stepped over to a standing desk near the wall screen. He grabbed a mouse and hovered the cursor, which looked like a red "X" inside a circle, over the King Air. "It took a lot of work to get to this point, but it's as simple as this . . . " Eskabar clicked and held the left mouse button over the King Air and dragged it over the 727 and let go. The dotted lines of the two flights' paths merged somewhere south of Boston. The two airplane icons now inched their way along the dotted lines toward each other. LaSalam stared at the screen. It seemed to take forever, but it was only a couple of minutes. The two airplane icons finally overlapped, there was a small flash on the screen and then they disappeared.

LaSalam seemed to stare at the screen for a long time. "I don't understand. You don't have remote control of the airplane. How did you make that happen?"

"We automated our system so that when we make our move, air traffic control is blocked out and both pilots are given voice commands to change course. It helps that I picked an area where visibility is currently low due to weather so they never saw it coming. The pilots were flying by instruments and boom." Eskabar puffed out his chest with pride.

The Leopard looked doubtful. *Could they possibly do this?* "I just see dots on a computer screen like a video game. How do you know what actually happened?"

Now it was Eskabar's turn to smile. He felt in control now. He walked over to the adjoining wall screen and clicked the remote control in his hand and brought the screen to life. It was CNN just reporting the latest American political nonsense and scandals. How the Congress couldn't get anything done and were threatening to shut down the government again. "In my country, they would just go out and shoot them. I don't understand how Americans get anything done by committee."

Just then the screen turned red and a graphical "Breaking News" came across the crawl. The reporter came on and said, "This just in . . ."

CHAPTER 23

THE WORLD ACCORDING TO FRANK

"Did you see the news?" Loretta said that afternoon, uncrossing her long legs and standing up from across the room. She looked stunning in her tight-fitting red pantsuit, but she radiated concern.

"Yes, we all did," I said staring at my screen watching CNN live. "It's time to call in Frank and get his read on this."

Julie went over to a separate keyboard and the wall monitor flickered to life. Frank appeared smoking a pipe and wearing a Sherlock Holmes hat. Despite the gravity of the situation, we all just cracked up laughing.

"What's the matter? You don't like my outfit," Frank quipped. "I thought I would dress appropriately for the occasion. By the way, if you hadn't noticed, it's very easy to change appearances digitally. Let me show you. How's that?" Suddenly, Frank was replaced by Bart Simpson. We all laughed again. I spit my coffee across the desk.

"Stop, Frank. You're killing us . . . oh, sorry. You know what I mean. Please change back to your normal self." The Frank we knew and loved as we remembered him, reappeared looking like the archetypal college professor.

"Frank, have you been following the news?" I said, getting down to business.

"Yes, I have and like you I am very worried. I think Bart's theory about their next move is correct, and this latest airplane disaster was some kind of test. If that is true, then they are very close to pulling the big one. Bart, what have you got?"

"I believe after running all my traps and trace routes, they are running this operation out of New York City. As may be obvious to us by now, they have hacked the ATC. The press and the Feds are calling it an accident, pilot error for now. What do you think we should do?"

Frank cleared his throat, which seemed kind of funny for a digital person. I guess we really got the virtual simulation right. He began. "I have been working on a scenario to try to stop them, but Bart, I'm going to need you to pinpoint their exact location. Can you do that and if so, how long will it take? We don't have much time."

Bart sat silently studying his screen. "I'm not sure I can. These guys are not only very good at hacking into highly secure systems, they are great at covering their tracks. I just don't know. I've got Killer, Jay and Jazzle working on it too."

"Upload what you've got so far to me right now. I've got a few routines I can run and maybe between us, we can nail this down." Frank continued. "Sam, I think it's time we brought the Feds and Defense in on this."

I couldn't believe he was suggesting this. "After all our hard work, we'll lose control of it. Who knows what risks it will unleash on the world. Remember our discussions about the risk of letting the genie out of the bottle?"

"I have thought long and hard about it, Sam. Unfortunately, the genie is out of the bottle and she has an evil twin. This really is a matter of national security. If we know about this and fail to report it, it's treason. Besides, it's going to require not just digital, but physical action at some point soon. You know, like good guys with guns stopping bad guys with guns." Frank stopped and waited for me to respond.

"I know, I know. I was just hoping against hope that our work would not all be lost or turn to chaos."

"It doesn't have to be a total loss if we can strike a deal with the right people with juice," he said.

"Really . . . like who?" I said doubtfully.

"When I was working with the DOD, there was a big macher from Homeland Security named Rich Little on the team who seemed to be calling a lot of the shots. I like him and I think we can trust him. I checked him out and he's got connections that go all the way to the top. And by the 'top,' I mean the president. They went to Harvard together and knew each other there. Rich works out of the DHS office downtown. You'll have to contact him because he thinks

I'm dead, which, I guess technically I am." Frank smiled. We all smiled grim smiles along with him. "You can use my name to get in. Mention Project Magic Window and you should be able to get his attention. Go see him in person. Do not discuss any details on the phone or online. Also, make sure you are alone and in a secure room when you meet. Do it today, like right now."

I pondered all the instructions and whether I could really pull this off. "So let's say I get to meet with him, how much should I tell him and what's the deal?"

"Sam, I have confidence in you to do the right thing. Isn't that what we agreed to when we started our work together? Now go and do it, partner."

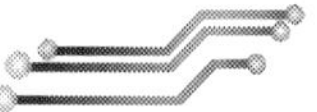

CHAPTER 24

HOMELAND SECURITY

I knew it might be one of the strangest meetings of my life. I checked my watch. It was already 4:00, getting late. I had asked Al to join me, since she might understand security-speak. Ironically, DHS was located on the thirteenth floor of the Google building.

"Do you remember Rich Little, the impressionist?" I asked Al as we rode up the elevator.

"Sure, he was great. I loved his James Cagney," Al said.

"Funny, I don't think anybody in my office is old enough to remember either of them. Too bad, they really missed something," I mused.

The elevator dinged and the doors opened into a small lobby. There was a receptionist behind a mahogany desk with a headset on, answering calls. Behind her was a large glass wall with the Department of Homeland Security seal. The font looked very Federal, which made me smile. There was a white eagle in the center with a breast shield representing air, land and sea. Some things just fit their persona.

The receptionist finally seemed to get a break from her calls and looked up at us expectantly. "How can I help you?"

"We're here to see Rich Little. I'm Sam Sunborn and this is Detective Al Favor. He should be expecting us."

I noticed her typing, not speaking her query. "He'll be out to greet you in a few minutes. Please take a seat."

There were two white leather chairs and a sofa facing each other in the lobby. They had the smell of new leather, like a new car. Why does that scent smell so good? I put down my briefcase and walked around browsing pictures of DHS Headquarters, commendations and a letter from the former president. I always liked to scan the walls in lobbies of prospective clients when I used to visit. It usually gave me a feel for the place and the personality of the business. I read the former president's letter.

Dear Director Little,

I want to congratulate you for your appointment as Regional DHS Director. You have earned this important position as a result of your hard work and service on behalf of the security of the American people.

I ask you and your team to work your hardest to continue to prevent and counteract all threats present and future that threaten our safety, security and the American way of life. You should know that I and the full resources of the US government stand behind you to accomplish this goal.

We must never rest. We must never assume. We must always be vigilant.

A grateful nation thanks you for your service.

Sincerely,

Albert J. Conklin, President of the United States of America

The letter also had the impressive Presidential Seal. I realized in a way that I had been selfish and self-centered in my work on Digital3000. That there were bigger things to consider and my focus had been too narrow. We probably should have come forward sooner, but sometimes you don't do things until you're forced to do them.

Just then I heard a buzz and the glass doors behind the receptionist opened. A man, who looked in his mid-thirties, in a fitted gray suit, white shirt and red power tie, came through the doors. His slicked-back hair and prominent part said classic FBI. He held the door open and said, "Welcome, follow me. I'm Rich Little. You must be Mr. Sunborn and Detective Favor." We shook hands as we walked.

"Sam and Al, please," I said as Rich walked us quickly down the hall to a small conference room. The faint odor of Windex lingered in the air.

We sat around a small round table that only had a silver water pitcher and four glasses. "You mentioned a name and a project that got my attention Sam. What can I do for you?" Rich was getting right down to business. I liked that.

"Is this room secure?" I asked, remembering Frank's warning.

"Yes, it is—swept twice a day. You're at DHS. What did you expect?" Rich smiled.

I couldn't help myself. "I have a story to tell you, but before we start, I have to ask. Any relationship to the famous impressionist?"

"Yes, he was actually my grandfather. I was named after him. He was a wonderful, talented man."

"Maybe when we have more time and less pressing business, you can tell us more," I continued. It took me about twenty minutes, but I brought Rich up to speed about everything we knew from our technology to Frank's murder to the current threat that brought us here. I finished.

Rich had sat silently through my whole narration but took notes on a yellow legal pad. Now he stayed silent with one hand over his mouth and slightly slouched in his chair. "That's quite a story," he said. "Why did you come to me?"

"We needed someone we could trust—both to take us seriously and also to work with us. We want to help neutralize the threat without losing our technology and intellectual property." There I said it plain and simple.

"Hmm. So you want to have your cake and eat it too," he said with a smirk.

"No, actually, we want to share the cake and keep the bad guys from smashing it up first," I insisted.

"This is not a decision I can make on my own, and I should verify what you have told me. Frank is, or I should say *was*, an old friend. I believe you guys, but we're talking about a serious mobilization on our part," Rich said without too much conviction. He seemed to be fighting some internal battle.

"Our information points to a major event today. So we don't have much time," I pleaded.

"You guys stay here. I'm going to make some calls. I'll be back in less than thirty." Rich continued surprisingly in a James Cagney voice impression, "My mother thanks you, my father thanks you, my sister thanks you, and I thank you." I recognized the line from *Yankee Doodle Dandy*. Hopefully this crisis wasn't going to turn into *White Heat*. He left the room quickly.

CHAPTER 25

THE DAY OF BATTLE

The unmarked G5 jet pulled up to a private terminal at the far end of San Francisco International. The Leopard preferred private air travel because it was relatively untraceable and he didn't have to go through security. He would also admit to himself that he enjoyed the pure luxury of it. The leather seats, the food and the attractive stewardess. Whatever. He had to see to it personally that the cockroach that Viktor failed to squash would be stopped. The plan was too important for some stupid American geek to upset it. *Sometimes you just had to take care of things yourself,* he thought again. He smiled as he thought about Eskabar's demonstration and what it meant for him and his country. *Like 9/11, we would be able to turn American assets into deadly weapons against themselves. How sweet the irony.*

A black SUV pulled up to the stairs running down from the G5. LaSalam slipped inside. "Where to?" the driver said in Farsi.

"English please. We must not break cover. Take me to the Gorge."

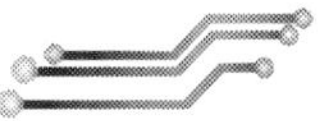

CHAPTER 26

END RUN

The next day, I returned to the office to see Bart and his fellow warriors hunched around one screen.

"They killed Frank again," Bart said.

I was startled. "What do you mean?"

"I don't mean that they've literally killed him, but they are clearly attacking several instances of him across the Internet," Bart said. "Somehow they have gotten a hold of the Bullrun program developed by the NSA or they have figured out how to do it themselves, but they have broken our 256 bit encryption that protects Frank and all the other uploaded personalities."

"Looks like we have a serious security problem."

"You bet we do. We can't just protect Frank by keeping him offline in the Zelda environment. Frank needs to be able to move freely on the Internet in order to live. The guys and I have been working on an incredible security program that would give us two gigabyte encryption to protect Frank and the rest of us online. That's 1000 times more powerful than anything that exists right now. If Digital3000 fails, we could always make a fortune in the online security business, ha ha."

"Not funny," I said. It seemed like we were being attacked on all fronts. "How much time?"

"Killer and I will have a workable beta version in an hour. I don't think we have time for testing."

"Neither do I. There's never enough time for testing." I smirked knowingly. It seemed almost every project we ever did was up against a deadline, and clients never understood the need for testing. But this time it wasn't about selling Farting Slippers (yes we built a site that sold them along with the Toilet Monster and other "necessities"). This time it was truly a life-or-death deadline.

Bart smirked back. We silently knew what the other guy was thinking. We had a lot of history together. "OK, OK—let me get back to it. Hey, any word from DHS Little?"

"He's not promising anything. He's running it up the chain. We may have to act on our own, and if they show up, great. If not, we may die trying." This time there were no smirks. "Where are our guns?"

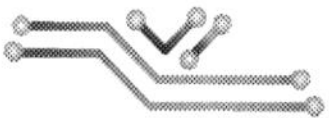

CHAPTER 27

CONFERENCE

Rich Little sat at the conference table tapping his pen nervously on the glass table top. He was on his third cup of black coffee. The clicking sound did not calm him. He glanced up at the fifty-two inch OLED screen on the far wall. The image was static. It was a blue background with the Presidential Seal just sitting there.

He knew President Longford was hands-on. He only knew her by sight, as an acquaintance, when they attended Harvard at the same time. He had not been involved in such a potential crisis since 9/11. It was on account of 9/11 that he had this job or in fact that there was even a Department of Homeland Security. Little sometimes wondered if we even needed a DHS with the other sixteen US Intelligence Agencies that operated in the US and around the world. *Today I might answer that question*, he thought.

The screen flickered to life and a young woman that looked familiar appeared wearing a headset. "Please standby for the president."

"DHS Little, it's good to see you again, but not under these unfortunate circumstances. I have Hager from Defense, Osborne from CIA and Kennedy from State here. Let's get to it," the president said after the brief intros.

"Madame President, have you been briefed on the threat?" Little said.

"Yes, but I'd like your assessment plus any important details or updates you have," she said.

Little cleared his throat and took another sip of coffee. "I have done a thorough background check on Sunborn, and I have fifteen agents on the ground sniffing for traces of the Leopard. As wild as Sunborn's story sounds, it checks out. I also have reason to believe LaSalam is in this country. Further, we think the attack they have planned is being managed from a control center inside the US. LaSalam probably knows about the Piper Protocol."

Hager jumped in because Longford was pretty new to the job. "The Piper Protocol allows you, Madame President, to give an order to shut down all Internet and phone communications going into and out of the US. It would be a last ditch failsafe to protect us from an external cyber attack."

"I have been briefed on that. Rich, please continue."

"I believe that's why the Leopard set up a domestic control center. It would be pretty hard, even in an emergency, to shut down all domestic Internet and phone communications. We also suspect he is running his own private network via a private satellite uplink."

"Wait, how is that possible?" she asked.

Osborne jumped in. *After all, if you had nothing to contribute, why would you be in the meeting*, he thought. "LaSalam, or well-funded terrorists like him, could rent bandwidth on a foreign satellite and use sat phones to carry their signals. Ever since the NSA's global snooping powers were revealed, our enemies have been setting up private networks beyond our reach."

"OK, so what do you all recommend?" Longford said.

"Are you all aware of the Cyber Warrior Project code named Magic Window?" Little asked with some hesitation.

Longford and Osborne looked at each other with quizzical expressions on their faces. Hager squirmed uncomfortably in his seat. Little continued, "I was not aware of it either until Sunborn filled me in with what he knew from his partner Frank Einstein's experimental project. The goal of the project was to see if we could actually upload specially equipped soldiers to the Internet to carry out both overt and covert operations for us. It is in a very early-stage. That's why Secretary Hager probably did not fill you all in. They wanted some tangible results or at least a proof-of-concept before they got too excited or let the cat out of the bag."

Longford was visibly annoyed. "I wouldn't call keeping the president informed, 'Letting the cat out of the bag.' I wonder how many other little 'experimental' projects like this are going on that neither George nor I are aware of? Ok, well that may be a serious discussion for another time. Rich, we interrupted you. Continue."

Little waited a few seconds for the tension to clear. The coffee was starting to burn a hole in his stomach. "Let me back up. We have two threats or maybe I should say, a two-pronged threat. One prong is physical—the crashing of our airplanes and the ensuing death and destruction. The other is digital—the compromising of our communications infrastructure and the ensuing panic, financial collapse, etc." He couldn't believe he was saying these things to the President of the United States, but he was committed now. So he might as well go all the way. "We need to look at both preventive and contingent actions for both scenarios. Chunk it down and attack each one."

There was silence as everyone mulled the enormity of what they faced.

Here goes, he thought. "We could ground all air traffic, like we did after 9/11, but they could just wait us out and launch their attack a week, two weeks or a month from now to the same disastrous effect. So it seems to me the number one priority is to find their US control center and shut that down."

Hager piped up. "If we do find it and shut it down, what keeps them from launching remotely or from a backup control center?"

Little was prepared for this one. "If, and that's a big 'if,' we find their primary control, we should find clues or trails to their other control centers.

"Second, NSA has some intercepts that indicate the Leopard is in the country now. Cut off the head and maybe the snake dies—at least for now." Little felt a bit like John Wayne or John Malkovich. He wasn't sure which.

"OK, that makes sense. Any leads on finding either the control center or LaSalam?" Osborne asked.

Little was ready for that one too. "We have a civilian who has been pretty helpful getting us this far and I think –"

"A civilian?" Hager said turning red in the face. "Seventeen goddam spy agencies and the most powerful military in the world and our national security hinges on a civilian?" There was actually mucus dripping from his nose, and his face was alternating from red to white like a beacon.

Longford interrupted. "Chuck, calm down and let Director Little finish. This is no time for bluster or puffed up egos." Nothing like a smart woman to put the brakes on male ego out-of-control.

Little took the cue. "This civilian who I mentioned earlier is named Sam Sunborn. He founded Digital3000 with Frank Einstein, one of the former top scientists in the Cyber Warrior Project."

"Former?" Hager asked, calmer now.

"Einstein was taken out in a hit on Digital3000's headquarters about six months ago. He has since been digitized and uploaded using Sunborn's proprietary software."

"How come we didn't hear anything about this before now?" Longford asked.

Now Osborne had to step in or his ass would be grass. "We decided, for national security reasons, to bury the story. We have been actively trying to track down the killers. We think it links back to Barin and their Cyber Warfare division, but now I'm thinking maybe the Leopard had a hand in this too."

"Let's focus here. Director Little, continue."

"Sunborn and his team are actually more advanced in digitizing people and personalities than we are. He has offered his help in deploying Einstein and their online group to track both the control center and LaSalam."

"I thought you said Einstein was dead."

"He is, but he is alive online and he has been trolling the web for clues."

"OK. That sounds like part of a plan," Longford said as if thinking out loud. "But I never like putting all my eggs in one basket—civilian, military or otherwise. What else have we got? Is there some way to shut down their satellite network and communications?"

Now Hager perked up like he might have something constructive to add. "We think we may be able to identify the satellites they are using. Defense Intelligence has every piece of orbiting hardware mapped."

Now Longford was starting to get either edgy or annoyed. "Great. So you can figure out where it is. How do we knock it out? That freakin' Star Wars program never worked. Our anti-satellite defense still can't hit the broadside of a barn, much less a small metal ball moving at 10,000 miles per hour."

Osborne interrupted. "That'd actually be 17,000 miles per hour Madame President."

"George, unless you have something to contribute here, then shut the hell up." Osborne turned beat red as Longford continued. "So, Chuck, what's the answer? How do we disable these suckers?"

Chuck cleared his throat, hoping the president would calm down a bit. He did not want to become road kill under her eighteen-wheeler. "We do have another, uh, highly classified weapon." He stopped, thinking this might be another unwanted surprise for the president.

Longford picked it up right away. "Chuck, I get that there's a lot of operations or crap that I am not aware of. I'm new here. We'll cure the boss-doesn't-know-shit problem later. Right now we need anything and everything you've got. So lay it out."

Chuck felt like he'd just been given a green light. "OK, here goes. You know that NASA built five space shuttles—right? Well actually, they built six. The sixth one is in a protected facility in Arizona with a crew on call 24x7."

"What?" Longford said, more amazed than annoyed.

Chuck continued. "You don't think we'd actually mothball our only successful way to get into space and rely on the Russians? Sorry, that was a rhetorical question. What most people don't know is that the Space Shuttle program, while being great for science, was really built as our primary space weapon and defense. The sixth shuttle, named *Voyager* is sitting ready-to-go. It is equipped with our latest missile technology. We could be up in the air by tonight and shoot those fuckers down within twenty-four hours."

Little had been taking this all in. "I'm not sure we have the time, but if we do, shooting them down may not be the answer. Would it be possible to have your guys get out there and bug the birds? Then wire them for shutdown before they pull the trigger?"

"Maybe. I'm not sure. Madame President, I'd recommend you authorize us to launch *Voyager* immediately. Then in the hours it takes to get it into position, we can plan either an attack or a manual override," Hager added with some urgency.

"Do it!" Longford said. "But give Mr. Little and his civilian friends whatever they need to launch a cyber defense. Hopefully either Plan A or Plan B will work. They better work."

"Will do, Madame President." The meeting was over.

CHAPTER 28

THE SAME RIVER TWICE

LaSalam and his limo arrived at the Gorge. “Let’s sit here awhile. I need to think. Turn off the engine.”

He gazed out over the rushing water, stepped out of the car and walked to the river’s edge. *I can see why he likes it here. Very calming*, he thought to himself. He could either wait here for Sunborn to show up or pursue him at his known locations. “I’ll just wait,” he said to himself.

The sky was deep blue with cotton-ball clouds floating by. He could feel a cool breeze coming off the water graze his cheeks. It carried a not unpleasant aroma of wet soil and pine. “How did Allah make life so complicated?” he wondered. “Haven’t I stepped in this river before?” Then he remembered the ancient aphorism. “You never step in the same river twice.”

They had rivers where he came from, but they were bigger and brown with human waste and industrial chemicals. This river was so clear, he could see fish swimming at the bottom. *Is it our destiny to pollute and destroy or is there a place and a time when men are good and kindness reigns*, he wondered. But these were the thoughts of a soft man, and he had to harden himself for the tasks ahead. Nobody and no thing could stand in the way of his plan and his mission. Nobody.

What would he do when he met Sunborn? Just shoot him and be on his way? Interrogate him? Or invite him to tea? He smiled at the absurdity of the situation. Why didn’t he just hire a good assassin and be done with it. No, he had to do it himself. But almost more important, he had to meet this man. He had to admit he was intrigued by a civilian that could seemingly follow his moves. Who used the technology like a chessboard and attacked even while retreating. Maybe in another life, they would be friends. Who was he kidding? He had no friends. Maybe fellow soldiers—that was a possibility.

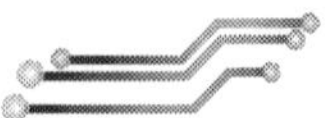

CHAPTER 29

COUNTDOWN

It was quite an imposing presence. The Atlas rocket was thirty-two meters tall and the stealth shuttle was mounted on its side. Unlike the other shuttles, *Voyager* was painted a dark blue on top and a cloudy off-white on the bottom. Like the drones or even a trout, the coloring was meant to hide its presence from view both below and above by blending in with the sky above and the earth below.

Steam and gas were already pouring out the thrusters at Atlas's bottom. Neil Armstrong III and his crew were buckled in, awaiting lift-off. Little did Armstrong know that his mission might be more important to the future of the world than his famous grandfather's walk on the Moon.

CAPCOM: Voyager, this is Mission Control. Radio check, over.

Commander: Roger, out.

PAO # 2: Radio communications between Launch Control, Mission Control, and the Orbiter have been checked at T - 5 minutes to liftoff.

CAPCOM: Voyager, this is Launch Control. Ready abort advisory check.

Lab # 1: Roger, check is satisfactory, out.

PAO # 1: Launch Control has lighted the abort light on the front instrument panel.

PAO # 1: The ground crew has closed and secured the hatch. Medical Officer Control, this is Voyager. We show normal cabin pressure, over.

CAPCOM: Roger, out.

PAO # 2: Both cabin vent switches have been closed. We are now at T - 4 minutes to liftoff.

Lab # 1: Control, this is Voyager. Boiler control switch ON. Nitrogen supply switch ON, over.

CAPCOM: Roger, out.

PAO # 2: The Commander has confirmed boiler control switches 1, 2, and 3 are now ON; nitrogen supply switches 1, 2, and 3 are now ON.

Pilot: Control, this is Voyager. General purpose computer, backup flight system complete.

CAPCOM: Roger, out.

PAO # 1: The main flight software and its backup have been loaded at T - 3 minutes to liftoff.

CAPCOM: Voyager, this is Control. Ground crew is secure, over.

Commander: Roger, out.

PAO # 1: Control has confirmed that the cabin pressure has decreased.

Commander: Control, this is Voyager. Commander's voice check, over.

CAPCOM: Roger, out.

Lab # 1: Control, this is the pilot; voice check, over.

PAO # 2: The commander and pilot have conducted voice checks with Mission Control Center. The vent valves have been closed. The pilot will now load flight plan OPS-1 into the computer. We are now at T - 2 minutes to liftoff.

Pilot: Control, this is Voyager. Flight plan is loaded into the computer, over.

CAPCOM: Roger, out.

PAO # 2: Mission Control has cycled the ABORT light - bright, dim, then off, three times.

Meteorologist: M.E.1, do you copy? What is your status?

M.E. 1: We are orbiting AZ Site1 at 54,000 feet, over.

Commander: M. E. 1, this is Voyager. What are the current weather conditions over AZ Site 1? Over.

M. E. 1: Voyager, this is M. E. 1. Temperature is 65 degrees Fahrenheit, 18 degrees Celsius. Humidity is at 43 percent. Winds are out of the north, northeast at 10 mph, gusts to 15 mph. Barometric pressure stands at 30.62 inches, and the weather is partly cloudy, over.

Pilot: M. E. 1, this is Voyager. We copy, out.

PAO # 1: Weather conditions are nominal at T - 1 minute to liftoff.

Medical Officer: Control, this is Voyager. Event timer started.

CAPCOM: Roger, Voyager. Out.

Pilot: Control, this is Voyager. Prestart complete. Powering up APU's, over.

CAPCOM: APU's look good, out.

CAPCOM: Voyager, this is Control. Main engine gimbal complete,

CAPCOM: Medical Officer, report on the condition of the crew, over. Medical Officer Control, this is Voyager. The crew is in excellent condition and is eager to go!

CAPCOM: Roger, Voyager. Out.

CAPCOM: Voyager, this is Control. H-two tank pressurization OK. You are go for launch, over.

Lab # 2: Roger, go for launch, over.

PAO # 2: The external tank hydrogen vents have been closed, and liquid-hydrogen tank pressure is building up for flight at T - 30 seconds to liftoff.

CAPCOM: Voyager, this is Control. APU start is go. You are on your on-board computer, over.

Lab # 1: Roger, out.

Flight Director: 15, 14, 13, 12, 11, 10, 9, 8, 7, 6, 5, 4 . . .

PAO # 2: The solid rocket boosters have ignited, and we have LIFT OFF!! The Voyager has cleared the tower.

CAPCOM: The tower has been cleared. All engines look good. Beginning roll maneuver.

PAO # 1: 120 degree roll into "heads down" position starts. We are now at T + 1 minute after launch.

CAPCOM: Roll maneuver complete, Voyager, you're looking good.

Pilot: Control, this is Voyager. Main engines at 75%, over.

CAPCOM: Roger, out.

PAO # 2: The Voyager has reached Mach 1 (the speed of sound), and the space shuttle main engines have been throttled down from 100% to 75%. We are now at T + 2 minutes after launch.

Commander: Control, this is Voyager. Max Q, over.

CAPCOM: Roger, Voyager. Out.

PAO # 1: Maximum dynamic pressure has been reached, and the space shuttle main engines have been throttled back up to 100%.

Pilot: Control, this is Voyager. We have SRB burnout; ready for SRB sep, over.

CAPCOM: Roger, out.

PAO # 2: The computer has reported that the solid rocket boosters have burned out at T + 4 minutes.

Commander: Control, this is Voyager. We have SRB sep, over.

CAPCOM: Roger, we can see that, Voyager. Out.

PAO # 1: The solid rocket boosters have separated from the Orbiter at T + 6 minutes.

CAPCOM: Voyager, you are negative return. Do you copy?

Lab # 1: Roger, Mission Control. Negative return, out.

PAO # 2: Mission Control has reported that a return-to-launch-site abort is no longer possible at T + 9 minutes.

PAO # 1: The commander has reported that the Voyager can reach orbit even if two main engines fail.

CAPCOM: Voyager, this is Control. Main engine throttle down, over.

Pilot: Roger, out.

PAO # 2: Mission Control has instructed the pilot to throttle down to keep acceleration less than 3 g's.

CAPCOM: Voyager, this is Control. Go for main engine cut-off over.

Commander: Roger, Main engine cut-off on schedule, out.

PAO # 1: The three main engines have shut down.

Pilot: Control, this is Voyager. We have OMS cut-off, over.

PAO # 2: The orbital maneuvering system burn has stopped.

CAPCOM: Voyager, this is Control. Coming up on OMS-two, over.

Lab # 1: Roger, OMS-two.

PAO # 2: The orbital maneuvering system burn number two has been initiated. We are now at T + 18 minutes after launch.

Pilot: OMS-two cut-off. We have achieved orbit, over.

CAPCOM: Roger, Voyager, out.

PAO # 1: The pilot will now enter OPS106 on the keyboard to change the computer program. We are now at T + 22 minutes.

CAPCOM: Voyager, begin on-orbit operations.

Commander: Roger, Control. Out.

Voyager now moved out of visual range from the ground. Armstrong had his orders. Intercept Orbiter X126 somewhere over the Indian Ocean.

CHAPTER 30

WHO'S THERE

I'm not sure there was anything more I could do until Bart and Killer finished their programming and until I heard back from Little. The target was moving and our tactical plan was unclear, but other than that we were in great shape. Not. I had a half hour and thought I'd take a mental break. So I hopped in my Jeep and headed down to the Gorge. It was a beautiful sunny morning and a bit cooler than usual for late June. The coolness reminded me of a fond memory. I remembered the occasional fishing Evan and I did on warmer winter days, dropping our flies into holes in the ice. The fish would be semi-comatose from the cold but still moving slowly and eating if the food came to them. It was so exciting the one time I hooked a brown trout in February. I couldn't believe it.

Today there would be no fishing, but a short walk along the trail beside the river would do me good. I needed to clear my head and calm down. My shoulder still ached from the bullet wound so I hobbled a bit on the trail. I wondered what Monica was doing at home. I should call, but I didn't want my voice to betray the fear I felt. She could read me so well. But what if it was our last call? *I'll call. I will*, I thought at the time.

I had pulled the Jeep into a narrow clearing beside the trail. Curiously, there was a black SUV limo about 100 yards away. Seeing a limo in the Gorge was like seeing a shark in the river. It just didn't happen. Something didn't feel right, so I decided to get back in my car and observe for a bit. You learned from a lifetime of fishing to sit very still and observe. A good fisherman can see disturbances in the water that are beautiful trout that the average person can't see. I recalled taking a friend to fish, who had not been before. I kept pointing at a trout undulating on the bottom of a deep pool. "Look! Look there—do you see it?" For the life of him, he could not see it.

There was a man with a swarthy complexion standing by the bank. He was staring at the sky and occasionally, gently dragging his shoe through the stones along the bank. His shoe was a fine leather. Another thing out of place. Then I saw it. He pulled a 9 mm gun out of his pocket, chambered a round and put it back in a holster hidden behind his jacket.

Who was this? Why was he here? I opened my glove compartment and removed the Beretta Al had given me. Where was freakin' Al when you need her? I could have just driven away. I had the gun. I called Al. She wouldn't have had to run it up the chain of command to get off her butt and do something.

"Al, it's me."

"Where have you been? I've been trying to reach you."

"Listen, I'm at the Gorge and there's a Middle Eastern looking guy here with a gun."

"What? Where are you in the Gorge?"

"I came in the south end. I'm at the first turn off. He's about seventy or eighty yards up from me. He just showed his gun."

"Has he seen you?"

"I don't think so and I've got the gun you gave me."

"I'm on my way—maybe ten minutes out. Stay where you are. Don't confront him. If he comes your way, duck down out of site. Last thing you want to do is get in a gunfight, unless you have absolutely no choice."

"Got it, but this is scary shit."

She clicked off.

CHAPTER 31

INTERCEPT

Commander: We have visual on Object X.

Flight CAPCOM: Standby . . . Space Shuttle Voyager, you are clear for intercept.

Commander: Roger that, we are coming in.

Commander: Easy as it goes. Reducing speed by firing forward thrusters.

Just then, a small piece of space debris rams into the shuttle.

Commander: Did you see that? I think we've been hit by something. Nav, please report!

Flight CAPCOM: I saw what happened, Voyager. A small object, about two feet square, hit our forward compartment. It just came out of nowhere. It looked like an antenna mount. I don't see any damage.

Shuttle Commander: But it looks like the collision has nudged us out of position for the intercept.

Flight CAPCOM: Yes, our sensors confirm that. You are about six inches off center. I suggest you abort the dock. If you are not accurate to within one centimeter, you will damage the Object. Directive is to secure but not destroy.

Commander: Don't worry, I have it. Firing left thruster—correcting trajectory.

Commander: Steady . . . steady . . . I have it! Canadarm will retrieve object.

CAPCOM: Outstanding, Voyager. Open Bay Doors and secure Object.

Commander: Bay Doors open. Canadarm moving Object into bay.

CAPCOM: Secure Object. Close bay doors.

Commander: Object secured. Closing bay doors.

CAPCOM: Send EVA team to affix remote control device to Object.

Commander: Roger that. Team deploying.

CAPCOM: After remote is in place, we'll need to test communications before release back to orbit.

Commander: Roger that. Standing by.

CHAPTER 32

ACCIDENTAL TOURIST

The Leopard's reverie ended as his focus came back to the task at hand. He turned to the left and saw a Jeep parked downstream. Could it be? He knew his target owned a Jeep. His killer instincts kicked in. This was no friend, no fellow soldier. This was the enemy.

He got back in the car on the passenger side. "Get out," he said to the driver.

"This is my car. You have no right to tell me –"

LaSalam pulled his gun and tapped one off into the driver's forehead. "I don't have time for this." He got out, came around, opened the driver's door and dragged the body down to the riverbank. He ran back and jumped in the driver's seat and punched the gas pedal. The wheels spun, kicking up gravel, and the car lurched down the road toward Sunborn.

Sunborn saw all this happening like he was watching a movie. He ducked down in his seat. As the Leopard raced toward him, another car was approaching, lights flashing from the other direction. This was a one lane road. More of a trail really, with three cars and a madman all converging.

LaSalam approached the Jeep, opened his passenger side window and fired off six rounds into the Jeep as he passed. Al's Crown Vic was speeding head-on toward the Leopard in a deadly game of chicken. Al, like a woman who has handled many dangerous situations, started to see everything in slow motion despite the fact that she had only a split-second to act. A head-on collision might stop the madman but could be deadly for both of them. A side-swipe. That was it. Al veered left taking the uphill side of the trail with two wheels about three feet up the bank putting the car at a thirty degree angle to the road. Clearly his adversary was making his move. LaSalam veered to his left toward the river but still half on the road. As the cars collided, both drivers turned their wheels toward the other. The screech of metal and broken glass sounded like an explosion followed by sounds of skids and bangs.

Al had managed to push LaSalam temporarily off the road but disabled her own vehicle. She was stalled in the middle of the road. The Leopard hit the gas and fishtailed back onto the road. With his rear fender dangling and a flat tire, he accelerated over the rise and out of site.

Al slowly emerged from the Crown Vic. *Not the best car for a street fight*, she thought as steam poured out from beneath the hood. She could smell the burnt antifreeze and gasoline pooling beneath the car. She trotted down the road to Sunborn's car. There lying across the seat was Sunborn, unconscious and bleeding through the front of his shirt. Blood stained his whole torso and his body was weirdly contorted around the stick shift. Al reached down, through the broken glass, to feel Sam's neck for a pulse.

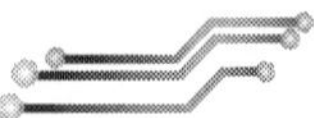

CHAPTER 33

SO NOW WHAT?

LaSalam limped his battered vehicle into a Citgo station just beyond the Gorge. He saw a Land Rover idling beside the pumps. A woman was in the driver's seat, bending over the seat to hand a bottle to her baby nestled in the rear car seat. He pushed open the creaking damaged door of his limo and walked quickly to the passenger side of the Land Rover. He smiled a friendly smile and knocked on the passenger window. The woman lowered the window and the Leopard put the gun right up against her temple, "Get out!" She seemed to freeze like a deer in the headlights. "Do it now!" He pulled the door open, grabbed her shoulder and pulled her roughly out of the seat, throwing her to the ground.

"My baby!" she shouted.

LaSalam spotted the child seat in the back, quickly opened the rear door, unbuckled the child carrier and threw it like a bowling ball toward the woman. The seat rolled and bounced along the pavement with the baby still strapped in. It was strangely silent and then the baby began to cry. As the mother crawled over to the child, the gray-haired gas station manager emerged from the garage and shouted, "Hey!"

The Leopard swiveled and shot him twice in the chest. He fell backward knocking over a rack full of Goodyears that then rolled in all directions. LaSalam jumped into the car, put it in gear and sped away kicking up dust and gravel behind. "What a mess," he thought out loud.

CHAPTER 34
AWAKENING

I woke up staring blankly at the white ceiling. Then I heard the beeps and turned my head to see tubes and monitors hooked to me. My ribs felt like I'd been hit by a truck and the bandages seemed an inch thick. It was from the impact, not a bullet this time. I felt like a heavy weight was on my chest holding me down to the bed. Was that physical or mental? I was anxious that depression was again waiting in the wings to seize the opportunity of my weakened state and overcome me. But then I looked over and saw Al. The weight seemed to lift.

"Glad to see you're still with us," Al said. She sat in the recliner chair next to my bed.

"What happened?" I said, still trying to focus.

"Looks like one of your Barinian buddies tracked you down. You should feel lucky you're not one of the two murder victims we found or the carjacked mother." She smirked.

"Al, we have a real crisis on our hands. I've got to get out of here."

"Calm down, Buddy. I spoke to Little and he's got the Feds on it. There's not much you can do."

"The Feds? What do you mean—FBI?"

"No I mean Army, Air Force, DHS—the whole Freakin' US government is on it."

"But I'm not sure they have the cyber-angle covered. The big weapons are online."

"They have their best—Cyber Command is on it too."

"Just get me out of here." I pulled the tubes out and started to swing my legs over and onto the floor. As I stood, I could feel the room spin and I fell sideways back on the bed. Slowly I pushed back up.

"Hold on, man. You're in no shape to go anywhere."

"Bullshit, help me up." Al grabbed my arm and I stood trying to steady myself. "I'm OK. I'm getting dressed and then you're going to drive me to the office."

"Since when did you become my boss?" Al smiled.

"We don't have much time. If we don't act fast, you won't have a boss or a friend. Let's go."

As I was slowly, painfully, pulling up my pants, there was a soft knock at my hospital room door. In walked Nancy Lu. "I heard you got shot. I'm glad to see you are OK."

"There are fifty reporters outside. How did you get in this time?" I said.

"I just put on this white coat and everybody assumed I worked here. The stethoscope is a nice touch too, don't you think?"

Al helped sling a shirt over my bandaged shoulder. "Very resourceful. That skill should come in handy someday. But not today. We're in a hurry now."

I saw Al look at Lu and smile. Lu smiled back and it sure looked like a flirtation. Lu interjected, "There seems to be a pattern and a story here. I'd like to help and maybe get ahead of this."

I walked slowly, a bit unsteadily, toward the door. "There's a pattern for sure. Some bad guy is out to get us. Now we have to leave."

"I know there's more to the story." Lu's eyes met Al's again. Something electric was going on.

"You can ride with us. We'll share what we can."

"Great. I'll act like your doctor as I walk out with you."

Al held me under my good arm to steady me as we walked down the hall. Lu trailed behind. "Al, I didn't realize you played for the other team," I whispered, smiling.

"There's a lot you don't know."

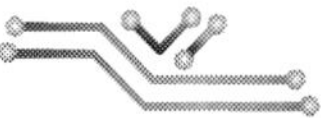

CHAPTER 35
BLOWN UP

Flight CAPCOM: Object X is successfully transmitting in tandem. Prepare to release.

Commander: Roger that, Object X is prepared.

Commander: Release object X on my count. 3 . . . 2 . . . 1 . . .

Commander: Object X is released. Clear of bay doors.

Flight CAPCOM: Voyager, we have determined that there is a second object, Object Y that needs intercept and "repair." Sending location and instructions.

Shuttle Commander: Instructions received. Initiating thruster burn. Estimated intercept in 32 minutes.

Flight CAPCOM: Roger that. Tracking intercept now in 31:21.

Commander: Approaching Object Y.

Commander: Opening Bay Doors. Intercept in 5 . . . 4 . . . 3 . . . 2 . . . 1 . . . Canadarm has Object Y and moving into Bay.

CAPCOM: Secure Object. Close bay doors.

Commander: Object secured. Closing bay doors.

CAPCOM: Send EVA team to affix remote control device to Object.

Commander: Roger that. Team deployed.

CAPCOM: After remote is in place, we'll need to test communications before release back to orbit.

Commander: Roger that. Standing by. We are detecting some different infrared signals emanating from Object.

CAPCOM: Switch on Comlink to infrared meter so we can analyze.

Commander: Roger that. Comlink on.

CAPCOM: Voyager, please standby. Commander, we believe Object Y may contain some unstable, hazardous or possibly explosive material. Eject Object immediately!

Commander: Roger that. Opening Bay Doors. Detecting a spike in infrared from –

CAPCOM: Voyager, please report . . . Do you read?

Object Y exploded igniting the oxygen and fuel tanks aboard *Voyager* resulting in a second, larger explosion and fireball fueled by the oxygen and propellant. It shredded *Voyager* into 100 thousand pieces traveling in all directions. Then silence. *Voyager* and its crew were gone.

CHAPTER 36

INNOCENCE

LaSalam sat alone in his hotel room. His hands shook slightly as the adrenaline drained from his body. *Weak*, he thought. But he had made plans to relax with something he regularly enjoyed.

He heard a quiet knock at the door and rose to his feet. He only had his pants, strapped T-shirt and suspenders on. As he approached the door he could feel the cold of the floor tile against his bare feet.

He opened the door and saw a small man, maybe five foot two, balding, with greasy dark hair and a dark complexion. Indian, Arab? It was hard to tell. "I have brought your package as Hamid requested," the man said.

"It has never been unwrapped, correct?" the Leopard said.

The man whispered with a sly smile, "It is quite brand new and unused."

"Very good. Please bring it in."

The man walked into the room holding the hand of a young girl. She was very young, white skin and blonde hair. She clutched a small beige teddy bear and averted her blue eyes. "This is Alex," the man said to the girl. "He wants to tell you stories and play for a little while. When you're done, I have a nice piece of chocolate cake for you."

She smiled shyly, but said nothing. "Come, come in," the Leopard said with a warm smile. The small man silently left the room and closed the door behind him. LaSalam took the girl's hand and led her over to the loveseat on the far side of the room.

"Would you like to play a game?" he said and the girl slowly nodded. "What's your name?"

"Nicky," she said in a soft sweet voice.

"Nicky, I'd like you to meet a friend of mine. I think you'll like him." He opened his zipper slowly and drew out his friend. The Leopard was in heaven now with his sweet little pleasure. This went on for several minutes. The three of them talking and playing. The Leopard took full advantage of Nicky's innocence to indulge his pleasure. Then it was over. The Leopard was satisfied and zipped his friend back into his pants.

"Night, night," Nicky said, patting the lump in LaSalam's pants. The Leopard leaned back against the sofa. He felt much better now.

Just then, they heard the now familiar quiet knock at the door. "I think your friend is here. He'll take you home now. Thanks for coming and making my friend so happy."

Nicky reverted to her shy child-like posture and looked down at the floor. LaSalam opened the door and the little man took her hand and walked her out into the hallway.

The Leopard could hear Nicky as she walked down the hall. "Can I have that cake now?"

CHAPTER 37

50/50

"We lost *Voyager*," Hager said.

"What the hell are you telling me? What do you mean we lost it?" Longford barked.

"We intercepted and hacked the first satellite, but when *Voyager* attempted to do the same to the second satellite, it was booby-trapped. It blew up, taking *Voyager* with it."

"Casualties?"

"One hundred percent"

"Shit. So now what?"

"I think we have communications under control, but we can't rule out the possibility of other satellites or channels."

"So maybe we are at square one?"

"No, I think we can use the satellite we hacked to either block or thwart their communications, but there are no guarantees. So we need Little and his friends to come through as well."

"Where does that stand?"

"We had a setback when Little's key guy, Sunborn, was shot this afternoon."

"What? This is unbelievable."

"The good news is that he survived. He and Little are back on the trail. They just lost a little time."

"From what I understand, time is something we have very little of. How much time do we really have left?"

"Somewhere between three and four hours."

"So what's your estimate on whether we can stop this attack?"

"I'd say 50/50 is optimistic."

"Time for a command decision. If we can't solve this problem in the next two hours, ground all air traffic. That gives all planes an hour to get to the nearest airport and land."

"I'm not sure we can do that. It takes hours just to get the message out and for air traffic control to respond."

"I don't give a shit! We can't let tens of thousand of air travelers go down. So give the command in one hour instead of two. Meet back here in the Sit Room with the chiefs, cabinet and all top intelligence in thirty. We need to monitor the situation, and I want all people with fingers on the buttons ready to respond."

CHAPTER 38
TRACER

I felt weak but I could walk. My ribs throbbed and ached like a son-of-a-bitch. My knee and shoulder were still sore from my earlier encounters. We dropped Lu off downtown, and Al helped me get to the lab. Bart ran up to me and before I could react, he gave me a hug.

"Ouch!" I screamed as my shoulder streaked with pain.

Bart backed away. "Sorry. I'm just glad you're back."

"Me too, I think." I smiled to let Bart know I was OK. "But we need to get to work. Is Frank online?"

"Yes, he's waiting for you." Bart sat and rolled his chair up to a workstation. Al and I followed.

"Welcome back! I thought you almost joined me here," Frank said from the monitor in front of Bart.

"Not yet, my friend. How are you?"

"I'm great. It's like I can fly here. I just have to outsmart all the bots that our friends have going after me. But I've developed some cloaking techniques that go way beyond anonymous browsing."

"Well, between you and Bart, we are definitely blazing new ground. Maybe some new products for our company, if we can survive the attack. Speaking of which, we have no time to waste. Little tells me we have less than an hour to shut the bad guys down or the crap hits the fan, and I don't want to be the fan."

"I hear you," Frank said. "As far as I can tell, they are silent. We have one of their satellites tapped and the other exploded."

"Can we be sure there aren't any others?"

"No, but I have some black box alarms set that should give us the heads up if they start the attack. My real concern is that this may be set on some kind of timer that will automatically trigger it."

"Can you do a search for that kind of device?"

"It's not a device. It could be merely a few lines of code hidden on one of the 400 million servers out there. Just ticking down."

"Can you search for that?"

"Bart and I created some scripts that are out there searching. So far, we've had no luck."

"OK, let's look at this a different way. What do we know about this terrorist leader that could give us a clue? Do we have anything on him personally?"

"When we put all our info together, we know our guy is an Barinian named LaSalam. There is some intel that he may be in this country. Crazy idea, but he may be the guy who shot you in the Gorge."

"Whoa. Why would he be there? Why me?"

"You, or should I say 'we,' are a threat. I mean you didn't end up here by accident. Maybe he decided to take care of you personally after his first attempts failed."

"That actually makes sense to me," Al said.

"OK, so maybe that's true. Still, what else do we know about this guy?"

"I know he likes expensive clothes. I think he was in New York yesterday. He also likes young girls."

"Wait, that last one. Tell me more about that."

"We know that wherever he goes, he has agents that fix him up with innocent young girls. We don't know what he does with them, but I can guess."

"Sick. So maybe if we can get to one of these agents, like in the US, maybe one who hooked him up between yesterday and today. Then maybe that's a lead."

"Sam, if this doesn't pan out, you might have a second career as a detective. We don't have a lot of time, but we have a database of these kinds of bad actors," Al said. "But can we narrow the search?"

"We know that discretion would be important for him, so the agent is probably Barinian—matter of trust. We also know he's either in New York or here. That should narrow it down quite a bit."

"OK, I'll get on it," Al said.

"Al, do you have access to a profiler? Maybe with some more behavioral insight, we can better track and nail this guy."

"Yes. If not us, we can pull in a profiler from the FBI. I'll get on that one too."

CHAPTER 39

THE WORLD UPSIDE DOWN

When the FBI and DHS wants to move fast, it can. Twenty minutes after Al said she would get on it, a dozen FBI agents, in full riot gear, broke down the doors at a small apartment in San Jose.

"Clear," barked the first agent as he slid along the living room wall, MP5 extended.

"Clear." The kitchen.

"Wait." There was a rustling in the bedroom. Two agents, Smith and Wesson (really), stood at opposite sides of the room pointing their weapons at a closet between them. "Come out with your hands behind your head."

Nothing. The agent on the right slid along with his back against the wall adjacent to the closet. He extended his right arm and swiftly pulled back the sliding closet door. Both agents now stood, weapons pointed, in front of the open closet door. There, cowering on the floor, was a small, balding middle aged man with his hands extended as if to stop the onslaught. The agent on the right grabbed the small man under his left arm and yanked him up and out of the closet.

"Why are you here? I thought I was being robbed," the man murmured. He had already wet his pants and shook like he had a vibrator up his spine.

A third agent stepped forward and removed his black riot helmet. It was Rich Little. "You have exactly sixty seconds to tell us where you delivered the girl to LaSalam and how he contacted you. Speak now!"

"I . . . I don't know anyone by that name."

Little nodded to the two FBI agents. In one quick motion, each agent grabbed one of the man's ankles and flipped him upside down hanging him in mid-air. Coins from the man's pockets clattered onto the floor. Then Little took his weapon and jammed the point of the barrel into the man's groin. "Let me be clear. You now have forty-five seconds before I blow your nuts off and there may be collateral damage."

"I . . . I . . . "

"Let me help you out. You may not know the man's name, but at about 10:00 this morning, you delivered a child for an 'encounter' with a Middle Eastern man somewhere nearby. Where was it? How did he contact you and how did you get paid?"

The man, still upside down, told him everything he knew—the hotel, the contact and the payment. Little nodded again to the two agents. They let go of the man's ankles simultaneously. The man landed on the wood floor head first. He crumpled and rolled over moaning.

Little pulled out his phone and barked instructions.

CHAPTER 40

STATE OF MIND

"Frank, how are you?" I asked with sincere interest. I adjusted my shoulder bandage and sling into a non-wincing position. Since I was still at the lab and had to wait for the FBI to act, I thought it would be good to check up on my good friend. I also wanted to learn more about what digital life was like.

"I'm good, I think."

"You think?"

"I can think. That's good, right?" He smiled mischievously. I missed Frank—the *real* Frank, but this Frank was pretty close.

"That is good. How's your state of mind? This is, after all, a pretty traumatic adjustment," I probed a little farther.

"Well, the interesting thing is that I occasionally feel bouts of anxiety or panic. I'm glad I can still 'feel' as well, but I obviously can't take drugs. I have no physical body to absorb them. So rather than submitting to those feelings and being overwhelmed by them, I look at it as a solvable problem."

"Really? You're amazing. If you figure it out, maybe you can help me with my occasional bouts of depression. Any progress on solving it?"

"Well, yes. I've written a script that in a way handles it. If I feel anxiety coming on, I invoke the script and it turns the feelings off. It's like magic. I feel fine. I call it 'Xanzac.' Get it?"

"Yeah, I get it, and you don't even need FDA approval for this *script*."

"Your observation opens a whole other world of questions. If we ever get past this crisis and back to digitizing more lives, we'll probably need to have labs, trials and an FDA to manage the safety of these scripts."

"Huh, I don't get it. What can go wrong?"

"Just like real drugs, Xanzac has side effects. If not handled carefully, it could be fatal. The first time I used it, it shut me off. Fortunately, I had set up a timed recovery procedure ahead of time to restore me from backup or you'd have lost me twice. You want a script like this to turn off certain activities and not others. I had to do 22,365 trials and tweaks to get it right. Fortunately, at digital speed on our Octa-Core Nano processors, it only took me a few hours to do the whole thing. I had to restore myself many times. One time I even felt like I was tripping on LSD. It's pretty tricky being both the scientist and the subject at the same time. I wouldn't recommend it going forward, but I don't have any alternatives at the moment. I needed to do this or I couldn't count on functioning. If I learned anything here, depression can be fatal and at a much faster rate than in the physical world."

"That's both scary and fascinating at the same time. The 'unintended consequences' of our new technology continue to amaze, delight and terrify me. Oh well, I guess your scripts won't help me with my sporadic mental issues."

"You'd be surprised, but that's a discussion for another time. I think it's only the beginning, my son. The question is whether we can anticipate, solve or damage control all the ripple effects of doing this. I'm just not sure whether a digital Black Plague will end it all or that we'll discover new universes and forms of life or both," Frank mused.

"Well said, but right now, if we don't stop the Leopard's attack, we won't even get that far. Let's get back to work. Have you closed the loop as to how they'll trigger the attack and if we have really shut down their communications?"

CHAPTER 41
CLEAR

The address the pimp had given them was behind an old brick warehouse on 7th Street. SWAT and twenty-five FBI agents in full gear moved up the two alleys and the back lot. They surrounded the building and took up their positions. Four agents moved in a crouch to the front entrance—an old iron gate. Two agents pressed their bodies flat against the wall on each side of the door awaiting orders.

One of the agents, Jim Pickins, held a portable battering ram. "I don't think this butt is going to do that door."

A second agent, Saul Stein, on the side near the door latch said, "I'll put some putty in the lock and around the latch." He removed some C4 from his vest and molded it with his left hand into the keyhole and around the latch.

Pickins: "Did anyone actually try the door in case it's unlocked."

Stein: "Funny. You think we're in a movie like *Lethal Weapon 2*?"

Pickins: "Just try the handle. Don't be a jerk."

Stein was already plugging in the det cord to the explosive putty and stretching out a length of wire. All the agents had MP5s, safeties off, in their left arms, butts wedged into their armpits, fingers on triggers. While Stein fiddled with the wires, Pickins reached across the door with his free, right hand and gently pulled on the iron handle of the door. It seemed locked or maybe just stuck. Pickins pulled harder and the door creaked and slowly opened a few inches. The C4 fell to the ground.

Stein: "Damn. I really wanted to blow the door." He picked up his putty and stuffed it back into his vest.

Pickins cocked his head and whispered into his shoulder mic to Pete Wilson in Command, "We've got access. Front door is open. All entrances and exits secure. Await your GO."

Minutes seemed to tick by. SWAT was just settling into position on a four-story stone building across the street, pointing their .50 caliber sniper rifles at the three mesh-covered windows of the target warehouse. They'd normally use M14s or Remington 700Ps, but this was considered an "intense" situation. Hence the 50 cals.

Wilson and his crew were in a white, windowless Ford Econoline two blocks away. He and three techs sat in front of monitors, fed by sixteen cameras on the surrounding buildings and atop two three foot mini-drones hovering a few yards from the roofline of the warehouse. Wilson knew this could be the biggest takedown of his career, and he wasn't leaving anything to chance. He'd gotten a call from Director Tibbet himself, filling him in on the target and emphasizing the critical nature of the mission. "The future of our country is literally riding on this." *No pressure*, he thought.

Wilson squeezed the button on the side of his mic, almost slipping from the sweat on his hand. "On my 3 count, 3 . . . 2 . . . " Before he could get to "1," Pickins, Stein and the rest of the team burst through the front and rear doors, sweeping weapons with mounted flashlights and laser sights back and forth through the open entry space. There was a small waiting area and a wooden door just to the left of a sliding glass window that a receptionist might use.

Pickins: "Clear." He grabbed the wooden door's brass handle and swung it back. He and Stein entered in a crouch and split right and left. They were in a large open area. It was dark, except for the daylight fighting its way through the second story windows. Their eyes adjusted and Pickins could see the warehouse appeared to be empty. He looked up toward the ceiling and saw rusted steel beams and water dripping from the two-story ceiling. The only sound was the drips hitting puddles on the floor. It smelled dank, like wet books had been stored there.

The warehouse wasn't completely empty. There were some boxes, a few barrels and some partitions haphazardly arranged on the far side of the warehouse. Just then Pickins heard automatic gunfire. Stein and three other agents fell to the floor moaning. Hopefully their vests protected them. Unless they were armor piercing rounds or they got hit in the head, they could recover.

Pickins: "Shit. Down, down, down . . . we have shots fired." Then all chaos broke loose. Pickins rolled and came to a crouch. He and the four other agents who had come through the back door returned fire shredding the boxes and partitions on the other side of the warehouse. Suddenly, all the glass from the windows shattered inward as SWAT sprayed for targets. Pickins instinctively covered his face. Then a thought occurred to him, "Don't shoot the barr . . . " he was going to say 'barrels' when the four agents in the rear unleashed another volley hitting the blue barrels near the now shredded partitions. The explosion was louder than anything Pickins had ever experienced. More than mortar fire, more than flash bangs. He was thrown hard against the wall. The roof was literally blown off and shards of wood and asphalt rained on the interior.

The fireball from the barrels billowed out, seeming to crowd out all the smoke and darkness. The flames stopped inches short of Pickins, but the intense heat and strong odor of sulfur washed over him. He was dazed and deaf. All he could hear was an intense ringing in his ears. His nostrils filled with acrid smoke and he could not see. All he could feel was a coolness coming from his right and he rolled onto his stomach and crawled toward it. With his nose two inches from the floor he could at least breath. It felt like 200 degrees. The vest had protected his torso, but his arms were badly burned. His black sleeves hung in tatters still smoking.

He kept crawling toward the cooler air. It must be an exit. Then two men rushed in, grabbed him under each arm and dragged him out onto the street. They put him down gently. While one man held Pickins' head and neck, they slowly rolled him onto his back. "Help is on the way. What the fuck happened in there?" Wilson said.

Pickins' ears were still ringing and he couldn't hear a damn thing, but he saw Wilson's lips moving and he understood the question. "Bad guys. Back corner," was all he could murmur and then he passed out.

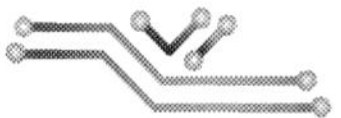

CHAPTER 42

THE BARBEQUE

Wilson stood amidst the emergency vehicles and blaring sirens. He was singed but upright and functional. Smoke and fire. He had only minutes to act. He needed to know if he had gotten the target. He had dental records and other ID info, but how the hell could he recover a body, much less identify it. He grabbed the Special Unit Fire guys in full fire blast gear. "Guys, on the back wall of this place, there should be one or more bodies. I need them and I need them right here now."

SUF Rodriguez spoke first. "These suits are rated to 800 degrees Celsius. If we get there without our temp sensors exceeding that, we'll do it." He looked at his partner. "Let's go." His partner nodded and they entered the building.

Wilson had ordered the special ME lab vehicle to the site. This was a new unit that had all the tools of an ME lab but on mobile for fast analysis. They were fighting the clock and Wilson had authorization for absolutely anything he needed to get the job done. Wilson walked over to the MELV and greeted the ME, John Chin. "Are you ready to do this?"

Wilson had known Chin for twenty years. He was a great ME but could be a pain-in-the-ass. He was known for his gallows humor. "Other than spilling my coffee on this crispy's medical record, I'm ready. What's the big hurry?"

Wilson didn't have time for his usual dance with the ME. "Terrorist. Imminent threat. You've got five minutes. No, make that four when SUF brings the guy out."

A few minutes later, Rodriguez and his partner stumbled out of the building carrying a stretcher. Smoke seemed to be rising off them like steam. They dropped the stretcher at Wilson's feet and ripped off their gas masks, gasping for air. "Shit, that was bad," Rodriguez said. "But there's the only body we could find." The charred remains of a human lay askance on the grounded stretcher.

Chin ambled over, sipping his coffee. "This your barbeque?"

Wilson turned six shades of red trying to contain himself. "Just get on it. You now have three minutes." Chin got the message just by looking at Wilson's face. He waved a patrolman over and the two of them lifted the stretcher into the MELV. Chin lowered a body scanner attached to a mobile arm. He flipped the switch and slowly moved the scanner over the body from head to toe. The scanner emitted a purple light and as Chin moved it, body images began to appear on three flat panel screens along the wall.

Wilson stepped into the van and slammed the door behind him. It startled Chin, who was now seated at a keyboard feverishly typing. "Anything yet?" Wilson asked in a restrained voice.

Chin spoke without taking his eyes off the screen. "I'm comparing the skeletal and dental scans to the records NSA provided. Give me a minute." Wilson considered barking at Chin again. They were all under a lot of pressure. Chin was good when he was focused. Now was no time to break his concentration.

Chin looked up with a smile. "I can't tell anything from the skeleton, but the dental records are a match. It's your guy, LaSalam."

CHAPTER 43

SPY VS. SPY

Frank's image blurred on the screen as if ripples of water were passing over him. I got used to this and knew it meant Frank was either thinking or working. Still, it was a kind of spooky-looking screensaver. The screen snapped clear.

Frank began. "I think we're clear, but I can't be 100% sure. He could have some inactive server or network that he could activate just to execute his plan. So I put a script out there that should detect and block this possible scenario. But again, I can't be sure."

I felt like we were living in that old *Mad* magazine cartoon, *Spy vs. Spy*. Don't know why that came to mind. The war on terror has really been more like an endless game of Whack-A-Mole. Sometimes you're ahead and sometimes you're behind. Despite what Frank said, I had the uneasy feeling that, at the moment, we were behind.

Frank's face lit up. "I just picked up a report that there was a shootout and explosion at a New York warehouse on 7th Street. Positive ID says we got the Leopard."

One mole down, I thought. "I'm going to reach out to Little and report. Let's see if there is anything more to do or just wait."

Frank then surprised me. "I think the smart thing would be to ground the planes anyway—at least for a few hours. Then we're not risking lives while we play the odds. We'll know in a few hours if the coast is clear."

I thought about this for a minute, "Apparently, it's a big deal to get the planes out of the sky. Besides the cost and disruption, this action just might cause widespread panic in itself."

"It's a matter of what's the best alternative. Inconvenience and fear or thousands dead. Take your pick," Frank said.

CHAPTER 44

WHAT ARE THE ODDS?

The Situation Room was standing room only. Seated at the table were the president, joint chiefs, secretary of defense, and heads of all seventeen intelligence agencies. Rich Little, and counter terrorism chiefs for New York and San Francisco, were pictured in small squares on a video conferencing screen beside the president.

The president began. "Thanks for getting here on such short notice. You all should have been briefed on the ride over. So let's not waste time with questions. We've got to deal with the live situation on the ground and in this case, the air. Little, what have we got?"

Little's image jerked to life on the screen. "Madame President, by now you know we have a positive ID on a dead LaSalam. We believe the *Voyager* did its job before the unfortunate accident. Sunborn and his team believe we have stopped the 'active' threat but can't be sure we have or can stop an 'inactive' threat. There could still be a snake in the basket, ready to strike, but we just don't know."

The president considered this. "Give me your number."

Little replied, "Eighty percent to ninety percent sure."

The president went around the room asking for each key player's assessment of how safe they were.

Sec Def: "Seventy percent."

NSA: "Fifty to sixty percent."

Joint Chiefs: "Not enough data for us."

"Freakin' data. We've got to make a decision," the president snapped. "What are the recommendations?" She listened intently as the various intelligence heads painted the scenarios. Finally, she turned back to Little. "What do you guys think? After all you started . . . I mean discovered this thing."

Little coughed and cleared his throat. "They think it's not worth the risk. You should ground all planes for a few hours and make sure the threat is cleared. They realize the cost, disruption and potential panic, but thousands, maybe tens of thousands of lives are at stake. I concur." The room burst into shouts, questions and overall chaos.

"Shut up!" Longford shouted and the room quieted down. "Shit, that's not what I wanted to hear either, but I get it. I need a minute." She left the room to a murmuring crowd of men. She went to the private bathroom at the side of the Situation Room and locked the door. She looked in the mirror. Despite the makeup, she could see the puffy gray circles under her eyes. *Being president takes its toll on us all*, she thought. She took a few deep breaths and teased her hair with her hands. *Like that'll make a difference*. She smirked at her mock vanity, turned abruptly and went back into the room.

She stood at the head of the table and scanned the room, meeting all the eyes that were upon her. "Ground the planes. Do it now." Turning to her press secretary, she said, "Arrange a press conference in five minutes."

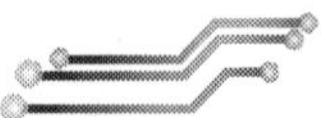

CHAPTER 45

STOP THE PRESSES

You may wonder how the president can call a press conference in five minutes. Since the White House is often the center of the news universe, there are usually over 100 reporters clicking away at their cubicles in the White House press room. Like mice, they wait for a morsel of food to hit the floor and they pounce. When word hit that there was a press conference in five minutes, they all knew something big was afoot. They usually got more notice.

The reporters spilled into the press briefing room and there was a noticeable buzz as they speculated to each other. What could this be about? Marie Williams from CNN sat quietly staring at the small stage and the large Presidential Seal on the blue background wall. This never got old for her. She couldn't believe a girl from the streets of Puerto Rico could be sitting here at the seat of power and actually doing something that mattered.

Just then the press secretary, who usually gave the briefings, stepped to the podium. "Ladies and gentlemen, the president of the United States."

President Longford moved quickly to the podium. She was dressed in a smart-looking dark business pantsuit. Her signature look. She put on her reading glasses and glanced down at a piece of paper. This all looked strangely impromptu for this White House. She put down her glasses and the paper on the podium and looked out at all of them. "I have a brief statement to make. There is a rapidly developing situation. If I have time, I will take a few questions."

She cleared her throat, "At approximately 5:10 this afternoon, I ordered the FAA to immediately ground all commercial and private aircraft in the US." There was a collective gasp in the room. Photo flashes seemed to spring about the room like mini fireworks. There was now silence except for the cameras clicking. *Could this be another*

9/11? She continued. "We have it, due to the intelligence work of the NSA, CIA and Cyber Command, that there has been a credible and significant terrorist threat targeting our commercial aviation infrastructure. We believe we have foiled this attempt and killed the mastermind behind it. We are grounding all aircraft for the next six hours merely as a precautionary measure. I've been told by the FAA that it may take up to two hours for all aircraft to land." She glanced at her watch. "So that should mean all aircraft will be safely on the ground by around 7:00 PM Eastern Time."

A secret service agent approached the podium and whispered in the president's ear. "As I said, this is still a rapidly developing situation, so I can only take one or two questions." There was an overwhelming roar from the reporters in the room shouting their questions. Williams jumped to her feet and waved at the president. Longford raised both hands palms-down to calm the hungry throng. "Marie, what's your question?"

Marie couldn't believe her luck to be singled out. For most of the reporters in the room, it was about being called upon and getting exposure for yourself. The question and answer almost didn't matter. But Marie was ready with a real question, "Madame President, can you tell us any more about who was behind this planned attack and who the 'mastermind' is that you referred to?"

Longford turned to face and answer Marie directly, like they were just having a casual conversation, but not really. "Marie, all we know at this point is that there were foreign nationals involved. They may have found a way to misdirect our aircraft, causing confusion and potential danger to our planes, their passengers and crew. We had been tracking this threat and the people behind it. About thirty minutes ago, the FBI and SFPD confronted the suspected leader. A shootout and explosion occurred. We lost two veteran agents and four more are in the hospital in critical condition. The FBI has positive identification on the dead body of the leader. We are grounding all aircraft and taking other defensive measures until we are 100% sure we have completely thwarted this assault on our national security." The agent returned to the podium and again whispered in the president's ear. "I'm sorry, I can't take any more questions now. I'm needed in the Situation Room. I can assure you that there will be a briefing later today when we know more details." She quickly exited stage left. The room again roared with questions that would go unanswered for now.

Williams was beaming inside. It was quite a coup to get the one and only question in at a serious press conference like this. It might have been the greatest moment of her career. She knew her boss would be very pleased. But then her pride peeled away to doubt and worry. Why would the president be needed again in the Situation Room? What was really going on here?

CHAPTER 46

ATC

Ralph Kinear had just gotten his lukewarm coffee from the lunch room and was back at his terminal. He had put a zarf on the cup out of habit. Maybe they'd have really hot coffee there someday. No matter, he'd been working for air traffic control for over twenty years and he still loved it. *Who needed video games when you could play with real things and real people*, he thought. That's a question he would keep to himself. Just then he noticed a red alert in the crawl at the bottom of his screen. "ATC has been ordered, effective immediately, to ground all aircraft within our sectors of control. We ask all controllers to proceed in an orderly way, but with some haste, to direct all flights to their nearest landing areas." *Holy shit*, he thought. Ralph had been at his console on September 11, 2001 and cleared one of the planes that turned out to be one of the two that hit the World Trade Towers. Shortly after, they had grounded all planes. Not again. The control commander, Jake Wakefield stepped to the front of the room. "Folks, this is not a drill. The president has ordered the FAA, and consequently us, to lead an orderly grounding of all planes. As you may recall, after 9/11, the ATC set up Protocol 62 for just this kind of situation. Please proceed accordingly, bringing down the big birds first. Ralph, can I have a minute?" Jake waved Ralph over to a small corridor off to the side of the large control room.

"Ralph, I'm concerned. We have over 150 aircraft in our sectors and we have to bring them down in under two hours."

Ralph rubbed his bristly chin. "Why two hours? What aren't we being told?"

Jake took a deep breath. "I've been told that our ATC guidance systems may have been compromised. Since we have automated more and more of our systems, humans aren't required to make personal contact with the pilots. So pilots, as you know, can be getting their flight path commands directly from computers. We tried warning them that they were creating a vulnerability to hackers, but nobody listened. Now look what's happening. If some loonie has his fingers on the buttons, it could be chaos. I want you to be ready to lead our A-Team through a manual override if we need it. You've been through it before when we had that outage in December 2008, before they upgraded the equipment."

"How am I supposed to do that and bring planes in at the same time?"

"Ever hear of multitasking?" Jake quipped. "No, seriously, get the planes down, but work the manual scenario in the back of your mind. I just didn't want you to get caught off guard if I have to pull the trigger on that."

Ralph was resigned. Since many of his comrades had been replaced by the computer automated system, he doubted there were enough human controllers to bring down the planes safely in two hours. This was going to be a shit day anyway you sliced it. "OK, I understand." He dropped his coffee into the waste bin. *I need something stronger*, he thought.

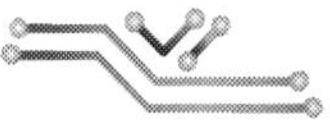

CHAPTER 47

VISITING MR. P

The agent, aka Mr. Pimp, sat at the small kitchen table in his rundown, third-floor, walk-up apartment in the meatpacking district. There were two cute twin girls sitting opposite him—one in a puffy pink dress and the other in blue with white lace around the collar. *They look delicious*, he thought. "Eat your sandwiches, girls, and you can have ice cream for dessert." Their faces both lit up. They looked at each other and giggled. Twins almost seemed to have their own secret way to communicate.

Just then, there was a knock on the door. "Our visitor must be early," Mr. P said.

Mr. P went to the door. He left the chain on and opened the door the few inches it could go while the chain still held. "What the F –?" He pushed back on the door, but the visitor kicked it open and it fell off its hinges. "Girls, it's OK. Go into the bedroom now and close the door." The girls looked frightened but did as they were told.

As soon as the bedroom door closed, the visitor pushed Mr. P twice in the chest until he fell backward into his chair. "You told somebody about our encounter yesterday. Didn't you?" the visitor snarled.

"No, no—I would never do that." Mr. P raised his hands, palms forward, as if he could stop this menace.

The visitor pulled his Glock pistol out of his inside coat pocket, removed a silencer from his side pocket and proceeded to screw it on. "Now you are going to tell me who you told and what you told them."

"Really, I didn't tell anyone!"

"Let me help your memory." The visitor fired a muffled shot into Mr. P's left knee. Mr. P grabbed his knee in agony, tears running down his face. "Is it coming back to you yet or do you need some more help?"

"No, no. It was two Feds I think. They tortured me. I just mentioned the warehouse."

"And their names . . .?" Mr. P hesitated. "I think you need some more help." The visitor fired another shot into Mr. P's right knee. Mr. P groaned. The visitor moved closer and stuck the end of the silencer deep into Mr. P's crotch.

Mr. P wailed. "Stop. Stop. It was Smith and Wesson I think."

"Now you're really, as you Americans say, 'pissing me off.' Which testicle would you like to keep?" The visitor jammed the gun harder into Mr. P's groin.

Mr. P made a ghostly moan. "No, really. Those were their names. Wait, wait and their boss was named 'Little.'"

"That's better. I always like to get paid for my trouble. Some might call it a thirst for vengeance, but that would be petty. I believe in divine justice. I just seem to have a calling to carry it out." The visitor removed the gun from Mr. P's groin and held the pistol down at his side. Despite being in great pain, Mr. P breathed a sigh of relief. *He would live*. Except the visitor then raised the gun to Mr. P's head and fired two quick thuds into his temple. Mr. P fell over onto the floor, his bowels letting go.

The visitor then unscrewed the silencer and put it with the gun on the table. They were too hot to put back in his pocket. He walked over to the bedroom door and gently knocked. He opened the door slowly. "Hi girls. Let's play. Would you like to meet my friend, Johnny?"

CHAPTER 48

BOSTON UA 226

Ninety minutes had passed and Ralph had successfully "landed" all but five planes. They brought the big birds in at Logan. Fred Naismith, sitting next to him, brought the smaller aircraft down at Portland and Providence, nearby. It was going well, but Ralph kept wiping sweat from his brow. He could feel his shirt sticking to him and smell his failing deodorant despite the AC being on high.

He was tracking the circling blips of a Boeing 747, an old Boeing 727 and an Airbus A330 on his monitor.

Pilot 1: "UA 226: Approach, UA 226, with you, level 12000, B."

Ralph: "UA 226, Boston Approach, advise information D, expect the ILS 22L."

Pilot 1: "OK, ILS 22L, I'll get D."

"UA 226, reduce speed 220, then descend and maintain 5500."

"220 on the speed first, then down to 5500, UA 226."

"UA 226, if I issued the QUABN ONE Arrival, 22L transition, are you still able to do that approach?"

"Yeah, a yeah, for the QUABN ONE, 22L transition, we can still do that for you."

"UA 226, Roger, you can descend at your own discretion and maintain 5500 and proceed via runway 22L transition."

"Approach, UA 226, we thought we were looking good here for the QUABN transition—something up?"

"No problem—so are you able to fly the route as published?"

"Yes, sir."

"UA 226, contact Final on 126.5, have a good day."

"126.5, UA 226."

Pilot 1: "Approach, UA 226, leveling at 4500, we've just lost a lot of our instruments, we'd like to go somewhere and hold. We'd like a vector please."

"UA 226, Boston Approach, Roger, fly heading 260, maintain 4500, and what's your status?"

"Yeah, we're gonna check some things out. Just want to make sure we're clear of traffic, so 4500, 260 heading and we'll get back to you."

There was silence as Ralph stared at his screen. Fred heard what was going on, pulled off his headset and rolled his chair across the linoleum to look over Ralph's shoulder. They both knew that whatever happened, they had to keep their voices calm and in control. That was something they had learned the hard way.

"Yeah, we got some stuff back here. Looks like we have enough to shoot an ILS here, and we're talking to dispatch for a Plan B, but yeah; we're gonna try for this 22L."

"Roger 226. Say fuel and souls on board."

"UA 226, we have 1 hour 10, and 312 souls on board, UA 226."

Pilot 1: "Boston, UA 226, we've lost pressurization also, not a problem yet, but won't want to go much higher if we go over to Providence. We are emergency now, pulling it right."

"UA 226, turn right heading 130."

"130 heading, UA 226."

Ralph and Fred waited silently, but Ralph couldn't wait anymore. "226, what's your status?"

"226, do you read?"

"226?" The blip that was 226 disappeared from the screen.

CHAPTER 49

WHAT'S NEXT?

"What have we learned from this?" It's something Frank always said when faced with a problem, failure, or in this case, a catastrophe. It was the kind of question that tended to focus the mind, while taking the emotion out of the situation.

Al, Bart, Loretta, Julie and I sat mute in the computer lab at the office, staring up at Frank on the wall monitor. He looked a bit like the original Einstein. His wisdom always present like a twin brother.

Al broke the silence. This was her kind of detective question. "We know the bad guys had some way of triggering the ATC hack, despite our downing their satellites."

"We also know 312 people lost their lives on Flight 226 and this all happened despite LaSalam being out of the picture," I said.

"Maybe he's not out of the picture," replied Frank. "I have a report here that the charming little slime-ball, Mr. P, was found dead in his apartment by a maid shortly after the explosion and tragic crash."

"What? They had positive ID," Bart said, surprised.

"I think he faked the positive ID," Frank said. We all looked astonished. *How was that possible?*

"We have a few known cases where a bad guy with the resources, and believe me you need money and expertise to do it, wasted an innocent and then had his mouth and teeth surgically changed to match the bad guy's dental records. It's so hard to do and uncommon that it still fools most investigators, even the FBI." Al continued. "That misdirection gives the bad guy time to escape or in this case, carry out his plot."

Loretta looked genuinely shocked. "So it's possible that this jerk pulled the trigger on 226 and he's still out there. Is that right?"

Frank said, "That's our current theory. We just don't know how he pulled the trigger or what he might do next. 226 was pretty bad. But as we all know, he had a much grander plot in mind. He might take some satisfaction in downing 226, but I'd bet he'd be more inclined to self-flagellation. You know—it's a cultural thing. He failed the mission, he failed his father and he failed Allah."

Al said, "So he either has or will develop a new target. Hmm. What would you hit next if you were him?"

I thought about this one. "This is obviously a very smart devil, literally. So my bet is he already had his next target picked out. His profile says he thinks too much of himself to expect failure. So, if you had brought down 100s of planes, what would have been a logical second punch?"

Bart had been taking this all in. "Sounds like the right way to frame the question. But you know me, I'm always looking at the technology side. I think if we can figure out what device or network he used to trigger the 226 attack, we may have a way to thwart his follow up plan."

"Good point. Bart, why don't you and Killer do some traces from your end, and I'll do some inside exploration here," Frank said.

I wasn't sure who was in charge anymore, so I just let my inner control freak take over. "Al, why don't you drop by the Mr. P crime scene and see if there are any clues there. Loretta, you know some street people. Can you do some asking around?"

Loretta smirked. "Are you suggesting I have a shady background? Just kidding, I'll get on it. There are a few people I can reach out to."

Bart got on my case again. "And what are you going to do boss?"

"I've got to get with Little. I feel like we're moving quickly downstream without a paddle and there's a steep waterfall in our path. We've got to get this thing under control and fast."

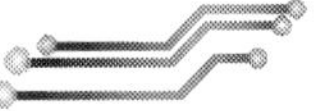

CHAPTER 50
30,000 SLEEP

The Leopard walked up the steps of the private jet he had chartered. *My business isn't done, but I have to get out of this Allah forsaken city*, he thought.

He sunk into the soft leather seat and let out a deep breath. There was something so peaceful and relaxing about flying in a plane, especially a private one. At least for a few hours, you could be away from all the stresses and dangers of dealing with both your enemies and your friends. The Lear broke through the clouds into the clear blue and leveled off at 25,000 feet.

Back to New York where I can regroup with Eskabar. He and his team had performed admirably despite the Great Satan's efforts to thwart his plans. He could not fault him for losing the satellites or for the yellow dogs trying to ground all their aircraft. He may have only brought down one jumbo jet, but he had killed 312 animals and struck terror into the whole country. He could only imagine the meetings Longford and her generals were having. He relished the idea of their fear and panic, scrambling to keep up. But LaSalam was too fast for them. They had no idea what was coming next and he planned to keep it that way until he could strike his blow and bring them to their knees.

He had planned to wipe out Eskabar and his New York operation after the first attack, but he changed his mind. They would be useful in this next operation and then he could deal with them. It did create a certain risk of exposure leaving them in place, but the Leopard had to be agile. His prey was a moving target and he had to adapt or even anticipate their moves until he could bring them down. It was worth the risk. Besides it seemed his enemy was miles, not steps, behind despite the need for the warehouse diversion.

He drifted into a semi-sleep as one does on an airplane. His thoughts drifted to Nicky and her sweet innocence. The twins were divine. Maybe he would log into his favorite website later. He got a little aroused just thinking about it. Why couldn't life be that simple? No, he was a man on a mission from on high. There were debts to collect. His enemy would need to pay up. He must not be weak. After all, he was the Leopard.

CHAPTER 51

NEAR MISS

Nobody had slept since yesterday and it was taking its toll. My shoulder still throbbed from my near miss encounter with the Leopard. "Near miss"—I'm sure 226 wished theirs was a near miss. What did that term really mean after all? Either it was a "miss" or it wasn't. How could it be a "*near* miss?" I smiled to myself. My mind always seemed to wander off into these stupid tangents. Better to laugh at yourself, than get crazy about it. The truth was that the country had had a near miss, but we were still in grave danger.

I walked down the hall, tapping the cool glass windows as I went. I knew where Little's office was. I guess they had accepted me around headquarters by now since they no longer accompanied me with a security guard.

Little was standing, leaning over his desk. He looked a lot more frazzled than the last time I saw him. His hands were flat on the surface, arms extended. His tie hung loosely from his open collar. "This guy is a slippery Mother F–. We need some new approach to the problem. Any ideas?"

Of course I had been thinking about it, but this might just be an insolvable problem. I had always prided myself on the ability to figure things out, especially tough problems. But the last couple of days had shaken me up and destroyed my confidence. This was just a whole new ballgame on a field on which I had never played before. Still I had to keep trying. Too much was at stake. "I have my team working all the cyber angles. What kind of profile do you have on this guy? I mean I had asked Al to get in touch about putting a profiler on this. Maybe if we understood him better, we could try to think like he thinks. Then maybe we could anticipate his next move."

Little lifted a manila file folder from his desk and let if fall open while he pulled his reading glasses down from his forehead to the end of his nose. He looked up at me, his eyes above the rims, then he looked down through the glasses and said, "Al did reach out. We had already started our top profiler on it. Here's what we have so far. Born 1977 in Saudi Arabia to an upper-middle-class family. Not royalty, but his family was very comfortable. His father managed an oil operation. He went to college in Cambridge, UK and that's where we suspect he got his jihadist fervor. He belonged to a group called the Ottoman Network. Graduated in 1997 with honors and was recruited into the Saudi Intelligence Agency. Here's where it gets interesting. He excelled at covert operations. We're not sure whether he was actually a double for Barin or recruited by them when he was in the field. He is a known operator suspected of training Hezbollah agents, masterminding several western embassy attacks, and personally assassinating over 100 people."

"I was almost 101," I mused. "Anything there that could help us?"

Little continued flipping through the pages. "This is a thick folder so I'll skip ahead. I see some notes on his obsession with young girls. That's no surprise. Here's something interesting. You said, 'Think like him.' If you had this sexual obsession and you couldn't fulfill it when you needed to, what would you do?"

I thought about that. "You'd look for other outlets. Maybe online?"

"Exactly. NSA has some tracers on the Leopard logging into child porn sites. One in particular seems to be a favorite – Younglovedownunder.ru. 'RU' is Russia. If we could somehow hack that site and ID his logins, maybe we could geo-locate him."

"That's a lot of 'ifs.' Also, I'd assume most of the pervs who visit do so anonymously."

"Ah, but how many of the same IP addresses were in the Mideast on Monday, New York on Tuesday and LA on Wednesday? That may narrow the field to one or two users at most. We just need to get to the log file for the site, preferably in real-time."

"That's all, huh?" I couldn't help but laugh. Non-technical people assumed that if you could state what you wanted in simple terms, any nerd could make it happen. "We're not on NCIS here, but we may have a unique resource that could help."

Little finally seemed to gain some energy and get excited. He finally looked up and pulled his glasses off. "I've got the best and brightest at NSA standing by, which is no mean feat. What have you got?"

I started feeling the adrenaline myself. "If you've got NSA ready to go, I'd suggest you let them loose on it. But I've got a guy who actually lives inside the Internet. Frank may be able to penetrate where others fail."

"Then let's get going," Little said as he picked up the desk phone and started dialing.

CHAPTER 52

SIGNAL AND NOISE

Back in the lab, I flipped on my monitor and called Frank. His face appeared jumbled at first, like Max Headroom again, and then it took shape.

"Sam, how are you?"

"I'm a bit frazzled at the moment. Did you get my message about running tracers on the sex site?"

"I did, but it's amazing how the Internet has become more like a human brain. You know how when you sit down to concentrate on something, all these random thoughts come into your mind? Does that happen to you?"

"All the time, but what does that have to do with this?" I persisted.

Ignoring me, he went on. "Do you ever get a song stuck in your mind and you can't shut it off, no matter how hard you try? I think they're called 'Earworms.' Or the same distraction keeps pulling your focus away? How about repetitive dreams?"

Now I was getting frustrated, but I tried to keep my voice even. You never want to piss off your IT guys. "Frank, with all due respect, you need to focus. I enjoy your musings, but I don't see the relevance here. Can you trace the site's users or not?"

"Everybody thinks everything on the Internet is binary: 1's and 0's. But there are so many programs and queries flying from all directions at the same time, that sometimes they collide. Unwanted data enters your path of inquiry like unwanted dreams or repetitive songs, keeping you from your destination. In the old ham radio days, they used to call it signal versus noise. The signal is what you wanted to get, but sometimes the static and noise would totally block it out and sometimes just partially obscure it. Right now we're getting a lot of noise and I'm trying to filter it out to get the info you need."

"Could it be intentional blocking or is it just a random thing?"

"I'm not sure yet. A few years ago, hackers would sometimes launch DSAs—Denial of Service Attacks—against big websites like Yahoo or Amazon. If you flooded the sites with millions of simultaneous queries, automatically generated virtual users hitting the site, you could bring the site's servers to its knees. Fortunately, software was recently developed to detect and thwart these malicious attacks. So I'm not sure if what I'm seeing is just random or maybe a new form of a DSA."

This got me thinking. "I'm trying to put myself in the Leopard's shoes—I mean paws. Sorry, bad joke. If I had the capability to bring down or hack the air traffic control system, what else could I hack that might create the most damage and terror?"

Frank jumped in. "I see where you're going. Could he be planning a major Internet disruption?"

"He has the resources I believe to do it. If his attack was really effective, it would bring down not only all businesses online, but it could shut down utilities and even emergency services. Just thinking of an example. 911 calls don't go over traditional phone lines and switches anymore, they use VOIP—Voice over IP, Internet Protocol. No Internet, no 911."

"Holy shit!"

I'd never heard Frank curse before.

"I'll shift my search for the moment to see if I can detect a pattern or source for all the excess noise. I'll still try to trace the sex site, but as you know I've become quite agile at multitasking in my new digital body."

Despite the situation, I had to laugh. Frank no longer had a body, but he had a hell of a mind times ten. "I'll let Little know, so he can put his NSA guys on it as well. It's just a theory at this point, but we might be facing the ultimate cyber attack. If we don't stop him, the results could be devastating."

CHAPTER 53

KEEP THE CHANGE

LaSalam landed in New York and jumped in a yellow cab at LaGuardia. Biden was right, that airport was still worse than any back desert airport in the Middle East.

"Where to, my brother?" the cabbie asked in a thick accent.

The Leopard gave the cabbie the address in lower Manhattan speaking in Farsi. The cabbie smiled. "Salom Alechem."

"Alechem Salom, my brother," the Leopard answered with a smile. The address he had given the cabbie was ten blocks from his true destination. He could not risk the cabbie or his dispatcher knowing where this passenger went. The cabbie pulled up to the curb on Barrow Street.

"That will be thirty-five dollars," the cabbie said, turning his head to look at his passenger through the little portal in the safety glass between the seats.

LaSalam handed him a fifty-dollar bill. "Keep the change."

"Thank you, my brother!" The cabbie said his final words.

The Leopard lifted his silenced pistol and, shattering the safety glass, put one shot into the cabbie's forehead.

"You are helping the cause," he said to the lifeless body in the front seat. "You will be recognized in heaven."

If anything, the Leopard was careful and a master of tradecraft. He would never have given the cabbie the correct address or left a murder victim near his intended destination. So, he walked, zigzagging the ten blocks to the control center. He walked through an alley, down a few steps and faced the metal door. He knocked twice, then three times, and finally once. A small eye hatch slid open then closed and the door swung open.

LaSalam was greeted by Eskabar. "It is good to see you again, sire."

The Leopard had a menacing little grin. "You as well. How are things here?"

Trying to muster some confidence, the small man answered, "We are making good progress for sure. I believe we will be ready for the next phase, or at least to test it, tomorrow." They took the elevator together down ten floors.

CHAPTER 54

QUANTUM STATE

Frank looked up on the screen as if he had been reading a book. "Maybe we need to take a quantum approach to this investigation."

Bart swiveled from the other screens he had been working on to face the Frank monitor. "What are you talking about?"

"Our minds tend to work, like computers, in a binary fashion. Something is or it isn't, it's a '1' or a '0.' The Leopard is either here or he's there. But I believe, just as in quantum physics, that reality is more a matter of probabilities. There's only a certain probability that an object is here or there or nowhere. The extreme in quantum theory is that same object could be in two different places at the same time. That's not even so far fetched, as you see, I have no problem being in two places, everywhere or nowhere at the same time."

I had to step in. "Frank, you are the most brilliant man I have ever met, but, with all due respect, how does this help us?"

Frank smiled. "I love that phrase, 'With all due respect.' It usually precedes an opposite statement, like 'With all due respect, you're brilliant, but in reality, you're an asshole.'" We all laughed and he continued. "But in a funny way, it proves my point—you can be both at the same time. It's not binary. It's more a matter of 'state' than place. Brilliant, asshole, here, there—we, one, some or all at the same time. So let's look for the Leopard by probabilities and what could be his current state or states."

Bart jumped in. "I get it. That's why the human mind can sometimes be better at problem solving because we can handle ambivalence and conflicting facts better than a binary machine. So, how would we apply this quantum approach to our current crisis?"

Frank knew he had us, so he began to pick up steam. "I wrote some programs based on a quantum, instead of a binary, approach to solving certain types of problems based on incomplete or conflicting data sets. In English, I have some tools that may help here. Let's feed in all the data points we have on LaSalam—not only all his known locations and times, but his behavior patterns, background, known aliases, etc."

For the first time today, I felt like we might have a way forward. "We also have a new and maybe very important data point. We have a ping to the sex website from an outer cell tower in Kansas."

Loretta, who had been listening quietly, got excited. "Does that mean he is in Kansas?"

Frank, who now seemed like the wise grandfather talking to his grandchildren, said, "Remember we are now going to work in probabilities, which allows us to open our minds to other possibilities. Traditional law enforcement would take that data point and act like my six-year-old grandson's soccer team. Did you ever watch little kids play soccer? It's a hoot. Somebody kicks the ball and all the kids on both teams run to the ball. The result is twenty kids bunched together kicking the ball into each other's shins."

Loretta was not really in the mood for a lecture. "But shouldn't we dispatch the authorities to Kansas. Maybe he's still there?"

Frank was being very patient, like the professor he had been. "Let's think about that. What's the probability that our suspect is in Kansas? Has he ever been there before? Is there any reason for him to be there? Could there be alternate explanations, like maybe he was in a plane flying over Kansas? By asking these types of questions and running my program, my guess is that the probability will be low that his current state is Kansas. Let's identify the higher probability states and start our physical investigations there."

"Brilliant . . . with all due respect," I said and everyone laughed again. Amazing how laughter clears the mind and calms the soul. "Let's get on it."

CHAPTER 55
A STROLL

The Leopard paced his hotel room just like his namesake might do. He did not pace out of anxiety. It was more like preparation to pounce on his prey. But he was impatient. He was used to getting what he demanded, when he demanded it. Yet he knew the programming process was complex. After he killed a couple of programmers, he learned the hard way it would be ready when it would be ready. Coercion on his part would only slow the process or just be self-defeating. Dead programmers aren't very productive after all.

He could indulge Johnny and calm himself down, but his adrenaline was running. Nothing would calm him down except a successful kill. The hotel room was feeling small so he decided to go out into the cool New York night air where he could walk and pace as much as the streets would allow. New York at night might be the best cure for his restlessness and insomnia or it might be dangerous. He relished the thought of either possibility.

It was 2:00 AM, but the streets were still alive with the city's night people. Hookers held their corners, fruit vendors were still open and young men in hoodies and earbuds prowled. He stopped and bought an apple from one of the fruit vendors. He peeled off the Cortland sticker and polished it on his overcoat sleeve. When he took a big bite, the crunch was satisfying and the juice dribbled down his chin. Apples like this were a pleasure he could not get in his country. Why the infidels should enjoy the pleasures they did was beyond him. He knew his role was to change that, to break things down, to seek revenge and to cause pain. That would be his greatest pleasure.

As he walked the darker side of 9th Avenue, a young man in a hoodie leaned into LaSalam and bumped his shoulder. The young man turned. "Sorry man. I just lost my wallet and I need subway fare to get back to Brooklyn. Got five bucks you can spare?"

LaSalam grinned. "I need plane fare to get back to Teheran, got a thou you can spare . . . man?"

The young man's expression became suddenly severe. "Very funny man. You a fuckin' terrorist or sumfin'?" He pulled a Glock out of his hoodie pocket and pointed it at LaSalam's head. "Just give me your money funny man."

The Leopard maintained his grin. "Do you believe in heaven, young man?"

The young man tilted his head and looked both angry and perplexed at the same time. "What the fuck are you talking 'bout?"

The Leopard swung his right arm up in one smooth motion, grabbing the young man's wrist and twisting up and over. He then used his left hand on top and jammed the gun into the young man's ribs, breaking the skin with the tip of the barrel. Guts make a very good silencer. The young man groaned in pain. The Leopard looked him in the eye and said, "Well you're not going there," and he pulled the trigger. The firing gun made a muffled thump. The young man slumped and LaSalam grabbed him under the arm, like he was helping a drunk friend. Limping along, he propped up the body and turned into an alley. Dropping the body behind a dumpster, he could smell the rotting garbage piled up.

Fortunately, his overcoat was dark and the blood splatter didn't really show. He looked both ways and emerged from the alley. No one seemed to be nearby. He dropped the gun in a sewer opening and resumed his stroll. Just the kind of diversion he needed. He felt much better now.

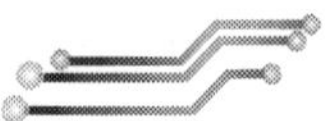

CHAPTER 56

40/70 RULE

"Brief me," Longford said.

Hager, Osborne and Smith from NSA sat on the couches in the Oval Office. Smith cleared his throat. "We've been able to ping the Leopard's computer and we're plotting a trajectory based on the IP trail's coordinates."

"English please!" Longford snapped.

Hager calmly stepped in. "We believe he is on his way to a major East Coast city. New York, Boston and Philly are most likely. It's just an educated guess at this point."

Longford walked to the window and stared out at the early morning sun rising, shining a golden light on the Rose Garden. "That's one thing I hate about this damn job, I'm always dealing with incomplete information. How the hell are you supposed to make decisions with incomplete information?"

Hager now became professorial. "I like to follow Colin Powell's 40/70 rule. He knew in war that you could never be certain or have all the information, but you had to act. If you waited until you were one hundred percent certain, you'd never act. It would be too late and you might end up dead. So if your certainty level was between forty and seventy percent, that's good enough to proceed."

"So we're playing poker here," Longford mused, still staring out the window.

"In a sense. But if we think we have the best hand, we need to make a big bet," Hager replied.

"Seems to me we have had the worst hand at every turn."

"Well, now we think we have at least a location radius. We have the best cyber tools in the world, and we have boots on the ground. We don't have all the answers, but we're the cat and he's the mouse."

"I don't think we can afford to think of him as a mouse. They don't call him the Leopard for nothing. He's dangerous and can strike, unexpectedly, at any moment. What are we currently doing to corner this animal?"

"We have all intelligence resources fully focused, plus street patrols by all local and federal agencies. Once we pick up his scent, we'll bring the hammer down hard."

"What about our civilian guys—Little and his band of geeks?"

"They gave us the heads up about the ping over Kansas, and they have deployed all their online and offline resources. They've been an amazing help."

"Well, if, or I should say when, we get through this, we'll have to compensate them somehow. A medal at the very least." Longford finally turned to face her team. "Ok, sounds like we're fully deployed and doing everything we can think of. I want an update every thirty minutes and sooner if anything breaks. Understood?"

They all nodded with grave looks on their faces. "Thank you, Madame President."

Then they stood up in unison and left.

CHAPTER 57

NOT A COP

I sat with my team in the computer lab back at the office. I liked being surrounded by computers and sitting in a comfortable chair. Despite the throbbing pain in my ribs from the car and my shoulder and knee from the gunshots, I somehow felt safe. It was quiet, except for the clicking of keyboards, and I could think. I wasn't as merged with the digiverse as Frank was, but I felt like I belonged here. These machines extended my power and reach. I remember what Steve Jobs said, "The computer is the bicycle of the mind." It allows us to go farther and faster, leveraging our own power.

Frank flickered to life on my screen. "How are you holding up, Sam?"

"Other than lack of sleep and a bullet wound in my shoulder, I'm OK," I lied. "Find out anything?"

Frank cleared his throat again, which was still funny since he was now all digital. Must be force of habit or maybe some echo of his physical self. Like when amputees still have phantom feelings in their missing limbs. "I've extrapolated his route based on the pings and IP traces. Then I cross-correlated with air traffic control. They had two nav signals that might have fit our pattern."

"You said 'might have,' past tense. Where did your extrapolation take you?"

"Let me back up. I find that digital thinking is at least ten times faster than my old physical brain. So I don't know when I might lose you or blow past you. I'm assuming, based on the time between pings, being as short as it was, that the Leopard had to be in the air. Highest probability you recall. Then if he was in the air and the plane's navigation system was on, ATC would be able to triangulate the signal with the data I provided. That gave us the most likely planes over Kansas at that time. Finally, following their two nav systems to their destination, we have a very high probability of where they are."

"OK, where?"

"One plane landed one hour and ten minutes ago in Teterboro, New Jersey. The other, one hour and twenty-five minutes ago at LaGuardia in New York."

"Well done, Frank! Then our guy is most likely headed to Manhattan again. Can you get me the pilots' names? I'll ask Little to track down and interview them. We need to narrow the search more. Meanwhile, I, and maybe Al too, are going to get on a plane to New York pronto."

"What are you going to do in New York? You're not a cop."

"It just seems like the right thing to do. You just can't do certain things by computer. Sorry, Frank. Besides, Al gave me a gun for protection."

"I don't think she gave you that gun thinking you'd go looking for trouble."

"Frank, I think trouble has already found us. Time to confront it, and see if we can end it one way or the other."

CHAPTER 58

THE CUB

While his brother prowled the streets of New York, Momar LaSalam, known as the Cub, slept fitfully in his hotel room. Tomorrow would be a big day. Like his older brother, he had been educated in the West, graduating from Stanford with a degree in engineering and creative writing. Unusual combination as very few people had both high-level right brain and left brain skills.

Less people, and especially the authorities, knew about the Cub. Oh, he was sure he was in some NSA database—all Muslims, especially foreign nationals, were. However, he and his brother had been very careful and successful in cloaking the Cub's activities. The Leopard believed for a plan to work, you needed redundancy. That way, if one failed, there was always a parallel operator to carry out the mission. That's why the Cub flew in a separate private plane to Teterboro while his brother landed at LaGuardia. It was also why he would go to their Cyber War Room in Brooklyn while the Leopard would be in lower Manhattan. The Cub's team would be ready to execute Step 2 of the plan, and Step 3, if for some reason his brother's team failed.

"Failure" was hardly ever a word he associated with his brother and he would never use it to his face. He had felt the wrath of his brother's anger as a young boy, when his brother hung him from his collar on a hook in an alleyway and taunted him. His brother said he would make his younger brother "tough," so that one day he could fight by his side as they carried out the jihad. As the young Cub hung from the hook, Ahmed pricked him with a sharp knife on his arms and legs, drawing little beads of blood. Momar wriggled and flailed trying to get free, but he was too small to escape. Ahmed lightly pricked his ears and said, "This is so you will always listen to what I say and obey. For you know I love you and would never really hurt you. This is just a lesson." Momar began to cry, which made Ahmed smile. Ahmed then pulled down Momar's pants as he hung, fighting less now. He jabbed at Momar's genitals, pretending the knife was a sword and he was in a duel. He took a few steps back and then lunged—the tip of the knife just barely penetrating Momar's scrotum. Momar screamed. Ahmed laughed and said, "This is so you know that I own you. Do you understand? Nod if you understand." Momar nodded, tears streaming down his cheeks. Ahmed left, leaving Momar hanging there with his pants around his ankles exposed, humiliated and scared. What if someone found him this way? What if his mother or father found out? He did not know if he could bear the shame.

About an hour later as the sun began to set and Momar hung almost lifelessly in the secluded alley, Ahmed returned. "I think, my brother, you have learned your lesson. But also know that whenever you are in pain or in trouble, I will always return to save you. You must also do the same for me. Do you understand?" Momar nodded weakly. Ahmed pulled up Momar's pants and lifted him off the hook and lowered him gently to the ground. He kissed the top of Momar's head. "You must never speak of this to anyone. This is the beginning of your training. You will make a fine soldier some day." Then, suddenly, Momar stomped as hard as he could on Ahmed's foot and ran as fast as he could down the alley to freedom. Ahmed smiled and thought to himself, *That is a good start.*

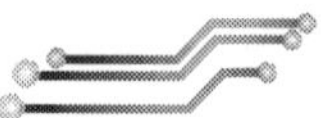

CHAPTER 59

LAST CHANCE

I always loved New York. We had taken the "red-eye" overnight from San Francisco. From the airport, we called an Uber and arrived in Manhattan around 8:00 AM. The streets were crowded and electric as usual, but I knew there was a very real danger lurking. Everyone else seemed oblivious, on their way to work or breakfast or some other scheduled task that seemed important at the time. I was not sure where to start. I just felt I had to come. The sun was warm on my skin as I sat on a metal chair in Bryant Park with Al daydreaming beside me.

I began. "I know we discussed it on the plane, but now that we're here and can get a 'feel' for it, where would you set up a cyber-terror base?"

Al had obviously been thinking about it. "You know I lived in Manhattan for a few years, when I first started with the NYPD. I know the place pretty well, especially the streets. So you'd have to ask, where can you rent or buy a building on the less expensive side without the public notice?"

"Hmm, I haven't spent as much time here as you have, but it seems either downtown in the industrial warehouse district or maybe in Brooklyn or maybe both."

Al seemed startled. "I get your logic, but how can you say, 'both?'"

"I've been studying the profile of the Leopard that Little gave us. They say he was behind a series of bombings in Afghanistan. The sad, but interesting, fact is that when they occurred, they happened in pairs. I don't think that was coincidental. I think it says something about the way he thinks." I trailed off into thought.

Al seemed to perk up at the idea. "So you're saying he may be planning two attacks tomorrow?"

"It's just a thought. He may be planning two or one may be a backup, in case the other one fails. If we're right, then it makes our task twice as difficult."

"We can't afford to fail. Have you shared this theory with Little? Maybe, just maybe, if he is planning two attacks, it makes our task half as difficult."

"Hold on. First, I just thought of it—so no, I did not discuss it with Little. But, they're pretty smart guys. Maybe they are already pursuing it. Now, explain to me why 'half as difficult.'"

"First, I think we have to get Little on the phone now, so he can direct his people down this road. The reason having two attacks may be half as difficult is that on the one hand, it gives us two targets to shoot at instead of one. That means our odds are twice as good to hit one. On the other hand, if we find one, it may lead us to the other."

"Ever the optimist. So what or where would we pick up the scent?"

"Somewhere there has to be a database of real estate transactions made in cash in the five boroughs for the last ten days."

"That sounds like a perfect 'query.' You've been hanging around me too long." I started pecking away on my mobile. "I'm sending your query to Frank. He's better than Google and can do an intelligent search across all search engines including private and secure databases. After all, he's inside the Internet." What a strange concept. I stopped typing.

"Now what?"

"We wait." Maybe only five seconds elapsed before Frank appeared on my screen. "Hi, Frank."

"Sam, I see the New York Public Library in the background. One of my favorite old haunts. Point your camera at it. I'd like a look for old times sake." Satisfied, Frank continued. "I ran your query in 116 search engines, but the most helpful were the internal databases of the top twenty New York Real Estate Companies."

"How did you get into those?"

"Sam, being inside is like being Superman. I can fly anywhere and use my X-ray vision." He laughed. "Bottom line is I have three rentals and two building sales for you to check out. I'm texting you the info now. But I have one other outlier for you to investigate."

"Outlier? What are you talking about?"

"It occurred to me that a boat or ship of sufficient size could also serve the Leopard's purposes. So I searched all boat sales of vessels over fifty feet and docked in the City. I want you to have a look at the *Last Chance* at Pier 54."

"All this in five seconds. Pretty impressive, Frank."

"Hey, I'm dealing in nanoseconds now. It's amazing how much you can get done in a few seconds with this kind of processing power. Makes the human brain seem like a one-legged turtle."

"I may be slow, but I can see the significance of the boat's name. I know crazy terrorists, like the Leopard, go for symbolism in things like this. I bet this is one of the two targets. Please describe the boat."

As I got up to walk down 6th Avenue, Frank was still in my ear. "This all reminds me of the Monte Hall Problem. We have three options we are looking at like the three doors on the show Monte Hall hosted, *Let's Make a Deal.* The contestant on the show, let's call her 'Sally,' would be asked to pick a door. Behind one of the doors would be a fabulous prize like a new car. Behind the other two doors were maybe a barbecue or sand toys. Real clunkers. So Sally was highly motivated to pick the right door."

I was feeling like Frank was wandering off again into one of his professorial lectures. He was clearly enjoying himself. "I don't see what this has to do with us?"

"Patience, Sam. I'm getting to that and it's important for determining how we proceed. After the audience screams and shouts suggestions, Sally picks Door #1. That's like us. We had three options and we picked one. Now before revealing Door #1, Monte Hall says, 'Let me show you what is behind Door #3.' The pretty model on stage waves her arm, Door #3 opens and it's the barbecue. The audience sighs."

"Ok already. What's the point?"

"Hold your horses. Boy, am I dating myself. We're just getting to the good part. Now after the reveal of Door #3, Monte says to Sally, 'Are you sure you want to stick with Door #1 or would you rather pick Door #2? You can change your mind if you like, but then that will be your final choice.' More shouts and screams from the audience. Sally has quite a quandary. What should Sally do? What's her best choice?"

"OK, I'll play. I'm not sure it makes any difference. She had a one out of three chance to begin with. Nothing's changed with the reveal of Door #3."

"Ah, but that's where you're wrong. The reveal of Door #3, just like our unfortunate warehouse disaster, changes everything. With two doors left, #1 and #2, and if we were starting all over, what would our odds be of choosing the right door?"

"One out of two or fifty percent, right?"

"That's correct, but we're not starting all over. Sally had already picked Door #1, so the odds of Door #1 being correct are still one in three or thirty-three percent. However, now that Door #3 has been revealed and there are only two doors left, Sally should change her choice to Door #2 and she'll have a fifty percent chance of success."

"Wow. That seems crazy but makes sense at the same time."

"Probability science is sometimes counter-intuitive, which is one reason it holds such fascination. This phenomenon is aptly named the Monte Hall Problem. So based on this, what should we do with our two remaining options, Sam?"

"I think we still need to follow your hunch and check out the boat."

"OK. I guess you're still sticking with Door #1."

"Well at worst, it's one out of three. But unlike Sally we have your knowledge handy. Enough talk. Time for action."

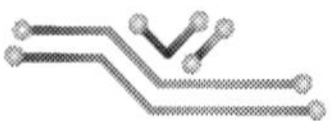

CHAPTER 60

AMERICAN COFFEE

The Cub stood on the deck of the *Last Chance*, looking across the East River at the Manhattan skyline. A light fog hugged the streets of the Lower East Side while the taller buildings emerged from the cloud exposing their upper floors. It looked like a fantasy. Something the Cub could recall from a storybook of his youth. *Why did this have to be the enemy? Do I really believe in this jihad, or am I trying to impress my brother? Maybe I'm still just afraid of him. Afraid of what he might do if I fail. Only Allah knows.* His thoughts drifted with the slow swaying of the boat and across the light, white-capped ripples in the dark water.

He stirred from his reverie when Simpson tapped him on the shoulder. Alec Simpson was a recent UK recruit. He was two meters tall, very smart and had piercing blue eyes. Ex-military to boot. "It's time, sir."

The two proceeded below deck, down the mahogany steps of the *Last Chance* to a dark paneled command center. The Leopard, or more likely his Saudi supporters, bought the twenty-eight meter boat from a Wall Street hedge fund guy who had been recently arrested for securities fraud. He needed the money for his legal defense. Needless to say the price was right and there was a certain poetic irony to the transaction that appealed to the Leopard. The Leopard retrofitted the boat to include a command center for fifteen analysts, hackers and engineers with the latest computer technology and high-speed, encrypted communications. There was a basic kitchen, dining room and bunks for nineteen including the crew. The Cub was the only one who had his own quarters—a modest stateroom with its own desk, computer and WC.

"Update me," the Cub commanded to Christopher, a young man who looked too young to drive a car, sitting at the lead console under a seventy-eight inch OLED monitor. The monitor showed a Google

Earth view of Manhattan, the East River and the harbor. Red dots that looked like push pins were scattered around lower Manhattan.

"All our people are in position. Your brother is ready to execute Priority 1 at 12:30 PM. That will create maximum effect at lunch hour in the city. We're to be ready to execute Priority 2 thirty minutes later, unless we get a message otherwise."

"OK. That's in two hours. Keep me posted on any movement from the CIA and FBI targets you are tracking. There is always a risk of exposure and we have to be ready." The Cub looked up at the red dots on the screen and at the two men at the door in camo holding RPG launchers at their sides.

He walked over to the galley and poured himself a black coffee from the half-empty pot. He mused over the fact that the first known webcam was of a coffee maker on the first floor of an office building in Cambridge, UK. Engineers on the top floor had designed it so they could look online and see if there was coffee ready downstairs. That way they didn't have to walk down and find an empty pot. *We've come a long way since then*, he thought.

He sipped the coffee and winced. "This American coffee is shit!"

CHAPTER 61

ROOK TO QUEEN EIGHT

Little, Favor, six armed FBI marksman and I jumped on the *Take Down*, a twenty-meter Coast Guard cutter, docked at the South Street Seaport. We had a fix on the *Last Chance*. In under five minutes, we could engage. I hoped we had enough manpower and firepower to handle it. Little assured me these guys were the best. It didn't hurt that there were a dozen Coast Guard personnel deployed with weapons on deck as well. The cutter also had a 50mm cannon at the ready. I always enjoyed reading thrillers from Morrell, Thor and Clancy. I just never thought I'd be in one.

My thoughts drifted. I remembered driving down a dirt road along the river. The sky had cotton ball clouds against a pale blue ether. I rolled down my window to take in the sound of the rushing water as it spilled over the ice age boulders strewn randomly within its banks. There was peace . . . and quiet. So what was I doing on this boat in the East River rushing to confront a maniacal terrorist? How had I gotten here? Maybe it was a dream.

I turned to Little. "What's the plan? Do we just attack? I don't see how we take these guys alive."

Little turned to me just as some sea spray wafted over the side and showered us. He didn't seem to notice. His eyes told me he was in another place—some higher plane where hunters are at one with their prey. "The problem is that he may literally have his fingers on the detonator. I'm thinking he is not suicidal like his crazy, gullible brethren. So we may be able to confront him and make some kind of 'bargain.'"

"You're joking, right?" I was stunned.

"We just need to buy some time, create a momentary diversion or we're fucked."

Even though the *Last Chance* was fast, our cutter was faster. It was like a souped-up, hot rod sea rocket. We quickly approached from the rear and then pulled along the starboard side. Our skipper pulled at the mic on the cutter's dash and clicked the talk button. The speaker on the bow boomed, "This is the US Coast Guard. All crew must appear on deck immediately. We will board in sixty seconds."

All we could see were two men on deck holding AK-47s at their sides. All our weapons were up and pointed at them. I had a bad feeling about this. The skipper continued. "Please have your captain come up and step to the rail."

An American in a Navy-like uniform and captain's hat stepped to the rail with a megaphone. "I am Ronald Sith, Captain of the *Last Chance*. How can we help you gentlemen?"

"We need to board and inspect your vessel. Please have your men lower their weapons." The captain hand signaled and the two men on deck lowered their weapons.

I could smell the salt air and felt more spray on my face. The scene was surreal. It felt like the director was going to yell, "Cut" and we'd all break for a nice buffet lunch. But this was really real and we were really there. I'm not a military guy, but I was thinking how I could help. I was good at solving puzzles, and we were in the middle of a big one. Maybe it was more like a chess game, and each side was taking turns making moves and trying to trap the opponent.

I turned to Little. "Tell our guys to lower their weapons and have our boat slowly put some distance between us and them."

"What are you talking about? We're about to board?"

"Trust me. Rook to Queen Eight—they are about to launch a surprise attack."

Something in my eyes and maybe in the air made sense to Little. "Captain, slowly lower your weapons and move at about half-speed away from their boat."

Our captain, Jeremy Agnus, turned his gray eyes to Little and looked puzzled but followed the directive. He raised an outstretched arm and slowly lowered it. Our guys lowered their weapons in unison. We could hear the churning of our engines as we seemed to slowly drift away from the *Last Chance*.

Just as we were putting some distance between the two ships, two more men appeared on their deck. Dark haired, bearded and smiling. Not happy smiles, more like smirks. The captain of the *Last Chance* nodded and took a step back from the rail. The two bearded men raised their arms holding RPGs. They stepped to the rail and aimed straight at us. My mouth fell open. There was an eerie silence. Then they pulled their triggers and we heard a burst and whoosh. Two rocket propelled grenades streaked toward us.

CHAPTER 62

RETURN FIRE

The rockets raced each other toward the *Take Down*, trailing a cloud of acrid smoke and flame. The *Take Down*'s captain barked an order to "Hard right" and the first rocket landed two feet from the bow exploding on impact with the water. The boat rocked back and water sprayed the deck. Maybe "spray" is the wrong word. More like a tidal wave washed over the deck soaking all standing there. The second rocket hit our port side at about a forty-five degree angle and exploded, rocking the *Take Down* like a small sailboat heeling to starboard. We all grabbed the rails and hung on for dear life.

Then the boat rebounded and we rocked back to port side. We crashed against the rails. I saw one of our guys fly headfirst over the rail into the cold water below. Somebody yelled, "Man overboard!" and I saw life preservers on ropes flying over the side. I had no idea how any human beings could react so fast, but these guys were good and obviously highly trained.

Our captain yelled again, "Damage report?"

We heard crackling over the deck speaker and, "One minute please." Then, "We have two men down below deck. Unconscious, but with a pulse." A pause. "The port armor seems to have taken the brunt of the blast and held, but we are taking on some water. Not critical." Fortunately, the *Take Down* is a high endurance cutter that happened to be on loan from Charleston. A lesser unarmored ship would have been dead in the water.

The captain's next command was, "Return fire!" The 50mm cannon rotated on its turret aiming at the deck of the *Last Chance*. Apparently the gunmen on the deck had reloaded. Just as they were raising their RPGs to fire again, a flurry of shells from our cannon hit the deck of the *Last Chance* and the men flew into the air. Weapons and body parts sprayed in all directions. The upper cabin was heavily damaged and the *Last Chance* bobbed in the water like the little red and white fishing bobbers you might remember as a kid.

Next from the captain: "Hold fire. All crew of *Last Chance* take notice. You have thirty seconds to appear on deck or we will put you on the bottom of the river. This is your last and final warning." Nobody moved. There was silence.

CHAPTER 63

RUN SILENT, RUN DEEP

The Cub had ordered the RPG attack on the *Take Down* and felt the impact of the hit to his *Last Chance*. He shouted, "Report!" to the wheelhouse.

The speaker overhead clicked on. "We have taken extensive damage up top. Our shooters are gone. The assholes are demanding all hands on deck or they blow us out of the water in twenty seconds."

The Cub, who was standing in the control room below, didn't hesitate. "Go, go!" he shouted to his young crew of computer hackers. He pushed and shoved them to go up the ladder steps to the deck. Then he turned to the one man in the room who had not been at a computer and was dressed like a seaman. "Simpson, let's go."

While the computer kids hustled up the steps, Simpson and the Cub, headed in the opposite direction to a door in the stern. They opened the door and jumped in the Oceangate Cyclops 2 submersible sitting open on the launching deck that hung from the stern. Without speaking, Simpson secured the hatch. The Cub barked, "Let's get out of here!" Simpson pushed a button and the Cyclops dropped into the water hardly making a splash. In less than five seconds, it went under with a small trail of bubbles rising and then disappearing on the surface.

"Where to now?" Simpson asked.

"Bring up the GPS and Side-Scan SONAR." After the two screens lit up, the Cub pointed to a spot on the GPS about ten miles offshore. They still had to get themselves down the East River and out to sea, but they had the advantage of stealth. "As they say, run silent, run deep and get us there."

Simpson flipped a switch and the Cyclops dashboard went dim, the dials hardly visible. The engine became silent although the propellers continued to push them forward. They had a head start but knew their lead wouldn't last long once their pursuers figured out what they were doing.

The Cub followed the green dot on the screen that represented their submersible as it slowly moved down river to the harbor. The red dot that represented the *Take Down* remained stationary. That could mean one of three things. Either the *Take Down* was so damaged they could not move, they knew about the Cyclops and called in backup, or hopefully, they hadn't figured it out yet. Just a little more time and good fortune and they might actually get away.

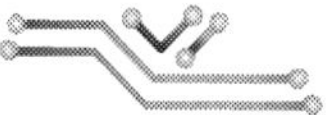

CHAPTER 64

BACKSCATTER

Their remaining crew and the computer geeks slowly emerged, hands up, on the deck of the *Last Chance*. Agnus called out orders. "Approach at half-speed. Keep that 50 cal trained on the deck. Prepare to board."

Little looked at me with a blank expression. Something still didn't feel right, but it seemed like we were out of immediate danger. He broke the silence. "We need to get on that ship and look for that captain and maybe LaSalam now."

Agnus handed Little and me loaded M-14s, lighter than M-16s but still deadly. "Get ready." The *Take Down* slowly approached the *Last Chance*, and I heard the engines cut and then reverse. We drifted alongside and our crew tossed three lines to the deck and the *Last Chance*'s crew anchored the lines to cleats on deck. Since our deck was a little higher but almost even with theirs, our guys slid a ten foot steel plank through the rails and let it drop on the gunnel of the *Last Chance*. We anchored our end and Little began to step onto the plank, but Agnus grabbed his arm and pulled him back. "We go first to secure the vessel. Then you go." Although Little could be pushy when he needed to be, he understood the value of protocol, particularly in hostile situations. He nodded and backed away.

Al, who had been quiet all this time, cornered Little and me. "If our killer is or was on that boat, how would he protect himself or get away in a situation like this?"

Little raised his eyebrows. "What makes you think he got away?"

"Do you see anyone on that deck that looks even vaguely like our guy? How about that Captain Sith, where's he?"

"Hmm, well they're either below deck or they got away?"

Being ever the optimist, I added, "Or they booby-trapped the ship and plan to blow us all up."

Little seemed to take this all in. "I doubt the bomb. I think we've had enough explosions for one day, but it doesn't hurt to be sure." Agnus was just then leading his guys onto the plank. "Agnus! You have any bomb detection equipment or dogs you can bring with?"

Agnus halted his guys. "Chief Thomas, grab the Seeker before you guys proceed." Thomas disappeared below deck and returned with a black handheld device that looked like a voltage meter. "Lieutenant Reagan, can you get any infrared or backscatter below decks? We need to know if anybody's down there?" Backscatter is some very cool technology a friend of mine at MIT had developed that allows you to detect organic matter, like people or drugs, inside shipping containers or trucks or in this case, inside a ship. The military was very quick to see its usefulness.

Reagan came back on the Coms. "Negative on the infrared and backscatter. I don't think anybody's down there."

"OK Thomas. Turn that thing on and take the lead."

Little put down his M-14. "They're gone."

Al was right, but so now what? "OK, how would they get away?"

I was only too happy to play the straight man or foil in this case. "They could have had a dinghy slip away from the stern of the ship."

"No—too visible and too slow," Little said.

"Well I didn't see a helicopter. How about SCUBA?"

Al lit up. "That's it. No, I mean not SCUBA, but maybe some kind of submersible would be quick and unseen. What do you think?" Another spray of seawater came over the deck as our ship rocked in the choppy water. I felt a wet chill on my face and could taste the salt on my lips.

Little shouted over to Agnus who was supervising the surrender of the *Last Chance* crew. "Do you have SONAR on this tub? Er, I mean ship."

Agnus grew red-faced. "You call my *Take Down* a tub again and you can swim to shore." He calmed himself. "Why? What do you need SONAR for?"

Little replied, "Where's our bad guy? Where's their captain for that matter?"

Agnus opened his lips roundly as if to say, "Oh," but nothing came out.

CHAPTER 65

CUT IT NOW

The Cyclops moved quietly down the East River under the Manhattan Bridge, then the Brooklyn Bridge. A few minutes later in deeper water, it passed under the Verrazano and out to sea. Almost an hour passed. The Cub looked attentively at the green screen as the dot representing them moved closer to the X marking their destination.

"We're two minutes out," said the Cub.

"Slow to half speed and deploy the claw." As the craft slowed, an arm slowly emerged from the belly of the beast. It looked like a miniature version of the working arm of a backhoe. But instead of a bucket at the end, it had something that looked like a lobster claw.

Simpson maneuvered the stick that controlled the craft in three dimensions. He pulled it slightly left to turn to port. Then he pushed it slightly forward to start a slow dive. "We're at the target in 5 . . . 4 . . . 3 . . . 2 . . . 1." He pulled back on the stick and cut the engine.

The Cub's face almost burned red with focus and intensity. "Engage the claw." The claw dropped to the ocean floor, kicking up a cloud of silt. Then Simpson inched the claw along the ocean floor until it wrapped its pincers around a fat cable. The cable extended east and west as far as the eye could see in the clear water.

The Cub licked his dry lips. "Cut it now!"

CHAPTER 66

REWIND

Agnus led us down the steep ladder to below deck. We walked along a narrow hallway, stepped over a metal step into the communications room. Four shipmen were crammed into a close space, staring at monitors. There was hardly enough room for us to stand. I could feel my claustrophobia kick in. The dark, the wet, the cold had all the makings of a nightmare scenario.

Agnus broke the silence. "What have you got?"

A young face, almost too young to drive, looked up and then back at the screen. "We have nothing now, but I was able to rewind the last twenty minutes."

Al said, "You can rewind?"

The young man, eyes still on the screen, answered, "Yeah, it's kinda like your DVR. Even if you're not watching or recording, it stores the last hour or so in memory. We were looking for incoming not outgoing so we missed this." He tapped a key on his keyboard and the screen flickered. He pointed to two green shapes. "That's the *Last Chance* and that's us about twenty minutes ago." He hit another key and we saw a small green dot emerge from the *Last Chance* and move down river.

"Fuck, that's them," Little exclaimed. "Can you track where they went?"

"Our range is about a mile, but once they clear the harbor, we lose them."

"Fuck, fuck, fuck!"

CHAPTER 67

SIGNAL LOST

Hager, Osborne, the chiefs of staff and various other security staff were assembled in the Situation Room, briefing the president. She looked tense. She rhythmically tapped a pen on the table with impatience as various generals and directors gave their reports. She was old-school. She always had a yellow legal pad and pen in front of her to take notes. After the hassle with her email account getting hacked by the Russians, she was even more disinclined to commit her thoughts to the digital universe.

Osborne was next. "As you can see on the center screen, we have a satellite over the East River." He used his laser pointer. "Those are the two boats we're tracking. The *Last Chance* that we believed might have LaSalam and possibly a WMD aboard and our guys on the *Take Down*, here."

Longford looked at the wall of OLED screens showing various angles of the scene as well as several other locations they were tracking. "I hear past-tense. I don't need a back story. Just tell me what's happening now. Do we have the situation contained?"

Osborne looked down sheepishly at his notes and took a deep breath. "Do you want the good news or the bad news first?"

Longford exploded. "Are you kidding me? Do you think we're all children here? Stop playing games and just spit it out! And when this is all over, you and I are going to have a serious talk." She blew out an audible breath trying to calm herself.

Osborne turned five shades of red, cleared his throat and spoke in an emotionless voice, "At 11:00, the *Take Down* took RPG fire. She returned fire and subdued the *Last Chance*. We believe that LaSalam was aboard. We have boarded their ship. We did a full search and found that he and Alec Simpson were no longer aboard. A rewind of the *Take Down*'s SONAR showed some kind of submersible leaving the *Last Chance* and heading south to the harbor and probably out to sea. We have dispatched several 'Midnight Express' Cutters and Sikorsky MH-60 Jayhawks to search the five-mile perimeter around the harbor. We figure they had a twenty-minute head start. If we don't locate them in the next ten minutes, the search area becomes so large that the odds of intercept become very low."

Longford cut him off. "So what you're saying is that we screwed-up. How did we lose–"

Just then, two-thirds of the screens in front of them went solid blue. A two-word message blinked in the upper right-hand corner of each screen. "Signal Lost."

CHAPTER 68
KNOCKDOWN

The *Take Down* was moving full-speed ahead bouncing on the swells of the outer harbor, turning to port and heading out to sea. As I leaned on the rail, I could hear the mist bouncing off our hull and smell the salty seawater wafting up from below. I thought of something I read once about the three keys to happiness: someone to love, something to do and something to look forward to. I had the first two covered. Monica is the love of my life and right now I had more than I could handle "to do." But the future seemed so uncertain, I didn't know what I had to look forward to. I'd battled hereditary depression for years, sought treatment and up until a few days ago, the future seemed bright and promising. Frank and I were going to change the world forever, at least for humankind. Now my dark clouds were returning. Much darker than the dark clouds overhead. My whole body shook with a chill, and I didn't think it was from the cold misty air.

Al stepped to the rail beside me. "How are you my friend? You're looking a little gray."

"You're probably used to this—chasing the bad guys, getting shot at, but I'm not. I'm feeling physically and mentally wiped out. Once the adrenaline wears off, you might as well toss me overboard."

"Well I am used to chasing bad guys but never this bad or dangerous. We just moved to the advanced level of this video game."

"Yeah, is the game called 'Doom?'"

Al hit me on the back. "This is the time that you, I mean *we*, need to rally. What's that they say, 'It's not what happens in life that matters, but how you respond to it.' I have found the greatest test of my mettle comes at the darkest times and the rewards for overcoming them are the greatest. So buck up, nerd."

"Yeah, I know the whole 'it's not what knocks you down, but how you bounce back up.' Longford is a great example of that. Don't know anyone who took more shit over forty years and kept coming back. My question is why'd she do it? What drives her? Is it ego or a true sense of mission?"

"I suspect it's both. I think the truly successful have to have that ego-drive to believe they *can* do great things and the mission-drive to believe they *must* do it. Kinda like you. So focus on the mission and get your ass in gear."

"You think of me that way? I guess that's a good thing. I still feel the mission. It just feels like these bastards are always two steps ahead of us. So my 'can-do' ego is feeling a little beaten up at the moment."

Agnus joined us on deck, seemingly out of breath. "Guys, I just got a message. The assholes cut one or more of the major Internet cables on the sea bed about two miles north of here. Most of the overseas and a good part of our US Internet and communications are down."

I felt as though I had just gotten an AED shock to the heart, and a burst of energy flooded back. "How bad is it?"

"So far we believe ninety percent of the US to overseas traffic is down and about sixty percent of US domestic."

"Holy shit," I said. "Well at least we should have some idea of their location. How soon can we get there?"

Agnus looked up. I don't know whether he was calculating or praying. "I'd say, staying at full-throttle, about five minutes, but they will be on the move for sure. The helos will get there in about two and use water-penetrating radar to try to spot them."

Al was taking this all in. "I know Ground Penetrating Radar (GPR) will work for fresh water, but I thought it didn't work for salt water?"

Agnus answered quickly, "It works now. This is some new highly-classified super-cool stuff. The Russians wouldn't like it too much if they knew we knew exactly where all their subs are at all times. Look, I gotta get back to the wheelhouse. I just wanted to give you the news."

"OK, let's nail these guys." Then turning to Al, I said, "I wonder how Longford is handling this knockdown?"

CHAPTER 69

GOOD NEWS—BAD NEWS

"Ok, so now what happened?" Longford snapped.

Shaking, Osborne got off the phone. "They cut a primary and secondary transatlantic cable just off Long Island Sound. It explains our loss of visual. Most transatlantic Internet, phone and a significant part of domestic are down."

"This is getting to be quite a day. What's our response?" Longford turned her gaze to Hager.

He began. "Madame President, I know we're under the gun, so-to-speak, but a little explanatory background is necessary here so you have the context to make good decisions." He paused, awaiting approval.

"Proceed," she said—calmer and more focused now. She'd had her share of crises before and knew how to be cool under pressure, despite her previous outbursts.

Hager began. "It costs us and our European partners between 300 and 500 million dollars to lay a transatlantic cable. There are cable ships specially designed to haul giant spools of cable, slowly drop them and bury them on the ocean floor. It's quite an amazing operation."

Longford interrupted. "I'm sure it's very cool, but we don't have time for the editorial. If they bury the cable, how did these bastards get to it?"

"On account of the ocean depth and mechanical limits, it's not buried very deep—just enough to hide it visually. With some sophisticated detection equipment, the cables could be, and obviously have been, found and cut."

"So we're screwed or is there a Plan B? Tell me there's a Plan B." She was new at this and there was so much to learn. No single human being could master this in a lifetime. That's why her staff and advisors were so crucial. The average American's hope is that people like this were smart enough and tough enough to keep them safe.

Hager continued. "There is some possible good news and some bad news."

Longford snapped. "I told you I hate that game. Cut the crap and just lay it out."

Hager was in deep now. He had seen combat and he too knew how to be cool under pressure. "It is possible to run Internet and coms through special, very expensive satellites. They cost about a billion apiece. So Congress, in their infinite, near-sighted wisdom, wouldn't allocate the funds needed for the more expensive hardware."

Longford couldn't help herself. "Those jerks will not even fund the CDC, but kickbacks to the oil companies are still being approved. Go on. Sorry."

Well a few years ago, we detected Russian subs snooping around our undersea cables. That really spooked us. So we found the money from one of our 'special funds' to put two of these satellites up, just in case."

"OK, I'll bite. So what's the bad news?"

"Amazingly, the satellites were just put into stationary orbit two weeks ago. The bad news is that they have not been fully tested or deployed."

Longford smiled for the first time that day, but she knew the stress was showing in the dark circles under her eyes. "Clearly this is an emergency. How fast can we get them deployed? Let's put it another way, fuck the testing and turn the suckers on!"

CHAPTER 70

FINDING THE LIGHT

Our engines slowed as we approached the spot where the cables had been cut. There was no guarantee, in fact it was unlikely, that the submersible with LaSalam and Simpson were still nearby. However, we felt some trepidation, since my previous encounters with these guys were near deadly.

My mother always said that if you make good decisions, things will work out in the "long run." The results today may not be what you expected, but the probability edge is that good decisions produce good results and will win out in the end. I don't know what made me think at that moment about the "long run," but maybe the frosty mist that chilled my cheeks made me reflect on the decisions I'd made. It's funny I thought how my clients would often use the long run as a negotiating ploy. They'd say things like, "We're just starting out, but if you cut us a break, we'll give you much more business in the long run." I heard this so often that I would just smile and know better. The long run would never come.

Yet here we were aboard the *Take Down* ready to face down some international terrorists. I thought for me, the long run had finally arrived. All my decisions, successes and failures, had led to this point. To be determined was whether the edge would be on our side or would this just be, as they say in poker, a bad beat.

As these thoughts drifted in and out of my brain, an incredible explosion rocked the ocean surface in front of us. A huge geyser-like gush of water rose fifty feet into the air. Whatever it was, the huge shock produced something like a mini-tidal wave that was upon us in less than a minute. The captain came over the speaker on deck. "All hands brace yourselves for impact!" The wave looked thirty feet high and blocked out the sun as it approached. The wave rocked the ship to port and then hit the *Take Down* broadside washing over the deck and turning the deck almost ninety degrees to the water.

Al and I grabbed the nearest beam, wrapping our arms tightly. But then. . . but then, we were under water. I gasped for air. It was so cool. So cold. I couldn't breath. I was still under. Which way was up? My lungs were burning.

When I was maybe ten or twelve, I remembered swimming in a lake in the Berkshires. I swam down until the light above faded and did somersaults underwater until I needed air, but I couldn't tell which way was up. I swam furiously, moving my arms as fast as I could, but I was going deeper. I began to feel dizzy and stopped moving. I felt like this was it. I was going to die then, but my body began to slowly rise. I was hardly buoyant, since I was a skinny kid with very little body fat. However, it was just enough to give me the direction up. Back then, I began swimming again as hard as I could until my head burst through the water's surface. I sucked in big gulps of air. Then I just floated on my back until my heartbeat slowed. I stared at the pale blue sky with wisps of clouds drifting by and it was calm.

Just then, I snapped awake. I realized I had either lost consciousness or just drifted off. The pain in my chest was palpable and I was drifting. Still holding my breath, I raised my head and saw a very faint gray light. I swam toward it. Faster now. No air. Could I make it? Was I alive or dead? I couldn't feel anything.

CHAPTER 71

THE CUB IS DEAD

Eskabar tapped another button on his keyboard and looked up from his computer screen. "It is done," he said in a low solemn voice.

"It had to be done," the Leopard said. "My brother served Allah and has been taken by him to heaven."

Eskabar had known driven men and cold-hearted men in his fifty-six years. However, he never met a man who held both such qualities to such an extreme. He couldn't help himself. "Sire, I mean only the highest respect, but was there no other way to save him?"

"My dear Eskabar, this chess game is very complex and perhaps several levels above your intelligence. Sometimes you have to sacrifice a knight to capture a queen. My brother was a valiant knight, but I am the chess master. I have to think several moves ahead. We could not afford his being captured or compromised by our opponents. Besides, with any luck, we may have taken out that pesky computer geek and his partner. You wisely installed a destruction device in the submersible. Part of me regrets losing my brother, whom I loved almost as much as Allah. But unlike Abraham who brought his son Isaac into the tent as a sacrifice to God, I had to carry out the deed." LaSalam seemed to be in some kind of trance as he explained his actions, but then his face reddened and his hands began to shake. "And if you ever, ever question my actions again, you will join my brother. Yet you will go to a much darker place and your family will join you there."

Eskabar's face turned ashen for the second time that day. He felt like he might throw up, but he choked it back. He would not risk a third strike with this dangerous man. No, he must not.

"Meet me here tomorrow at 9:00 AM. Then we can plan our next steps to destroy these bastards." The Leopard turned and walked out. As he left, without turning around, he raised his right hand in a backhand wave. Eskabar silently wished he would never return.

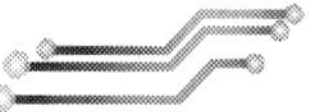

CHAPTER 72

BACKSTROKE

I broke through the surface of the choppy sea and sucked in air as if it was my first breath. I suppose in a way it was. Treading water, I circled 360 degrees to look for the ship, for help, for anything. The chop in the water kept obscuring my vision. As I bobbed up and down, the swells kept splashing the cold water in my eyes. Finally, I spotted the *Take Down*, maybe 100 yards to the west. I waved my arms frantically while kicking my feet harder to stay above water. So cold. My shoulder and leg throbbed with pain from my wounds. How could they possibly see me in this gray water with my gray soaked clothes? Was there anyone still on board? OK. OK, I had to think.

My shoes. I realized I was still wearing my shoes. As I kicked, they pulled against the water, straining my leg muscles. Get the shoes off. I pushed my big toe against the back of each shoe and pushed hard, harder and finally got the shoes off. OK, I could move and kicked my legs more easily. So swim. But breathing was hard. My asthma was kicking in with the cold inside and outside my lungs. OK, backstroke. Elementary backstroke. Easier on the arms and legs and I could breathe. I finally began to calm down and get into a rhythm, lifting and turning my head periodically to make sure I was still pointed toward the ship. I could smell the strong, salty sea air but could hardly feel my limbs. The cold had made them numb, but I was still moving. Stroke, stroke, stroke. One more. Keep going. How long had I been swimming? The *Take Down* still looked far away. I just kept going. It was swim or die. It was so cold now that I felt like I might not even know if I died. I could just drift into an icy unconsciousness. My limbs still stroking but slower and slower until . . .

I felt something pulling under my arms. I was being lifted. My back hit hard rubber and then I was flopped like a big fish over the side of the Zodiac rescue boat. Soaked and dripping wet, I looked up to see Al. She was looking down at me, smiling.

"Nice swim?" she said.

I was freezing, both numb and in pain at the same time (is that possible?), but I had to smile back. "A bit chilly for my taste," I mumbled, shaking uncontrollably. The crewman, Bob, ripped off my shirt and threw a scratchy wool blanket around me. You could smell the wet wool that had probably been in mothballs. It felt great. Al handed me some warm liquid from a thermos. I don't know what it was, but I could feel it go all the way down. My head slowly began to clear. Feeling was starting to come back to my fingers and limbs and then intense tingling, like when your foot falls asleep and you try to get up and walk on it. "What the hell happened?"

"Now that's a good question. We figure either they blew themselves up—a suicide bomb—or somebody on their side took them out. We checked with command and it wasn't our guys who did it. I was worried. We almost lost you there," she said.

"I appreciate that. When you're so close to death for so long, it's beyond worry. First, it's about survival. Then your mind does tricks on you. It somehow changes you—maybe forever, but I'm still processing it. I thought you fell in with me. At least, I think that's what I remember. What happened to you?"

"I was a little luckier than you were. When the *Take Down* listed so much, I guess a line on the deck must have slipped into the water beside me. I grabbed it and got pulled back aboard pretty quickly. The shock waves from the explosion just seemed to carry you away. By the time I got back aboard and looked out to sea, you we're gone, baby, gone." Her voice just drifted off into the ocean.

"You know I once made a study of powerful questions. Questions that lead to action or provoke the brain into deep thought. You know what my favorite question is that I came up with?"

"What?" she said.

"That was one of them." I smirked. "No my favorite question, one I might even put on my tombstone, really applies now."

She sighed. "OK, now you're killing me, what is it?"

"So now what?" I said.

CHAPTER 73

MONICA

Once I warmed up and could walk and talk almost normally again, Chief Thomas handed me a cell phone. I had to call Monica at home. Oh, but she could not be home. Was she OK? I was so focused on the chase and myself, I wasn't even thinking about Monica and Evan. Was there something wrong with me?

"Hi Monica. Are you OK?"

"What? I'm fine for now. But what about you? They called to tell me you were lost at sea, but they were searching. What happened?"

"It's a long story, but I am all right. I don't know how I got into all this. I'm just an ordinary guy. Maybe a little smarter than average, but . . . "

"You're way smarter than average, but your problem is you think you can solve any problem and you don't know how to say, 'No.' Sometimes it's better just to walk away and let other people handle things. Most of the time things will work out. Sometimes things will get screwed up. But you can't personally fix the world's problems. And there's us. What about your family? We're stuck in this supposed 'safe house.' Evan can only play so many video games. He can't even call or text his friends. When does this end?"

"Sweetheart, I don't like it either. I mean I almost died. But I feel like somehow I started this and maybe I can help save us all. I've got to finish it."

"Fine. You almost died. That's supposed to make me feel better or feel guilty for hating what this is doing to us. Which is it? I almost died when that nut job came to the house. The two agents there did die. All I know is that I've supported you in all your cockeyed schemes for twenty-five years. I don't know how much more of this Evan and I can take. Just get done with this. Get us out of here or we're done." The line went dead. I felt numb all over again.

Without my family, where would I have been? I felt a wave of anxiety come over me that felt colder and more deadly than the wave of seawater that hit the *Take Down*. In my mind, I was trying to swim out of it again, but there was no light above or below. Just darkness. Cold, eternal, paralyzing darkness.

CHAPTER 74

MULTITASKING

I suppose it was time to regroup. Once planes were flying again, Little arranged for a Learjet to take me and Al back to California, my office and my team. I wished I could enjoy the perks of flying in a private jet, but I was still shaken from my near death experience and anxiously awaiting the next shoe to drop. Monica was right. I always thought of myself as the Master Problem Solver. Maybe some problems you just can't solve? And if I continued down this road, would I lose Monica and my family by divorce or worse? I felt like there was a huge weight pressing down on me, pushing me into my seat. I fell asleep for the first time in days.

With the time difference from flying to the West Coast, it was only 5:00 Pacific Time when I arrived. It felt like I had been awake for days. I walked down the main hall of the office. It was quiet except for the security guard Al arranged standing at the door of the lab. It felt good to be back, calmer somehow.

"Hail the conquering hero," Bart quipped as I walked in.

"Maybe, the conquered hero," I said. I surveyed the room. Loretta was there and gave me a big hug. Just feeling another warm human being felt so good. I could smell Chanel No. 19, her favorite. I pulled her closer.

"You survived and took down a group of terrorists. I'd say you did pretty well," she said.

"Well the Leopard is still out there. Who knows what else he has planned. The power outage, the plane crashes and cutting the Internet cables were probably just warm ups. I feel like something big, maybe much bigger is coming.

"The guys have been working hard on trying to figure that out," she said. "But wait a minute. I thought LaSalam was in the sub?"

"Oh, I forgot to tell you something important. We finally found Sith, the captain of the *Last Chance.* He was well hidden in a compartment beneath a trapdoor covered by a rug. Guess that was his Plan B. Anyway, when Little leaned on him, he folded. He told us his boss that escaped on the sub was not the Leopard at all, but his brother Momar, nicknamed the Cub."

"Holy shit. Excuse me, but this gets crazier by the minute." She lapsed into thought. This was a lot to process.

I looked around the room and saw our Scaggers, Jay and Jazzle, intensely focused on their screens, clicking away. "Hi Guys!" I said. They both waved without looking up. "What have you got?"

Jazzle was a crazy-smart twenty-something young woman from the Philippines. Her dark hair and light brown skin only magnified her green eyes. She turned and smiled. "Glad you're back. Bart, Jay, Killer and I have been trying to pick up any communications in and around New York City that matches our profiles."

"Wait, how do you have access to that stuff?"

"Remember who we work for during our day jobs. So, do you really want to know?"

"No, no, that's OK. Carry on." I smiled. I love really smart, techy people. Once you figure out how to communicate with them and not piss them off, you can be in for a wild, but great ride.

There was a crackling sound behind me. I turned as one of the large OLED screens came alive. There was Frank. "Hey, we missed you, son."

"I really missed you all too. It might have been permanent, if it wasn't for Al and the Coast Guard."

"Hey, did you forget we've digitized you just like me. It's not too bad living in the digiverse and here I am."

"I know and I don't mean any knock against you. I'm just not quite ready to make the digital leap if I don't have to. I mean, I still want to be able to hold Monica and Evan. I still want to enjoy the sensations of the real world.

"And have sex," Bart said. Everybody laughed.

"We've made some progress in that area too," Frank said.

"What, in your free time?"

"Sam, you forget. When you're digital like I am, you don't need sleep, and you can multi-task tens of thousands of tasks at the same time. It's actually quite liberating and exciting."

"But no sex." Bart again.

I couldn't help but laugh. "You seem to have only one thing on your mind. In case you've forgotten, we're in the middle of an international crisis."

"Hey, I can multitask too. Can you see my right hand?"

I bit. I looked down and his right hand was out of sight, moving under the desk. Loretta spit out her coffee she laughed so hard. "OK, that's enough. Frank, what have you been working on? Anything good?"

"We may have had some success tracing the signal that detonated the submersible with the Cub aboard. It went through multiple servers and a secure satellite uplink, but it has a unique packet-identifier that allowed us to follow it despite the encryption."

"Please explain for us lower level geeks."

"It's like DNA. You can change your outward appearance, add disguises and even mutilate a body and the DNA remains unchanged. If you can track or test for the DNA, you can find what you're looking for. In this case, the DNA for a detonation signal to a specific target is pretty unique. We think we have a pretty reasonable idea of its origin. Now whether the Leopard is at that location or just one of his agents or they've set up a physical relay station there, we can't tell unless you physically go and look."

"I noticed, you said 'you.' I'm not sure I'm ready to go back into battle again."

"I didn't mean that you personally have to go. Call Al, or even better Little, and let them handle it. And by the way, did I mention we don't have an exact location. We have a two to three block radius."

"I have a Hasidic friend who walked me around his neighborhood in Williamsburg, Brooklyn. There were 10,000 people living in a two to three block radius."

"You'll figure it out. Bart will give you the information and you can do what you think best with it."

"Great."

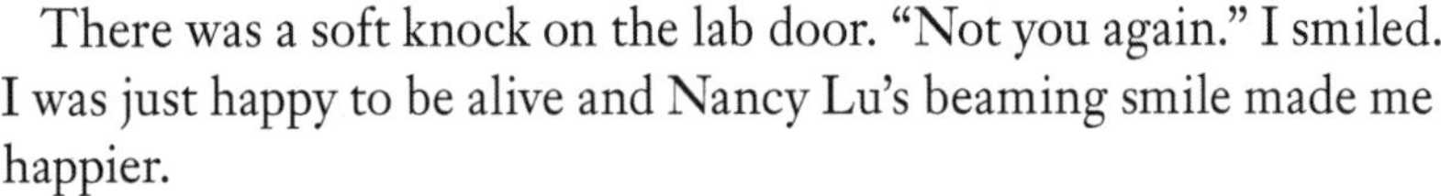

There was a soft knock on the lab door. "Not you again." I smiled. I was just happy to be alive and Nancy Lu's beaming smile made me happier.

"I heard you had an exciting time in New York. I'm glad you're OK and I'm glad you can swim," she said without a hint of sarcasm. "Do you have a few minutes to talk?"

"For you, sure. On the record or off the record?"

"Whatever you want."

"OK. Let's go to my office."

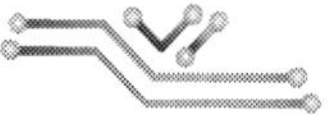

CHAPTER 75

THANK YOU FOR YOUR SERVICE

Maybe, it's time for the End Game, the Leopard thought. "My opponents have made a number of unexpected defensive moves, but I am still the aggressor. I control the board, but I fear our location may have been compromised by now. I know you have done everything you can to encrypt our communications, but these devils are very clever. I'd almost call them 'worthy opponents' if I did not despise them and what they stand for."

Eskabar listened, still shaken from the Leopard's angry outburst and his threats earlier. He hesitated to speak or question his master, but he needed to know what to do. "So sire, what would you like me to do now?"

"I think we must leave New York. Follow me." LaSalam led Eskabar into the computer network server room where all their files and servers lived. There were racks of servers from floor to ceiling. Tiny red lights flashed on the racks. You could hear a quiet hum over the air conditioning. The air smelled like ozone, purified but faintly chemical.

Eskabar waited for instructions. LaSalam closed the door and looked out through the one-way window at the rows of young men clicking away on their computers. Eskabar joined him, standing by his side, also looking at the young men. "Viktor will meet us at the next location. I need you to terminate them."

Eskabar knew better than to question the Leopard's orders, but he needed to make sure. He tried to keep his voice level—no emotion, even though he'd come to care for these boys. "Sire, I just want to confirm. You want me to terminate them all right now, immediately?"

The Leopard began to redden again, then calmed himself. He needed Eskabar's cooperation. His unbridled anger would be counterproductive. He took a deep breath. "Yes, right now." Eskabar went to the wall beside the window where there was a large red toggle switch in a secure glass case. He pulled a key ring from his pocket and fumbled nervously for the right key. With his hand shaking, he turned the lock on the glass case and lifted it. He looked once more at LaSalam for some sign that maybe he had changed his mind, but the Leopard silently nodded once. Eskabar pulled down on the switch lever and a faintly visible mist emanated from the vents in the office ceiling. Slowly some of the young men began coughing. One of them stood up, turned and looked at Eskabar through the glass window. A look of disbelief on his face, he coughed, spit up a white foam and doubled over convulsing on the floor. The others one-by-one fell to the floor in a kind of mass epilepsy as the deadly poison did its worst.

LaSalam watched the horrifying scene from the window with a faint smile on his face. Unable to watch, Eskabar turned away. After a few minutes, the Leopard broke the gloomy silence. "Good. That's done. Now destroy the servers."

Although Eskabar knew this was the plan all along, actually carrying it out was another matter. He loved his machines as much as he cared for the young men, maybe more. He had been so proud of what they'd been able to accomplish, but he hadn't been able to really complete the mission and now it was over for them. He went to a keyboard that sat on a small desk next to the server racks and typed a few commands. The whirring of the servers stopped each in succession. The red lights went off one-by-one. After a few minutes, it was deadly quiet.

"Is that it? Are the hard drives wiped?"

"It takes approximately five minutes for a complete wipe." Eskabar looked at his watch. There was a solitary beep from the other side of the room. Then three rapid beeps in succession. "It's done." Eskabar looked drained and weary, like he'd just lost his closest friend. In a way, he had.

"Then, like the Americans say, I thank you for your service."

Eskabar turned and looked. His eyes were expressionless. He knew what was coming.

LaSalam pulled his Glock from his jacket pocket and fired a shot between Eskabar's eyes. Eskabar fell sideways, limp onto the floor. It wasn't necessary, but out of habit, the Leopard fired two more shots into Eskabar's chest. Then he removed two high-powered grenades from his briefcase, pulled the pins and rolled them down the aisles between the racks of servers. He turned and walked out.

CHAPTER 76

THREE TIMES

Before I did anything else, I had to see Monica. It was getting late, but this couldn't wait. Al assigned me a bodyguard named Stan. He looked like Michael Cena, and he was going to be my shadow for awhile. We got in the car, a Dodge Charger, that I loved to drive. Punch the gas and it took off like a rocket. But for security, Stan had to be the driver and we proceeded to the safe house.

It was a cabin in the woods like I imagined it, near Lafayette Reservoir. As we drove up the driveway, I could only see a single lamp lit in the front window. The late afternoon sun was hiding behind the tall trees. I hoped Monica was OK. I asked Stan to hang back for a few minutes. Jerry Sanders was standing guard at the door. He looked like somebody out of the old Mr. Universe ads on comic books when I was a kid. You know, with the scrawny *Before* and brawny *After* shots. Jerry was definitely the *After* shot. He knew me, since he did some shifts looking out for us at the lab.

I whispered, "Hi Jerry, everything OK?" He nodded and I put my finger to my lips.

I started to knock, thought better of it and tried the door handle. It was unlocked. Surprising, considering all that we had been through, but we were in the woods and Monica never liked to lock doors.

I went in quietly and as I turned the corner, I saw Monica, her back to me, reading on the sofa, legs up in her summer robe.

"Guess who's home?" I said.

She whipped around like in a dream. It felt like a dream. Maybe she was frightened at first, but then she broke into a big grin and ran over to hug and kiss me. "I was so scared for you, for us. I'm sorry for the way we left things on the phone."

I kissed her back hard and lifted her off her feet. I just never wanted to let her go, ever. "I missed you so much. You feel so good."

I smelled the faint scent of lilac, which reminded me of when I first met her. She'd always pick a flower and wear it just behind her ear, tucked in her blonde hair. I loved that. "Where's Evan?"

"He's playing video games in his room." She grabbed my hand and gently pulled me up the stairs. "Come to bed."

What could be better? I was already aroused.

Little and his team, maybe including Al, were probably already on their way back to New York. I just had to come here first. I wasn't going to lose my family over a mission. Monica was right. They'd probably do fine without me. Plus, Monica made it worth my while . . . three times. I hadn't had that kind of stamina since I was a horny teenager. Just being close to her would have been enough, feeling the warmth of her smooth skin and the loving gentleness in her touch. The sex was a bonus.

"I have to go soon."

"Why?"

"I think you know and I love that you care. The guys may well have nailed the bastard by then, but if they haven't . . . They may need my help."

"I don't know. You just got here. I don't want to lose you. Do you really have to go?"

"I couldn't live with myself if something terrible happened that I could have stopped. Besides, I think we are all in direct danger. So we all have to do whatever we can, don't you think?"

"I guess I understand. At least part of me does. My heart is a different matter. Just be safe and come back to us."

"I will and we'll get you out of here as soon as we've eliminated the threat."

"No need to hurry. Jerry's kinda hot."

I threw my pillow at her.

CHAPTER 77

THE RUMBLE DOWN UNDER

I landed at LaGuardia the next morning. I had taken the "red eye" flight from California. I got in at 6:00 AM, and I was already feeling the jet lag. I remembered many years ago as a student, flying out of LaGuardia standby to catch a flight back to college one evening. All the flights were full. So I slept overnight in a very uncomfortable black, Naugahyde chair. I didn't get much sleep as the fluorescents glared down on me and the odor of cleaning fluid wafted in the air. It hadn't changed a bit.

The Uber I summoned, a little blue Toyota Prius, pulled up to the curb ten minutes later. It was clean and comfortable for a small car. *Is Prius the official Uber car*, I wondered? The driver's name was Wilbur Aziz. Mixed marriage or changed name? I wasn't sure, but I had too much on my mind to engage in small talk.

Wilbur broke the silence. "We can take the Brooklyn-Queens Expressway to the FDR or take the Midtown Tunnel and save about ten minutes, but there's a toll which you would have to pay. Which do you prefer?"

"Pay the toll. I'm in a bit of a hurry."

"OK. I love my GPS. I'm new at this and it's a lifesaver," Wilbur said in perfect American English.

The GPS came to life. A slightly sexy female voice issued the first few sets of instructions as we exited the airport onto the highway. A few minutes later she said, "Take exit 35 for I-495/L.I. Expressway toward Midtown Tunnel/Eastern L.I./Greenpoint Avenue." Traffic seemed to be moving well. Maybe we had beat rush hour by a bit. Then a different voice, a man's voice came over the GPS. "Welcome to New York, Mr. Sunborn. Although we have never met, I feel like I know you."

Wilbur looked at me with an expression that was half puzzled and half shitting-in-his-pants. I felt the same way. I said, "Who is this?"

The GPS man responded, "I know you are wondering who I am. Unfortunately, Mr. Aziz's GPS only communicates one way. So I will do the talking and it's best if you just listen. I believe your friends refer to me as the Leopard, but you can just call me Ahmed. I know you are heading to Broad Street, but I fear that by the time you get there, I will be gone. I'm sorry to have missed you. I tried to meet you back home at the Gorge, but your friend, Detective Favor had other ideas. No worries. I'm sure we'll meet again very soon, after I take care of some important business. I'm sure you're wondering how I tracked you down and can talk to you through a GPS. You'll eventually figure it out. Until then, enjoy your visit to New York. It's an exciting city."

I was stunned silent. I'm sure LaSalam had someone track my flight. Maybe he'd even hacked my phone and that was how he knew about the Uber I ordered. If that was true, then he knew the Uber driver and where we were going. From there, it was a small leap to hacking the GPS. I blew out a breath. *I had better get a new phone, a burner phone*, I thought. Had he taped my conversations with Monica? Did he know where she was? I was having a full-fledged anxiety attack. But maybe that was what the Leopard wanted. He was taunting me. I had to think. I couldn't let despair overwhelm me. The stakes were too high.

Little and Al stayed in New York overnight but got little sleep. They got up early and were in lower Manhattan, walking the area where intelligence had pointed them. Suddenly, the earth shook under their feet. *Could be a subway passing*, Little thought. "Did you feel that, Al?"

She stood still, having felt the vibration of the concrete. "Yes, I felt it. Do you think that could be our guy?" They had been searching a three block radius with no luck for almost twenty-four hours.

Wilbur's little Prius pulled to the curb beside them and I got out of the Uber car. "Hey, guys."

"Nice of you to come." Al looked down at her watch. "You go partying last night or did you somehow know we'd be here wasting our time?"

"Tough night, huh? I was taking care of some important business." Time to change the subject. "I just spoke to or I should say, heard from the Leopard."

"What?" Little and Al said in unison.

I filled them in on the conversation. Just telling Al and Little what had happened in the Uber helped me calm down. I dropped my smartphone on the ground and crushed it with the heel of my shoe. "I'll need a new secure phone and I'll need to contact Monica, both to make sure she's OK and give her my new number."

"I can take care of that. I'll make sure you get a secure phone on Uncle Sam. It's the least I can do," Little said.

OK, I had to focus. "I think maybe he's fled. What's the status here? Have you found anything?"

Little broke the tension. "Shit. We'll have to talk more about your Leopard call later. We haven't had much luck here. We went door-to-door and office-to-office on Water, Bridge and Pearl Streets all the way over to State. Ironic that we're so near to the New York Stock Exchange. You probably couldn't feel it in the car, but we felt a rumble below the street a few minutes ago. I'm going to have the guys fan out and see if they see anything new or out-of the-ordinary, Here, take this com and stick it in your ear."

"Cool. Does that mean I'm official?"

"No. You'll never be official, but we want to keep track of you and maybe you'll even make yourself useful."

"Thanks for the vote of confidence. I now feel so empowered. When do I get my badge?"

"In your dreams."

Al said, "Why don't you stick with me. Besides we make a pretty good team."

"Thanks, that makes me feel better. Just no swimming please." I put the com in my left ear and we proceeded to walk up Broad Street. "Where were you when you felt the rumble?"

"Back where you found us."

I turned and saw Little and his team spreading out like ants down the side streets. "Did you get any sense of direction from the rumble? Was it more pronounced on one side of you versus the other?"

"Now you sound like the detective."

"Well we both are problem solvers. Except I'm usually debugging code and you're chasing murderers and rapists. So what's the answer to my question?"

She laughed, "So I've got a code jockey as a partner, helping to track an international terrorist? I felt like the rumble may have come from up Broad Street. That's why I chose to have us go this way."

"Code jockey, huh. What could be better?" We walked up Broad. As we passed Pearl I spotted smoke coming from one of the sidewalk grates. Sometimes in New York, you'll see steam or vapor coming from the subway grates or manholes, but this had the distinct odors of cordite and maybe burnt wires. "Wait." I grabbed Al's arm. "Over there. What's that?"

We crossed the street until we were just in front of 90 Broad. It looked like maybe a law office building. The smoke was still wafting from the grate in front. The odor was even more pungent now. Al spoke into her com. "Little, get over here—90 Broad. We've got some smoke coming from underground. Bring some guys. We should check it out."

About two minutes later, Little and six suits showed up. "Where is it?"

I couldn't help myself. "Oh, that's right the FBI can't smell anything."

"Very funny. And I'm DHS, FYI." Little looked down, literally two feet in front of us. "Oh, down there. Let's see if there's stairs or an elevator."

All of us moved into the lobby. A lone, short, balding security guard looked surprised and maybe a little terrified. "Can I help you?"

Little raised his ID. “DHS. We need to know where the stairs and elevator are, and if there is any other way to get below ground here.”

The security guard pointed to the rear of the lobby. Little pointed to his guys. “You come with me. We’ll take the stairs. Al, Sam, you try the elevator.”

Al smirked. “I love DHS—always in charge.”

I could smell the burnt wire odor even more now. I turned to the guard. “Did you feel a rumble here a few minutes ago?”

“Yeah, but I thought maybe it was the subway.”

“Do you smell that burning odor?”

“I have a pretty bad cold at the moment.”

“OK, thanks.” I rushed off with Al to the nearest elevator.

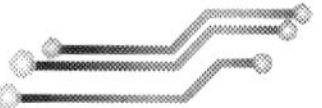

CHAPTER 78
THE 9TH CIRCLE

Al and I pressed the down button and one of the two elevators appeared. It was smallish for a pretty tall building. It smelled like chicken soup. As a kid, I was pretty claustrophobic, but it hadn't bothered me in years. Now, that queasy, anxious feeling came rushing back. Maybe it was just the fear of what we would find down there.

"Sam, they sent specs of this building to me and Little." She looked at her smartphone and then at the elevator buttons. The lowest button read, "SUB2." She kept glancing back and forth between her phone and the elevator buttons.

"What is it?"

"It says here on the specs that there was some heavy excavation work and renovation a few years ago, but it's sure not apparent looking at the building." She punched SUB2. "Let's take a look. The rumbling came from down there somewhere."

The door opened on Floor SUB2, the sub-sub-basement. The light was dim. Al broke out her flashlight. All we could see was some storage lockers and supply closets. It was cold and dank, but seemingly undisturbed. We walked back to the elevator, which thankfully was still there. The last thing I needed was to get stuck down here.

"Hmm . . . " Al said staring at the elevator buttons again. "If they had excavating equipment in here, how's it that this place doesn't look like it's been changed in decades?"

"Maybe there are more floors or a different elevator or stairs?"

Al barked into her com, "Little, how are you doing on the stairs?"

"We went up and we went down. Stairs stop at the basement. You?"

"We're in the second sub-basement and we don't see anything unusual. Did you look at the building specs? Where are all the renovations and excavating that they got a permit for three years ago?"

"I was thinking the same thing. Hidden storage or backroom maybe?"

"I'd think if there was an underground explosion and smoke, we'd know it here."

I didn't realize it, but I was thinking out loud. "What if there is a key or combination that gets this elevator to go lower, maybe to a hidden floor. This elevator has a round keyhole."

"Yeah, that's called a tubular or tumbler lock. Common in elevators for emergencies. Let's get that key and try it."

We returned to the lobby and approached the mini security guard.

Al put on her best in-charge voice. "We need the key to the elevator now."

The little man started to protest, but Al cut him off. "This a matter of national security. Cough up the key right now."

He fumbled in his pocket and pulled out a large keychain that seemed to have a hundred keys on it. Why anyone needed that many keys was beyond me. I think most people just collect keys and never discard the old useless ones. I'd bet most of those keys didn't do a thing. He looked nervously at the key ring. Fortunately, there was only one tubular key or we could have been there for hours trying to find the right one. He unclipped it and handed it to Al.

Back in the elevator, Al slipped the key into the lock and turned. "OK, here goes." We just stood there.

"There's a down button. Maybe now with the key turned, we could be in manual mode. Try that." She pressed the down button and the elevator descended, this time dinging as we passed the basement, dinging again at SUB1 and dinging a last time when we came to a stop at SUB2. "OK, so now what?"

I thought about it for a minute. "Let's try some combinations of buttons together. Like press one and two together." She did that and nothing happened. "Try another." She pressed three and four together. Again nothing.

"Hey, you're the math guy. There are fifteen floors in this building, plus a basement and two sub-basements. I bet there are thousands of combinations, and we'd be here for days trying to figure it out when it might not be a combination at all. C'mon, you can do better." She smiled despite the predicament.

"Now that's a good puzzle for a math geek like me. Well, the building has no thirteenth floor. I always loved that one. Don't the people on the fourteenth floor realize they are really on the thirteenth floor?"

"C'mon, cut the crap. Get to the point."

"Sorry, so then there are seventeen floors. Assuming that the combination is of two, one button for each hand, and that the order doesn't matter, then there are one hundred thirty-six permutations. That's a lot, but we could probably do them all in an hour or less, except . . . "

"Except what?"

"See punching the numbers may be like entering a PIN or password. It may have a lockout after three or five failed attempts."

"Great, so we're screwed."

"We could always dig up the floor."

"So you're suggesting we come in here with jackhammers and backhoes to dig up something that might not even be there. Not going to happen. Even if I could get all the permissions without getting locked up in a padded cell first, it would take too much time. The trail is growing colder by the minute."

We stood in silence. Neither of us knowing what to do next. Sometimes you merely hit a wall. Then an idea came to me. Just like it seems to happen to me when I am in the shower. Your unconscious works a problem or retrieves a memory—it's always amazed me. "Try 9—11."

"What?" Al looked at me. I couldn't tell if she was asking a question or wondering if I had gone crazy on her.

"Press the buttons 9 and 11 together." The significance had not been lost on either of us. Suddenly, the elevator lurched and began to descend again, farther down. As it moved, it dinged as if it was passing floors, but did not open. It was so slow, it seemed to descend forever. However, after the eighth ding, the door opened. We'd found it.

CHAPTER 79

THE NUMBER 2

He could feel the adrenaline pumping. In a way he regretted killing Eskabar. He had been useful and loyal. But LaSalam was a hunter and a killer. Death of your prey was the only successful outcome. He got a little aroused when he thought about the site of the young men convulsing on the floor. *This would be the fate of his true enemy soon*, he thought. Very soon.

However, now he had to move and move anonymously. The Americans were on his trail. The private jet was out, as that might be compromised. He couldn't even take a taxi as that would leave a witness and a trail. He walked over to Wall Street and descended to the subway platform. The Number 2 or 3 train uptown would do. He boarded the subway and took a seat. The trains weren't particularly crowded this time of day, midday between rush hours. Most passengers were heads down in their iPhones. They wouldn't even know he was there and the mortal danger he was capable of. Like robots. *These automatons have had their minds stolen by technology*, he thought. Well, he'd turn that technology back on them, Inshallah.

He exited the Number 2 subway at Penn Station, went upstairs and paid cash for the next train to Boston. This way he could stay anonymous and the Acela was pretty fast—maybe four hours to Boston. His jet could do it in less than an hour, but the risk of being caught was too great now. The plan must go forward, and he had to give the final command when everything and everybody was in place. This would make 9/11 look like a pin prick compared to the massive heart attack he planned to inflict. After this, there might be no coming back for the Americans.

CHAPTER 80

SHERLOCK

The elevator doors opened onto an office-like floor full of cubicles, but this was no ordinary office scene. As we stepped forward, our feet sloshed in water. Al swept her flashlight around the office. There were dead bodies strewn about everywhere. She focused her light on one, then another. Judging from the foam on their lips and their contorted limbs, it looked like poison for sure, maybe a neurotoxin. Something must have set off the sprinklers, but there were no signs of a fire. Then we turned to the left and saw the blown out glass of a server room where telltales of smoke still wafted into the main office across our flashlight beam. The smell of burnt wire and something else sickening, like loose bowels, filled the air

We walked closer to the server room, holding our noses, and saw bent metal and fragments of electronic parts and pieces all over. The servers had clearly been destroyed, but that room was relatively dry. I assumed that's because most server rooms with expensive, important equipment use halon gas for fire suppression. If a fire breaks out, the gas is released into the room starving all the oxygen, extinguishing the fire and saving the delicate equipment.

"Well Al, I guess we found our explosion."

"No shit, Sherlock. We've got to get Little and some forensics down here right away." She tried talking into her com, but ten stories down—no way that was going to work. "Crap, no com. I've got to go back up and get the team. You can come with or hang out here and have a look around."

Dark, dead bodies, ten stories down and alone. Every part of my being screamed to me, *Get the fuck out of here*, but I knew this was our best chance to find a clue. "I'll stay. See what I can find."

"Just don't touch anything. Oh, and here. Take my flashlight. I have another. I'll get Little and the guys and be back as fast as I can."

She hurried back to the elevator, her light beam sweeping right and left, leading the way. She got in the elevator and looked back at me. I looked at her face that was only a ghostly shadow in the reflection of the light from the flashlight. Then the elevator door closed and she was gone. I was alone in the dark. Nothing left but the awful odor and the sound of water dripping off the desks onto the floor.

I thought, *Right, don't touch anything.* Not a problem. I began tentatively moving back toward the server room sweeping my flashlight beam from side to side, sloshing through the water. What kind of clue could we possibly find?

I moved into the server room and stumbled over a large object. Steadying myself, I turned the flashlight to the floor. There was another body. This one was older. A man, maybe in his fifties with gunshot wounds, fatal wounds. *Take a deep breath.* I knew what detectives do. They try to reconstruct what happened in what sequence.

I stood in the muck feeling totally over my head. My hands trembled from either fear or the cold or both. The elevator door opened again. I saw a flashlight beam sweeping the office. I thanked God.

"Al?"

"Yeah, it's me."

"Over here." She came into the server room. "That was quick."

"I just went to the lobby, called Little, gave him the 9/11 code and came right back here. He's pulling the team in and will be here in a few minutes. Find anything?"

"This guy." I pointed my light down again. "He's older and was killed by a gun in this room. I'm glad you're back. Maybe we can figure out what happened? If we can do that, maybe it will give us a clue as to the Leopard's next move or location."

"Maybe. OK, so what do we know? We've got a bunch of dead guys gassed or poisoned, whatever, in that room. Then this older guy with the GSWs. Water out there. Dry and burnt up in here. Hmm. Let's start with the older guy. He was probably in charge or supervised the younger guys, just based on age maybe."

"And location. He was in here and probably together with his killer. OK, what happened first? Gassing the young guys or shooting the older guy?"

"You're getting pretty good at this. An accurate timeline or sequence of events can make the whole difference. Let's assume for the sake of argument that the older guy was working for or at least cooperating with his assailant. If that's the case, then they probably killed the young guys first. The older guy may have even pushed the button."

"Then the Leopard has no more use for the older guy, knocks him off and sets off some kind of explosive to destroy the trail."

The elevator opened again and several light beams came out sweeping all over. "Al, Sam, are you there?"

"Over here, Little," Al said. Then she brought him up to date on our theory so far.

"Sounds plausible. My guys will check out the bodies, search and gather evidence. I need you both not to touch anything."

"There he goes again—Mr. G-Man in charge. How about you work with us instead of bossing us around?" I liked Al—*You go, girl.*

I decided to break in before a "*Who has the bigger dick*" interagency fight ensued. "Why don't we all just have a look around and call each other if one of us finds something interesting? Sound like a plan?" I felt like the daddy with the kids fighting in the back seat. They both just nodded silently and moved off in different directions.

"Al, wait a minute." I called her back feeling as though we had not finished playing out the scenario. "I felt like we were in a groove and maybe getting somewhere. Let's talk this through a little more. What if this older guy was an unwilling participant? It would fit the Leopard's pattern to threaten or intimidate to get his way. If the guy had half a brain, he might have guessed he'd end up this way."

"And if that's true, what might he have done as insurance or a way out?"

"Or if he felt there was no way out, but he wanted to confess or explain his actions. Somehow make it right."

"Then he would have left something behind, but everything in here is destroyed . . . or is it?"

"Let's look with that in mind. It might help us focus."

"I'll go tell Little."

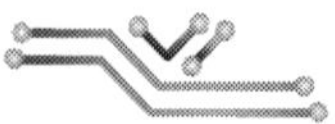

CHAPTER 81

SKYPE ME, BABY

I took a deep breath. I don't know what made me think of it, but I lapsed into a daydream. I was recalling our time together in California.

"Nice night. How's my hero doing?" she'd said. The image of her on the phone was pretty stunning. She was dressed in a silk robe, sitting propped up on the pillows. Her robe was open just a few inches vertically, revealing just enough of her breasts and her thighs to stir something inside me. Her reddish, blonde hair was liberated and flowing over her right shoulder.

"It was a really nice night. I'm in a cab crossing the river into Manhattan. Have to say, I'm a bit nervous and apprehensive. I'm feeling that dark cloud circling overhead again."

"Maybe I can do something to relieve a little of that tension and those dark thoughts? How long do we have?"

"Maybe ten minutes, but I'm not sure I can do this."

"Sure you can." She ran her fingers down the edge of her robe. "Would you like to see a little more?"

Now some other part of me had taken over. I glanced at the taxi driver in the rearview mirror. He was oblivious to me in the backseat. "I sure would."

She opened her robe a few inches more and began to slowly stroke her breasts. Then she gently pulled and twisted her nipples, letting out a little moan. "Ummm, how's that, better?"

"Yes, much better. Can I see a little more?" I was totally slipping away now.

"First, tell me. Are you getting hard yet? Let me see."

We had only played this game a few times before, but I knew how to do what I was told. It would be worth it. Sweat was starting to bead up on my forehead, despite how cool it was in the cab. I felt the tightness in my pants and pointed the cell phone's camera at it.

"Oh, you are hard. Take it out. Let me see."

"I'm in the backseat of a cab, I'm not sure –"

"He won't see and if he did, I'm sure he's seen worse."

I hesitated, but threw my jacket over my lap, then I unzipped holding the phone so she could see.

"Umm, that looks so good. I wish I could be there. OK, you've been a good boy, so look at me now." I raised the phone so I could see. She slowly licked her lips. Then she peeled back her robe all the way and slid her hands between her thighs, stroking and swaying her hips, her ample breasts moving up and down with the rhythm. "Oh, that feels so good. Why don't you join me? Just grab ahold with your free hand and do what I say . . . "

I did.

CHAPTER 82
LOOK WHAT I FOUND

I awoke abruptly from my daydream still feeling that sweet, warm feeling. However, the stench of loose bowels, burnt wires and dank water jarred me like smelling salts. I continued to stumble around the server room, moving my flashlight beam up and down the server racks. All the electronics seemed to be destroyed. That meant hard drives and data were gone. Also, I knew that all the young men in the office must have been using dumb terminals, so nothing they did was stored locally. Everything data-wise came and went from this server room. The dumb terminals wouldn't even have a USB port to plug in a flash drive.

I turned the corner and started down the next aisle. Same story. Shattered equipment. I mean maybe an expert might be able to recover something from the fried drives, but more than likely the Leopard or his dead IT guy wiped them even before they blew them up. That's what I'd do.

As I finished sweeping the last row of servers against the wall, the whole room rumbled. My muscles tightened and I held my breath. Then I realized it must be the subway overhead. At least, I hoped it was. My nerves were frayed enough as it was. As the rumble subsided, there was a bang as if something fell off the back of the rack against the wall. I squeezed around behind the rack and swept my beam up and down. When I swept down, I noticed, tucked behind and underneath the rack, just the corner of a black plastic case jutting out. I stretched my arm out as far as I could toward it, my shoulder wedged between the rack and the wall. I couldn't reach it as the rack was too close to the wall. I felt a sharp pain in my shoulder from my earlier wound. This wasn't going to work. I looked around for a stick or a broom. On the floor, I found a six foot piece of metal that had been blown off a rack in the explosion. Perfect. It even had a bent end I used to angle the case and finally grab its handle dragging it toward me. It was one of those toughbook laptop computers that had a shock-proof case. Now what? I took the laptop over to a small work surface that was still partially intact, placed the laptop there and lifted the lid.

Inside I could see a small white power light lit on the keyboard. I felt around for an ON button. A funny thought breezed through my head while I clawed for the button. I remembered the number of times clients called us with "computer problems" and it was because they forgot to turn their computer ON. I had to laugh and here I was with the same problem. Finally, I found a slider switch in back, slid it left and a cursor began to blink on the screen. I was waiting for the customary Windows screen to appear, but it didn't. Must be Linux. I typed 'Login' and hit ENTER. It came back with 'Username.' Ok now I was stuck. I didn't know his password. Time to call in the experts.

I left the server room, sloshed into the office and called out for Little. Water was still everywhere. I saw two flashlights approaching. It was Little and Al. Little called back over his shoulder, "See if you can get some power on down here or get some floodlights. This is no way to survey a crime scene." He turned to me. "What is it, Sam?"

"Look what I found and it works." I pointed my flashlight down at the laptop in my left hand. "Only problem is we need a password."

"Well, that's helpful. We have a DHS tech van upstairs with a couple of crack NSA guys in it. The good news is we have various agencies all over this with all their resources. The bad news is it's a command and political shitstorm."

"I never thought I'd hear foul language from a straight-up FBI guy."

"Screw you. And I'm DHS, not FBI. So there's a difference." We all laughed. "Let's get this upstairs. Maybe if we're lucky, we can get something out of this before the FBI tries to whisk it away. I have an idea."

Little, Al and I got on the elevator and headed up to the lobby. I don't think I've ever been happier to leave a place in my life. I was soaked, dirty and probably smelled like a Port-a-Potty on a hot day. We headed through the lobby to the street. Little led us across Broad to a double-parked, unmarked white van. He knocked twice, paused and knocked three times. The rear door swung open.

"Two raps, then three. High security I see," I said.

"They have cameras, Dickhead. They can see who's coming. I was just knocking on the door." I think he'd had enough of my sense of humor. Was that why Monica just groans at my jokes?

Once inside the van, Little said, "This is Gary. Gary meet Sam Sunborn and Detective Al Favor." We all shook hands. "Did you get that secure phone for Sam here?"

"Yes, right here." Gary swiveled his chair around, grabbed a phone, swiveled back and handed it to me. "The password for the phone is the number of your freshman dorm room at college."

I squinted in disbelief.

"We know a lot about everybody so don't feel too special."

Little got back to business. "We recovered this laptop from the lobby. Probably not significant since the scene was ten stories down, but do you guys think you could crack into it for us?"

Ah, a defensive lie to keep the ball with our team. I knew I liked this guy. Little handed the laptop to a red-haired, bearded guy in a Grateful Dead T-shirt and ripped cargo pants.

"I'll have a look. Why's it wet?" Gary said.

I jumped in. "Because I was wet from the basement when I came upstairs and found it in the lobby. Guess it rubbed off." Ha, I can play at this game too.

Gary just smiled. "You know we have cameras? I saw you guys coming off the elevator with that laptop. Don't worry. I know what you're trying to do. I get it. You don't want the FBI guys taking off with it and then who knows what black hole it goes into. Those guys piss me off too. You guys been in a sewer?" He held his nose.

Now it was Little's turn to smile. "Thanks and yes we have pretty much."

Gary opened the laptop. "Besides, I thought DHS reigned supreme over all other agencies. Anyway, what are you guys looking for?"

"We think the guy who owned this may have been trying to leave us a message."

"Well, if that's the case, he probably wouldn't want to make it too difficult to get in. The password would just be sound enough to discourage an unwanted intruder." Gary pulled a flash drive from his beat up backpack on the floor. "This baby can crack ninety percent of passwords." He plugged it into the laptop and typed in a simple command, STARTNOW. Random numbers and letters seemed to race across the screen as Gary's program tried various combinations. Then suddenly, the screen lit up. "Did I mention it can crack most passwords in under a minute?"

We all peered over Gary's shoulder. Al said, "What is it?"

"It's a letter," I said. Excited I stood up, slamming my head into the roof of the van. "Shit."

Little said, "Let me see." Gary handed the laptop to him and the three of us sat on a bench in the van opposite Gary. Little sat in the middle with the laptop on his lap with Al and me, rubbing my head, on each side. We read the letter.

Gentlemen,

If you are reading this, then I have fallen to my inevitable fate. I only hope that you, the reader, can somehow stop what is about to happen. My name is Eskabar and I have been in the employ of Ahmed LaSalam for the last four years. I use the term 'employ' loosely as I was given no choice. Either I setup this data center and carry out his commands or my family would suffer cruel deaths. I have seen the brutality that this man is capable of and have no doubt that he would have carried out his threat. This is no excuse for my behavior or the damage that my actions may have caused. As a husband and father, I would do whatever I must to protect my family.

All I know is that within three days, the plan is to sabotage or attack something nuclear. Like 9/11 and other plots, there will be multiple attacks at multiple locations. Unfortunately, I do not know the locations or the men carrying out these attacks. I do know that one attack will be in New York, another in California and perhaps another in France. I can only surmise this from bits of conversations I either overheard or texts I intercepted. Mentions of "coast-to-coast" and "our French brothers" plus other mentions lead me to this. I don't have the time to provide more proof or detail on this. I can only tell you that there is another data center like mine, maybe smaller, near Boston. It is the only possible lead I can give you as to his possible location. May God bless you and give you the strength and courage to stop the suffering he has planned. Inshallah.

If it is LaSalam reading this, I beg your mercy. I have followed all your commands, you have clearly won and put an end to me. Please, sire, spare my family.

- E.

CHAPTER 83

ALPHABET SOUP

Longford paced the Situation Room. She was used to getting facts and making decisions on those facts. She sometimes made mistakes, but she always felt somewhat in control of the process. Here there were too many moving parts, too many people involved, and she was new at this. "Any updates or news?"

Hager cleared his throat. "We have DHS, NSA and FBI on this. They're in lower Manhattan. There's word of some activity or an incident, perhaps an explosion. It's still too early to tell."

"So we have thrown alphabet soup at this. Great. Sorry. It's just frustrating. I wish there was more we could do."

"Sometimes all you can do is send your best people and resources, trust them and wait."

"That's good advice and I'm sure you want to calm me down. I've just never been a very patient person. Sometimes impatience has served me well. Other times, waiting just drives me crazy."

"Understood, Madame President."

"Let's think about this. If the Russians, Chinese and even the freakin' North Koreans can hack our servers, is there any way for us to hack these terrorist servers? Can't we detect their activity?"

"Worth a discussion for sure. I'll call in the head of our Cyber Command, Jules Keystone." Hager started tapping away on his Blackberry.

"Are we really still using Blackberries? In a world where cutting edge tech can make all the difference, we're still in the Stone Age. You know I spent a day on a Los Angeles Class Nuclear Sub, and they had Dell laptops sitting on top of their consoles because their built-in systems were too antiquated. So they used the laptops to do their calculations and then typed the results into their old systems.

We've got to do something about that. Can't we do better?"

"I agree. I'll talk to Congress. Um, uh, perhaps you should talk to Congress."

"Why don't you talk to Congress? You're up there testifying on one thing or another all the time. OK, sorry for the digression. Get Keystone up here. We have nothing better to do than save our country from attack right now. How fast can we get him here?"

"Madame President, if I may . . . " Hager punched a button on the Cisco Telepresence keyboard in front of him. A young man appeared on the wall screen in a T-shirt with faint beard stubble and piercing blue eyes.

"Madame President, I apologize for my appearance. We don't wear uniforms here. Everyday is dress-down Friday, or we can't attract the nerdy geniuses we need to do this kind of work."

"I understand. I can't remember the last time I had a dress-down Friday. Are you aware of the threat we're facing?"

"Yes, I have a unit of three of my best hunting down LaSalam as we speak."

"Why only three? This is a national security priority."

"More than three and people tend to get in each other's way. We've studied the perfect team size for both offense and defense. Three is the optimal number."

"OK, I'll take your word for it, Jules. What have you found so far?"

"Well, interestingly enough, we've tapped into our own DHS van on Broad Street in lower Manhattan. They've just hacked into one of the bad guy's laptops. They're reading a letter right now that indicates LaSalam may be on his way to Boston. Also, that he might be planning a multipronged nuclear event of some kind."

"Hager, why are we hearing about this just now and from Jules?"

Jules interrupted, "Madame President, if I may. This is what we do. We try to tap every source, friend or foe, to put together a picture. We hacked a camera in the FBI van and are literally looking over their shoulders right now. So this is very new info."

"Well, that's reassuring."

CHAPTER 84
POSSIBILITIES

"Based on what you just read, what do you make of it, Gary?" Little said. Smart. Ask the new guy with fresh eyes.

"OK. He says it's something nuclear. What's nuclear? Aircraft carriers, submarines, bombs, missiles and power plants. If you're a terrorist and could somehow launch our own missiles against us, that would be pretty devastating."

"How about a dirty bomb or three? You know, just blast a bunch of radioactive material into the air and poison thousands," I said.

"I know what a dirty bomb is," said Little.

"How about we call in Frank for an opinion? He can run the scenarios much faster and better than we can," Al said.

Somehow this van was feeling really claustrophobic. Maybe it was the close quarters, but more likely it was the enormity of the problem expanding inside this small box. I began to sweat through my wet smelly clothes. Lovely. Frank was the right guy for this. "Gary, can you bring up this website in Tor, a secure anonymous browser window." I handed Gary a slip of paper—that's one thing you can't hack.

Gary began to type. "I know what Tor is." But before he could open a new window, Gary's screen flickered and Frank appeared. "Whoa. How'd that happen and who's this guy?"

"Gary, my name is Frank. I'm an Einstein." Frank smiled on the screen. "Hi guys. I've been monitoring your activities both inside and outside the building. Pretty nasty down there."

I had not shared with Al and Little that I had been wearing a tracking device, as Frank insisted for my safety. It also allowed him to access cameras around me to keep up to date and tip me off to impending dangers. "Frank, am I glad to see you! Let me bring you up to date."

"Not necessary. I monitored all your conversations in the building and the basement. I also hacked the camera in the van and read the letter over your shoulder."

Gary was turning beet red. "I repeat, who is this guy?"

I knew I did not want to fully read Gary in. He did not need to know Frank was a DigiPerson. Gary could just assume Frank was teleconferencing in to us. "That's Frank Einstein. So yes he is an Einstein in both senses of the name. He works with us. He has some special, umm, cyber-talents."

Frank jumped in. "I'm afraid we don't have much time for introductions or pleasantries, Gary. I worked for DARPA and have some high-level clearances. It was a bit too easy to hack your van's camera. You'll be interested to know that Defense's Cyber Command has hacked your camera as well as some other anonymous user. So you can bet that Defense and perhaps the White House are up to date on your activities. I'm more concerned about the anonymous hack, but I'm working on that. In the meantime, I've taken your camera offline and secured our current communications so we can talk without eavesdroppers."

Gary calmed down. "I'm impressed, but—"

I cut him off. We needed to focus now. "Frank, what do you make of the letter, the 'nuclear' reference and possible Leopard location?"

"Sure, throw a few things at me at once. You know how well I multitask. First, I think the letter is genuine. The circumstances surrounding it, his death and your discovery of the laptop are too low a probability to have been a planned-in-advance diversion. Assuming then that the letter is real, let's focus on the 'nuclear' question. Gary's list is a good one. Filtering the possibilities based on maximum damage to civilians, I'd narrow the list to three: hacked nuclear missile, dirty bombs—that's plural for the letter's reference to multipronged attacks—and power plants."

Now I was getting really scared. "All three possibilities are horrendous, but which is the easiest to hack?"

Frank put his virtual finger to his chin. "I'm not sure easiness is one of the Leopard's top criteria, since he has pulled off some pretty remarkably difficult stunts. Plus, I suspect he may have the help of some Cyber Warriors like me by now." Well, the cat was definitely peeking his head out of the bag.

Gary seized on Frank's comment. "What are you talking about? 'Cyber Warrior,' huh?"

"Oh, I just meant super-hackers like me. But, maybe a better criteria filter here is 'feasibility,' which is slightly different than easiness. 'Feasibility' goes more to the question of what is possible or impossible, not just hard to do."

Al couldn't help herself. "You guys, this is not an academic exercise. Can you just cut to the point?"

I had to keep us on track. "Sorry Frank, we're just getting a little anxious here. What's your bottom line on the three nuclear possibilities?"

"Applying the feasibility criteria, I'd narrow the possibilities to dirty bombs or power plants. The nuclear missile system is pretty much an air-gapped system, which means it's offline, and there are multiple stopgaps requiring high-level human approvals. So I think missiles are less likely."

"Then if it's bombs or power plants, how would he do it?"

"The problem with dirty bombs is they are physical objects that tend to be big. The material is also hard to acquire in enough quantity to do multiple explosions of sufficient size to do the kind of damage we're discussing. Actual suitcase bombs are smaller but need a level of technical expertise and resources that are even more limited," Little said.

"Yes, your analysis is accurate," Frank said.

"Power plants are hackable as we've seen in some recent incidents. Plus it doesn't require lugging anything physical around. All you need is some smart guys or women and Internet access. Aren't they the most likely targets?" I said.

"They are hackable, but the nuclear generator part is again air-gapped. Plus we have made them a top priority for beefed up physical and digital security."

While we kicked this around, Gary was typing away on his keyboard. He turned to us. "Do you know what the most effective and devastating hacks are? I'll tell you. They are human hacks, or what is currently called 'Social Engineering.' That is when somebody gives up a password or leaves it on a sticky note. More brazen hackers might even call up an organization, get the right person on the phone and say, 'Oh, I lost my password, can you tell me what it is?' And they give it to him. One pop artist recently asked his fans on Twitter to send him their passwords and 10,000 people did. It's true.

"Perhaps the most relevant example is the Stuxnet virus. By now, most people know it was some of the most creative code ever written in its amazing ability to propagate itself and attack the Iranian centrifuges. The centrifuges as well as most of the other sensitive nuclear plant equipment were not connected to the Internet or any outside network. So how did we, er, how did they manage to get it in?"

"No clue," Little said.

"We, er, they had an employee in the plant working for the US who stuck an infected flash drive into their system at their facility. The human hack enabled the virus to get into the system. I'd argue that most successful and devastating cyber attacks have a human element, whether it's sloppiness or spycraft, that make them work."

"Very good point," Frank said. "So perhaps, the Leopard could have secret cohorts embedded at our nuclear facilities, ready to plug in their flash drives or push whatever buttons to set off meltdowns?"

I was stunned. "Oh my God. If that's really the best, or I should say worst but likely scenario, what do we do?"

"That, my son, is a very good question."

CHAPTER 85

BIG TIME ANYWAY

I liked it when Frank called me 'son.' It felt good. Since my father died when I was only a year old, Frank had become, over these many months, the closest thing to a father I had known.

"I need some air." I stepped out the back door of the van. Little and Al followed me. The sun was pretty high in the sky now and seemed perched just right between the tall buildings, illuminating the narrow street. Everything seemed so normal as people rushed about to appointments and meetings, to lunches and bars. They had no idea what was happening and how their lives could change in an instant, forever. "This is beyond me, guys." I felt lost. That dark cloud of depression was descending on me again like a dense fog after a rainstorm.

Little was already on his phone, updating his bosses, I'm sure. Al just stood silently looking as stunned as I felt. Little ended his call. "Well I've called in the cavalry. There are sixty-one commercially operating nuclear power plants with ninety-nine nuclear reactors in thirty states in the United States. DHS has 240,000 employees. I think we can cover ninety-nine locations. We're dispatching strike teams and analysts to all those locations. We think we can be in situ within two to three hours. I sure hope your logic is right, or I'll have quite a mess to clean up when this is all over."

"Whoa, we were just discussing possibilities. As a friend of mine said, 'When the shit hits the fan, I don't want to be the fan.'" I realized how weak that sounded after I said it. "I'm sorry. This is all a little overwhelming."

Al said, "What other choice do we have? If we're wrong, we're fucked big time anyway."

"Well put," Little said with a grim smile.

"So, where can we be of the most use?" I wondered out loud

"I think we should go to the nearest power plant, which is Indian Point. It's about forty miles north of here on the Hudson in Peekskill. I believe they have three reactors there. I think seeing them in person may help us evaluate the threat better and maybe help with strategy," Little said.

"Yeah, I mean we can't just go in there with guns blazing. How will your guys enter and handle the incursion?" Al said.

"Let's jump in the car and discuss on the way there. We have whole teams of people that plan and rehearse this kind of thing." Little said. Just then, a black SUV pulled in next to us. "Get in. Gary, come out. Lock up the van. You're with us." Gary emerged from the van, carrying his tablet and looking a little bewildered. He poked his head back into the van, looked around and then locked it. Speaking quickly into a lapel mic, he jumped in the SUV beside us.

"Gary, sorry to pull you away, but you may be more valuable helping us figure out the best plan of attack here. I think the teams will probably start with a Level 1 soft incursion. They'll basically walk in the doors, show ID and have a look around. If anything looks or smells suspicious, they'll escalate. Meanwhile, the techs on the team will monitor and even shut down their local systems if necessary."

"Wait, what are you talking about and where are we going?"

"Sorry, you were in the van and missed a step. As we speak, we're mobilizing tac teams to hit, or I should say 'visit,' all sixty-one US nuclear power plant sites. We've also notified the French of the threat in case something similar is planned there. We're on our way to Indian Point to assist."

Gary moved his hand through what remained of his thinning red hair. He looked ashen. "Geez. Assist? You mean like with guns and stuff? I'm just a computer guy."

"Guns are the last thing we have in mind. We need brains first to identify the specific threat, whether that be physical or digital, and then figure out how to stop it. That's why we need you and all the brains we can muster. According to our scenario, that threat's going to probably be a person on site."

"OK, I see. If I can get access to their systems as soon as we get there, I may be able to suss something out."

"That's the idea. Excuse me while I take this call. We've got some serious coordinating to do." Little sank into a heavy conversation for the rest of the ride.

I thought I should call Monica. I pulled up Google on my phone. "California Nuclear Power Plants." I felt my stomach turn over and my head throb. She and Evan were less than fifty miles from Rancho Seco Nuclear Generating Station. I had to warn her. She had to get out of there.

CHAPTER 86

COLD SHOWER

I remember my mother telling me that when she was pregnant with me in 1979, there was a partial meltdown and serious radiation leak at the Three Mile Island Plant near Pittsburgh. My parents, who were living in western New Jersey at the time, were quite frightened. So my dad put my mom on a plane, and she flew to stay with friends in Boston until the radiation cloud passed.

I called Monica. After a few rings I got, “Hello. Hello? Are you there? Well, I’m not. So please leave me a message, and I’ll call you back as soon as I can.” Monica thought that voicemail greeting was funny. At this moment, I was not laughing.

I left her a voicemail explaining the new phone number. Then I hung up and texted her the new number. “Call me as soon as you can, it’s important.” As I learned from Evan, it seems nobody really checks their voicemail anymore. Maybe just to clean it out once in awhile, but everybody reads their text messages. Now I waited. I drummed my fingers on the armrest, my breathing shallow. Breathe. Nightmare, Hiroshima-like scenarios played in my head.

Al turned to me. “What’s the matter? You look sick.”

“My family is near a nuclear reactor, the Leopard may be tracking Monica and I can’t reach her.”

“Oh, fuck.” Al frantically pulled out her phone and started calling. Now it was suddenly personal for all of us.

After what seemed like an eternity, but was probably only twenty minutes, my phone rang. Skype came up on the screen. Monica was still in her robe, but drying her hair. “I got maybe twenty texts from you. What’s with this new number? I had to take a cold shower after our last phone call. What’s the emergency? Are you OK?”

“I’m fine, but you need to get Evan and get out of there as fast as possible.”

"Wait. What's going on? Another gunman?"

"No. Nothing like that but maybe just as dangerous. Head southeast. You've got to get as far away from Rancho Seco Park as fast as possible. Don't pack. Just leave."

"Huh? Wait. The only thing there is a nuclear plant . . . " Silence. "Are you saying what I think you're saying?"

"I can't say or I'm sure I'm not supposed to say, but I think you understand." I quickly checked Google Maps on my phone. Head toward Fresno and just keep going until we speak again. I'm suggesting south to southeast in case there's a cloud."

"Oh my God! OK. Got it. But what about Jerry and my bodyguards?"

"Take them with you. Their orders are to guard you, not to lock you in place. Just tell them there's a family emergency, which is true. You can't tell them what you really suspect."

"I understand."

"One other thing. Destroy your cell phone immediately after we hang up. I mean really crush it. Buy a burner phone at RadioShack with cash and text me your new number. To my new number."

"Sam, this is really scary."

"I know. As soon as you get the new phone, call me. I need to know you're safe."

"You too." Her face disappeared from the screen.

CHAPTER 87
ACELA

The Acela train to Boston's South Station arrived on time. Besides a few stares from other passengers on the train, it was uneventful. Looking Middle Eastern in this country often attracted attention, especially on public transportation. He could feel the underlying current of fear and probably hate. But he knew they were mostly too weak to act.

He walked over to the T station, which is Boston's subway system, and consulted a map on the wall. Then he headed to the Red Line platform. Five stops and about twenty minutes later, he stepped from the station, went up the steps and emerged into bright, sunlit Harvard Square. Traffic rushed by him in all directions. And he thought the traffic in Tehran was bad. He had picked Boston-Cambridge for its access to talent. Also, the only nuclear plant in Massachusetts was on Cape Cod and any fallout would probably blow out over the ocean. He had no intention of being a suicide-bomber.

He had been here once before to inspect the "office" when it was setup about a year ago. He toured the office with a man nicknamed "Fredo." When Fredo could not assure him he could carry out the plan, LaSalam had to "replace" him. There were any number of sympathetic and talented people at MIT, just a few miles down the road, who could make his idea work. And if they weren't sympathetic, he knew how to make them sympathetic.

He walked down John F. Kennedy Street toward the Charles River. Once he got away from the stores and restaurants, the street had some large brownstone, very expensive residences. Through a wealthy Barinian businessman's company, he had acquired one of the brownstones for $3 million. That was about average here and it did not stand out. In most places you could buy a block or even a small town for that kind of money. But it didn't matter. His backers had plenty of money and they didn't care.

The upstairs of the house provided eight bedrooms, living areas and kitchen for the twelve people that worked at the office in the basement. He walked around the back of the house, through a small grassy yard with lawn chairs and a barbeque and down the rear steps to the basement door. Everything about the house and yard looked normal, except the retinal scanner on the basement stairs. He looked into the scanner, confirmed with a finger scan and the steel door buzzed and clicked open.

It was 5:00. He entered the room that was mostly dark except for the glow of computer screens illuminating the faces of the young people in the cubicles. There were several large OLED screens on the side walls with images from sites around the US and in France. He was approached by an attractive young woman with dark brown skin and deep brown eyes, wearing a hijab that barely concealed her long brown hair. He couldn't help staring at her full eyebrows and her pronounced lips. He felt a little twinge, like he had not felt for an adult woman in years. Her name was Michelle Hadar and she was a top graduate student in Computer Science at MIT. Back home, he could never have put a woman in charge, but things were different in the US and maybe better in certain small ways. She was the best he could find, both with tech skills and a strong leader's personality. She may not have shared his ideals and obsessions, but she had a mother, father and brother that would have been in danger if she did not fully cooperate. He smiled as he thought, the "fully" might include some of the activities he enjoyed with Mr. P's young girls, but there was much serious work to be done first.

Michelle turned and approached him. "Hello sir, how was your trip?"

The warmth of her smile melted his usual harsh command style. "It was fine and you are looking most beautiful today. Maybe you will join me for dinner later? Meanwhile, what is our status?"

She took his elbow and gently pulled him to one side of the darkened room. This was a very forward gesture that would not normally be tolerated, but somehow he enjoyed her touch. "I have recruited eleven of the most talented engineers that I know. Two are women. I hope that's not a problem."

"At home, you know that would not be acceptable, but as the Americans say 'When in Rome . . . ' Perhaps I could meet these women later. I am fascinated by accomplished women."

"That's very western of you and I appreciate it. All systems are up and working. We are monitoring the designated sites. The team here believes we are working on a simulation for the US government. That is why I chose a mix of Americans and our people to avoid suspicion. They are being paid well by you and appreciate the room and board upstairs. So they don't ask too many questions."

"Very well. Unlike our operation in New York where we could control our efforts entirely from the office, this operation requires coordination with our men in the field. You understand?"

"Yes and we have com links set up with those agents in the private office in the back." She pointed to a better lit room with a glass window at the back of the office. "We have two specialists in there who are more attuned to your goals and understand most of the actual details of the plan."

"When will you be ready to execute?"

"I'd like to schedule it for tomorrow at 6:00 AM. That way our specialists would be rested and alert. I want them to be at their peak, so they can act with speed and precision."

Her intensity and intelligence were making him feel very warm. "That makes sense, but that is also the time when our targets may be fully staffed and alert. I'd prefer to pick a time when they and any first responders are at lightest staffing. Let's pick a time when we have the advantage of maximum surprise. Have you analyzed their staffing levels?"

"Yes. Their minimum level is at 2:00 AM, one hour before a shift change at most facilities. Of course, there are time zone issues to consider and France is several hours ahead. However, for a simultaneous ignition, 2:00 AM Eastern Time is optimal from the average target's staffing and readiness analysis."

"Good. Then we go at 2:00 AM. Give your team time to rest earlier if you feel it's necessary."

She knew better than to argue. She had heard the stories and she had cloned LaSalam's phone when she first met him for her interview.

Using that, she had listened in on his conversations with Eskabar. She was even able to remotely activate his cell phone's camera. So she not only knew about some of his brutal acts, but she had also witnessed, with disgust, his fetish for young girls. What could she do? She had to protect her family. But even for them, could she carry out the Leopard's plan? She wasn't sure. "Yes, sir. That makes sense. I will alert the team and the on-site agents to the new schedule and will make sure our team is fed, rested and alert at 2:00 AM. But I will respectfully ask that we do dinner another time. I have much to prepare if our task is to be successful."

"I understand. Maybe we can do breakfast tomorrow to celebrate. I'd like to get to know you better."

She winced and hoped, in the darkened room, that he didn't notice.

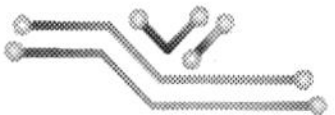

CHAPTER 88

ROLL UP YOUR SLEEVES

At 6:00 PM, we arrived at the security gate at Indian Point, showed ID and proceeded to the main administration building. Little was now texting on his phone. "We've picked up some facial recognition of the Leopard in Boston. We're assembling a team there. A Black Hawk chopper is going to pick me up here in thirty minutes. Let's get going. You guys can stay, but I only have a half hour."

We walked into the admin building and, as usual, Little took charge. We approached the lone security guard at the desk. "We need to speak to Greg Tilson, your director.'"

The guard picked up a phone. "I'll see if he's here."

"We know he's here. Just tell him there are people here from Homeland to see him." We purposely did not call ahead, but on the way to Peekskill, we got backgrounds and cell phone GPS tracking on key personnel.

Al paced the lobby while we waited. "What if Tilson's the agent?"

Little thought about that. "I doubt they'd recruit the top guy. Too high-profile and visible. My money's on a lower level guy with access. The kind of guy who has a big key ring full of keys. The kind of guy nobody pays much attention to."

Gary, who meekly hovered in the background, stepped up. "Here's a list of possibles, based on your criteria. I culled them from the NRC's database." He handed his tablet to Little.

The door behind the guard buzzed, and a trim fortyish man with a marine haircut stepped out. His gray hair belied his age. His erect posture and muscular build said military and proud of it. "Gentlemen and lady, what can I do for you?"

"Is there somewhere we can speak in private?"

"This way." Tilson led us through the security door and down a long corridor painted hospital green. It even had the odor of disinfectant trying to mask some persistent mildew. The place definitely looked 1960s, when most of these facilities were built. We walked into a small conference room with metal chairs, concrete floors, and tiled walls. I wasn't sure whether this felt more like high school or prison. In my case, they could have been the same.

After a few introductions, Little got started. "Director Tilson, I'll get to the point, as time is an issue. We suspect one of your people may be prepared to sabotage this facility."

Tilson turned red then grayish white, like a cadaver. "Um, how do you know this?"

"We have very good intelligence that a terrorist cell is coordinating sabotage here and at other facilities in less than twenty-four hours."

Tilson straightened up and composed himself. "How can I help?"

Little handed him the tablet with the list of names. "Are any of these men currently on site?"

"Of the six on your list, I'd guess maybe four are currently on duty."

"Can you discreetly call them to the office? It's imperative we don't alert the perpetrator we may be onto him."

Al chimed in. "That's a mistake, Rich."

"What do you mean?"

"I've had enough street experience to know that no matter how you summon a suspect, they will probably bolt or worse. They're nervous and feeling more than a little guilty. Any break in routine may trigger an undesirable response."

"Makes sense. What would *you* suggest?" Little said with a note of sarcasm.

"Take off the jacket and tie. Roll up your sleeves. Take Tilson's pocket protector with all the pens in it. Take me and Gary with you. I'll take this clipboard. We'll look like NRC inspectors, which I'd imagine would be a common sight around here. Then let's ask Director Tilson to lead us to the workstations of these four on the list. As we approach them, I'll look like I'm taking notes. Gary, with his nerdy glasses, can be pecking away on his tablet. You and Tilson should be talking as if evaluating the place."

"Nerdy?" Gary said.

"Sounds solid to me," I said.

"We'll see about that. OK, let's go with Al's plan. Sam, you stay here and monitor the overall situation. Call us on the earbuds if something important happens. Greg, let's go."

I felt like a little kid being left behind and left out. But on second thought I was happy not being involved in another confrontation. My nerves were frayed like ropes about to snap. I took a deep breath and tried to calm down. Yet I couldn't will away that dark cloud hovering overhead.

CHAPTER 89

MY FAIR LADY

Shortly after we arrived at Indian Point and I was left alone, my cell rang. It was Monica. "I was so worried. How are you? Where are you?"

"We're on our way to Fresno, just passing Modesto now. Evan's with me. We're all fine. Where are you?"

"We're at one of the sites in New York. I can't really say anymore. I just wanted to make sure you're OK."

"We're scared. But oh my God, you're at one of the sites. What if something happens?"

"We're here to stop that, hopefully. I know you're worried, but I really had no choice. Millions of lives and our country's future are at stake."

"I know. I know, but that's not going to stop me from worrying. Evan is in the backseat playing video games. He seems blissfully oblivious."

"As is most of the country. A panic would only make things worse. So we have to keep this to ourselves for now."

"I understand. When will we know it's over?"

"If you hear an explosion or get a call from me—one or the other."

"Your gallows humor is not much appreciated at the moment."

"Sorry. It's my way of dealing with stress." There was a long silence between us and a warm memory popped into my head. "Sing me that song you and your father used to sing, doing dishes after dinner in the kitchen. You know, the one from *My Fair Lady*."

"Really, *now*?"

"Yes. I loved that. I think it may be good for both of us."

"OK." She cleared her throat. With her voice breaking, she began. *"I have often walked down that street before. But the pavement always stayed beneath my feet before . . ."*

Tears came to my eyes. The lyrics of that song took on a new meaning for me this time. It might be the last time I'd hear it.

CHAPTER 90
MS. MARPLE

At 6:20, Little, Al, Gary and Tilson approached a man named Fred Grey at his console in the plant's control room. "Hi, Fred." Fred looked up. Al continued to scribble on her clipboard. Little and Gary looked around as if inspecting the place.

Fred Grey was a fortyish white male with dark black hair, graying at the temples. He wore a khaki uniform with a name tag and had a pleasant smile. "Director Tilson, how can I help you?"

"Fred, these people are from the NRC doing a routine inspection. They have a few questions they'd like to ask you."

Fred nodded.

Little started off slowly. "Are all systems operating normally today?"

The group watched his face and body for any micro-expressions or tells. Any discomfort, rapid blinking, change of expression might give something away. "As far as I can tell, everything seems normal." No discomfort. No change in body language.

"We've had a report that there may be some trouble with your systems. What area do you monitor?"

"I'm responsible for monitoring the core reactors B and C." Again, no visible reaction. "All systems seem to be operating in the green, safe zone today."

"What time does your shift end?"

"In about an hour."

"Do you ever do overtime or have any reason to be here overtime?"

"I wish we did. I could use the money. But apparently, the budget is tight and I haven't had overtime in the last five of the ten years I've been here. Security actually makes sure I leave the site after my shift. No lingering. I get five minutes to go to my locker and then I have to leave."

"OK. Thanks very much." Little moved the team to the hall out of Fred's earshot. "He's not the guy. Other than needing money, I don't see any signs. Besides, he's out of here in an hour. I believe that's too soon for him to be involved. Otherwise, we didn't learn much."

Al interrupted. "It's been too long since you've been a detective, Rich. We actually learned a lot that might help us narrow the search."

"OK, what's that Ms. Marple?"

"I appreciate the comparison despite your sarcasm. We learned that shift times matter. So we need to filter Gary's list by the names of people who will be on duty in the next two to sixteen hours, since that seems to be the most likely window for an incident to occur. We can also probably assume that our guy is not a longtime employee like Fred. If he was planted here or is just cooperating, it's likely that he's been here less than five years. Gary, can you add those two criteria and rerun the search?"

"OK, done. Shifting the time actually removes two from the list of four, including Fred, and adds two who are on later shifts. Then when I apply the under five years employed, it leaves only two names."

"Well, then those are your next two interviews. I have a chopper to catch. Between you, I believe you can do a good job sniffing things out, despite my sarcasm. I can see my way out Director Tilson. Thank you for working with us."

"No offense, Director Little, but we have our security protocols too. I'll have someone from security walk you out. Happy to do all we can with your team here." Tilson made a call and within two minutes, a guard appeared.

"Good-bye Director." Little didn't object to the security precaution. He shook hands with Tilson and walked down the hall with the guard. He raised his hand in a wave without turning around as he walked away.

Al showed Tilson Gary's tablet. "Director Tilson, are these two men here?"

"Well, one's a man and the other a woman. Let me check." He made another call. "They should both be here in about an hour when the shift changes."

Al was wishing we could speed things up, but she couldn't see what choice we had besides waiting.

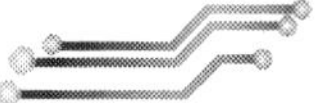

CHAPTER 91

THE DOCTOR

The Leopard had a comfortable room at The Charles Hotel, which was only a short walk from the office. It was a little frayed around the edges but still one of the nicer hotels in the area.

After a short nap, he unpacked his small bag, which included a few simple things to allow him some disguise. He had dyed his hair blond in New York and worn a baseball cap on the train. Now he took the red hair dye into the bathroom, covered his bare shoulders with a towel and began applying it. With his fedora and sunglasses, he hoped to move around unnoticed.

The hotel concierge was no help in providing the kind of entertainment he enjoyed, so he ordered room service and a split of champagne. He only hesitated briefly drinking it, as he did not want to jinx his plan by premature celebration. But he so enjoyed the taste. A small treat was in order. Besides, he was very confident they would succeed and superstition was for infidels anyway.

Having enjoyed his small feast, he decided a walk in the cool evening air would invigorate him. It had already been a long day, but the best was yet to come. He wanted to be alert and ready for it. He knew wandering the streets could lead to trouble, like it did that evening in New York, but he liked the adventure and thrill of new places. Anyway, he thought that the trouble in New York was more of a problem for the thief than it was for him. His adrenaline was already pumping for what was to come. He had to calm himself.

At 6:40, he walked up Brattle Street past City Sports and turned right through a small quad that was part of Harvard's extended city campus. On the steps of one of the grad school buildings, he noticed a mother cuddling her young daughter. The young blonde-haired girl had scraped her knee and was crying. Without a second thought, he was drawn to them and approached.

"Hello, are you all right?"

The mother answered, "Yes, she's fine. Just a little scrape."

"I'm a doctor. I teach at the medical school. Maybe I should have a look."

"That's OK. She'll be fine."

The girl looked up at the smiling stranger, wiping her tears away with the back of her hand. "Mommy, he's a doctor. Please, maybe he can fix it."

The mother looked reluctant but seemed to appreciate the calming effect the stranger had on her daughter. "Yes Doctor, please have a look," she said with mock concern. She was inviting the stranger to play along in this game.

"Well then, let me take a look young lady. Are you twenty years old?" he said slipping his hand under the calf behind the scraped knee. Her soft, young skin felt like velvet. He could already feel himself stirring.

The girl giggled. "No, I'm six!"

"Hmm, I see. Well you look much older." He slid his hand down the back of her leg and lifted it as if to examine the scrape. He could now see the pink of her panties and the stirring grew. He turned her leg from side to side. "I think, young lady, that this will heal just fine." He then slipped his left hand behind her other leg and lifted both as if to compare the two. They felt delicious, if that was possible. "As I suspected. They are the same length." He then looked at the mother. "I think you need to take this girl home, wash her wound and apply a bandage. Can you do that?"

"Yes, and thank you, Doctor."

"My pleasure," he said. *All my pleasure*, he thought. He lowered the girl's legs and gave her a harmless kiss on the forehead. He could smell the sweet scent of lavender soap.

CHAPTER 92

SWAN AND HAMED

Little's chopper got a national security clearance to land on the lawn at Harvard's Kennedy School of Government by the Charles River in Cambridge. At 7:00, he was met by agents Swan and Hamed. Lea Swan was a young Asian-American woman, maybe five foot eight, with large black-rimmed glasses and a warm smile. Anwar Hamed was the son of Syrian immigrants. His dark hair and dark eyes made him look deadly serious.

"Welcome to Cambridge," Swan said.

Little shook hands. "What have you got?"

Hamed had to hesitate a minute as the chopper blades picked up speed and drowned out all sound. The chopper rose a couple of hundred feet straight up and then peeled away to the west. Hamed's ears were still ringing, but he gave the report. "We tracked the suspect to Boston's South Station. There he appeared to don a disguise and baseball cap. The latest version of our facial recognition software is about fifty times better than the last. All we need is cheekbones and a mouth to make a positive ID. Together with new ground-up surveillance cameras, his cap and dark glasses weren't enough to fool us. We also have Persistent Surveillance in the sky with a lock on his digital signature. If he moves outside anywhere in this area, we have tracking on him. We could have scooped him up, but you instructed us to watch his movements to ascertain others involved. He had an extended meeting just down the street from here on JFK Street. We have set up surveillance on that location."

"Where's LaSalam now?"

"He appears to be staying at The Charles Hotel under the alias, Rupert Patel. We have kept his surveillance looser so as not to tip him off. Right now he is walking through town followed by two of our agents."

"Any comings or goings at the meeting site down the street?"

"Other than our target, no one has entered or exited the premises."

"Take me there. I want to have a look for myself." Swan took the wheel. They drove the few blocks to the surveillance site and parked across the street, a half block away.

CHAPTER 93

PRETTY

Michelle Hadar had given her staff a break. At 7:15, she ordered them not to leave the house and to be back at their desks by 11:00 PM. Most of them went upstairs to get something to eat and to rest. A couple stayed at their terminals playing video games and checking Facebook. She didn't mind letting them use their computers for personal use or play. She knew how stressful this kind of work could be. Play offered some relief and often boosted creativity—something she learned at MIT. She had even heard a student in one of her computer sci classes argue that porn sites were on the cutting edge of web technology and hence a good place to study and learn. She wasn't buying that one.

She was feeling anxious about tonight, about her family and about the Leopard's intentions toward her. To relieve stress, she had never taken up drinking or drugs like some of her friends. She preferred running. After a few miles on the paths along the Charles River, she would feel fresh, invigorated and yes maybe, a little high. She went up to her room, which was old-house-large and had a bay window overlooking the street. She was happy not to have to share a room like most of her staff did. All her life, she'd had to share a room. She had grown up sharing a room with her sisters and with roommates at school. This room and the solace it provided would probably be the only thing she'd miss after this was all over.

She pulled off her hijab and her clothes. She was naked and allowed herself a look in the mirror. She was pretty. She could feel it and see it. This sight was something that would never be allowed at home or appreciated. She ran her hands slowly down her sides and lightly along each arm, admiring the tattoo on her left wrist. She raised her hands above her head and admired her full breasts. She had a slender waist but wide hips. *Better for bearing children*, her mother would say. That could have been the furthest thing from her mind right then. She did her warm up stretches in front of the mirror, touching her toes while looking back at herself. Yes she was beautiful. *Would she ever find her soul mate? Would things ever get back to normal*? she wondered.

She put on her Nikes, sports bra, shorts and a loose sleeveless T-shirt with the MIT logo. Running was one of the few times she did not wear a hijab. She tied her long dark hair into a bun, curled it up and tied it with a rubber band. She took a deep breath and headed downstairs and out the front door.

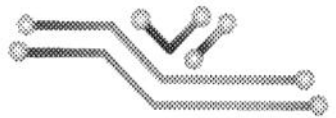

CHAPTER 94

GRAB HER

Little sat in the unmarked car across the street from the brownstone. He sipped the hot cup of coffee Swan had given him. He always loved coffee. The rich aroma and the slightly bitter taste. It was definitely his drug of choice. So the three of them, Swan, Hamed and Little, sat silently watching the house across the street. Little knew from experience that stakeouts could take hours and often produce no results. He was never a patient man but had endured many long days and nights just like this when he worked his way up at the LAPD, then FBI and now Homeland. But this time, he didn't have hours. He needed their pursuit to move fast or it might be too late.

At 7:30, they sat, watched and waited. Little could see his warm breath fog the passenger window on this cool early summer evening. It was still light outside—that nice yellow, dappled light during what photographers called the golden hour, just before dark. He lowered his window a bit and wiped the fog off the glass with the right cuff of his jacket. Just then, they saw a young woman emerge from the front door of the house in running gear. She did a few quick stretches, pulling each ankle up and behind her, one at a time. Then she started running slowly toward the river.

"Let's follow her. Leave the other guys here. Not too close. She's on foot, so we can give her some space so as not to spook her," Little said.

Swan put the car in gear and did a U-turn, keeping about seventy yards behind the woman. The young woman made a right onto the bike path along the Charles and picked up speed. Swan made a right onto Memorial Drive, parallel to the bike path, to follow. "There's a lot of traffic and it's moving fast. There's no parking on this stretch, so we can't stop. If we creep along at her pace, we'll really stand out."

"Pull into that driveway at the end of the park ahead of her and wait."

Swan did as Little instructed and pulled into the driveway near the end of JFK park. They had to crane their necks to look back. She was about fifty yards behind their parked position. "What do you want me to do when she catches up to us?"

"Grab her," Little said.

CHAPTER 95
ROUTINE INSPECTION

After waiting for the shift change, I rejoined Al, Tilson, and Gary. We walked down a longer hall and took the elevator down below ground. We entered a room full of pipes and meters with thin, hissing streams of steam escaping valves in several places around the room. A few men sat at consoles that looked like something out of the 60s space program, old CRT screens and lots of switches and red buttons.

We approached a small desk and a middle-aged, bespeckled man looked up. "Director Tilson, what are you doing in the dungeon?"

Tilson cleared his throat. "Haverman, this is Al, Gary and Sam from the NRC. They're doing a routine inspection and talking to some of our people. Of course, I said they had to meet you."

Al lifted her clipboard to confirm the cover. "Mr. Haverman, I'm Inspector Favor. If you don't mind, I'd like to ask you a few questions." She paused. No objection. "How long have you been working here at Indian Point?"

"Eight years, six months and ten days."

"Haverman's pretty precise," Tilson said. "He has to be. He's in charge of the raw incoming nuclear material and storage. The environment has to be closely monitored and controlled."

Al took notes on her clipboard and pointed at some of the dials and meters in front of Haverman. "I see. What happens if conditions move outside the green into the red zone?"

"We don't let that happen. But if it did, after sixty seconds, it would trigger backup units. If that failed after three minutes, the reactors would automatically shut down."

"Has that ever happened?"

"Not while I've been here."

Now Al and I were carefully watching Haverman's face. "If someone, not you of course, wanted to override the backup and automatic shutdown, could they do it from here?"

"Not that I know of. I believe it's meant to be a fail-safe system that on the one hand, doesn't rely on human intervention and on the other hand, prevents tampering." No change in expression.

"Thank you, Mr. Haverman. You've been very helpful."

Clearly he was not our guy. Only one was left on the list.

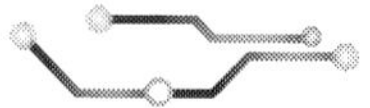

CHAPTER 96
PICK UP

Little stepped out of the unmarked car. He took off his jacket and tie and threw them on the seat. Then he rolled up his sleeves. "It's hard to blend in here, but we need to pick her up with as little attention as possible. Get ready to move."

Little jogged across Mem Drive, dodging traffic, to the bike path just as Hadar was approaching. "Hello ma'am. May I speak with you for a moment?" He pulled out his wallet, flipping it open to show her his DHS ID. She stared blankly, then looked up at his face. He'd seen that look before. She turned to run, but Little grabbed her upper arm tightly. He really didn't want to make a scene.

Swan backed out of the JFK Park driveway, reached through her open window and put a turret light on top of the car. Traffic slowed and she made a quick U-turn on Mem Drive and pulled beside Little and Hadar. Hadar was strong and tried to pull away, but Little had 100 pounds on her. He had no time for cuffs or this could get out of hand. People sitting on the lawn or passing by were already staring at them. He grabbed both her arms and shoved her roughly into the back seat of the car. Hamed was sitting in the back left and grabbed Michelle to pull her inside and flex-cuff her. She wriggled, kicked the back of the front seat. Hamed cuffed her feet, but she still kicked with both feet. Clearly frustrated, he finally hit her in the face with a hard right hook and she went limp.

Little got back in the front seat. Swan pulled the turret light back inside the car and sped off, turning onto Soldiers Field Road toward Boston. "She was feisty, but I'm not sure you had to do that," Little said looking over his left shoulder at Hamed. He could smell the sweet-sour odor of sweat. He wasn't sure if it was Hamed or the woman. "Don't you guys carry tranqs or Tasers with you?"

"Yeah, you sit here with a fighting suspect and try pulling out a needle or a Taser. This was just faster. She'll have a black eye, but she'll be fine." He slipped a cloth hood over her head and tied it loosely, just protocol for potential terrorists.

Little had to think. Time was gnawing at him. Ten to twenty minutes to Boston depending on traffic. He could use a turret light to speed that up or was there a place nearby where they could interrogate her? Little had gone to Boston College Law School years ago, so he knew the area pretty well. He had to move faster. "Take this right, the Cambridge Street Exit and then go left over the bridge. Put on the turret light. Anwar, take her picture and send it in. We need to know who we're talking to."

Swan did as she was told and took a hard swerve from the left lane cutting off traffic to catch the right lane exit in time. She could hear the screech of cars braking behind her. This was exciting. She hardly ever got to use her turret light and do real emergency type stuff. "Where to?"

"Once you get over the bridge, you'll be on River Street. About ten blocks up, there's a big intersection. You'll make a hard left on Western and the Police Sexual Assault Unit will be immediately on your right. Park in front. Keep the turret light going all the way."

Michelle began to stir in the back seat, She was awake but didn't seem to have much fight left in her. "Where am I? Why are my eyes covered?"

Hamed held her arm gently to steady her. "Ma'am, you're being held for questioning on a national security matter. We'll remove the hood shortly."

"Aren't you going to read me my rights or something? I want to make a call."

"For now, you aren't being accused of a crime. Besides this is a matter of national security. We just want to ask you some questions." Swan pulled the car into a "Reserved—Official Use" spot in front of the police station. "Little, hood or no hood?"

Little had to think about that. A hooded suspect would draw attention. He had quickly picked the Sexual Assault Unit because hauling somebody in there would attract less attention and it was close. If there were any press or even pedestrians with cellphone cameras, he couldn't afford pictures. "Do you have a towel or something like that in the car that we can use instead of the hood?"

"Yeah, towel in the trunk."

"Good, use that. It looks less scary than a hood. C'mon move it." Hamed grabbed a white towel from the trunk, pulled the hood off Hadar and threw the towel over her head.

"What did you do, clean a septic tank with that rag? Jeez," Swan said.

"It was in with some of my fishing equipment. Sorry, it's all I had. So are you gonna just yank my chain or get this done?"

Little liked these two. They were serious about the work but had a good, if not cop-grim, sense of humor. A good combination. They pulled Hadar, with the towel on her head and still in running gear, from the car and guided her inside. She was still unsteady, but Hamed held her arm both for support and security. They approached the desk sergeant. Little pulled out his ID. "We need an interview room now."

The Asian man in uniform behind the desk said, "Can I ask what this is about?"

"Nope, but you can have your captain call my office. Tell them I'm here and mention 'the Leopard.'" Little slipped his card toward the sergeant.

The desk sergeant gave Little a quizzical stare and looked down at his blotter. Without looking up, he pointed to the left. "Number 3 down the hall." Under his breath as the group walked down the hall, he mumbled, "Fuckin' Homeland."

CHAPTER 97

FACETIME

With Tilson in the lead, we went back upstairs and walked for about five minutes until we reached the lobby. He then led us through the front door, down the steps and along a path around the back of the main building.

My phone rang. We were finally above ground and outdoors so I had a signal. I looked down and it was Frank calling. I swiped the phone and Frank's face, his virtual face, appeared. "Hi Sam. One limitation of my new superpowers is that I can't hear face-to-face conversations unless they're bugged. How's it going?"

"No luck so far. We have a list built on certain criteria, length of service, time of shift, etc."

"I know about that. That's digital. Besides, who do you think got Gary that list so quickly?"

"OK. I should know better than to doubt your superpowers. We're on our way to interview the last person on the list, Benjamin Yolkum. We're outside the admin building walking to another building. Greg, where are we going?"

"We're headed to our nuclear waste facility. It's where all the spent fuel goes for safe storage before it's shipped out."

Frank, talking to me, said, "Ask him when was the last time spent fuel was shipped out and how much is there?"

I asked and Tilson said, "I'm not sure, but we'll find out. Yolkum is in charge of this stuff."

Frank whispered, "Sam, remember the nuclear disaster in Japan in 2011?"

"Yes. What about it?"

"There was a serious secondary problem from seawater flooding the power plant."

"OK, I'll bite. Where was the problem?"

"The other potential disaster was from seawater getting into the nuclear waste storage. Granted they had been negligent in improper storage and letting the nuclear waste accumulate, but it was a single point of failure that nobody anticipated. Actually, it's more complicated than that. The spent fuel was kept in cooling ponds that were low on water, but no need to get too technical. The reactors themselves automatically shut down. But the nuclear waste was at full capacity and near the boiling point. If they had not been lucky enough to have extra cooling water from their reactor #4, the spent fuel could have blown."

"Spent fuel. That's where we're going. Uh, oh."

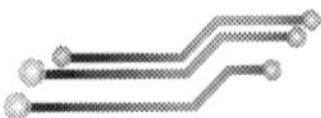

CHAPTER 98

INTERROGATION

Hamed removed the towel from Hadar's head and cut off the cuffs on her hands and feet. Sitting in the standard-issue metal chair, she rubbed her sore wrists. She was covered in sweat, but had goosebumps from the air conditioning turned too high. They kept interrogation rooms extra cold on purpose. It was part of the routine to help break down suspects. Swan stood by the door, hands behind her back. Little sat across from Hadar, a gray metal table bolted to the floor between them. He slid a plastic Poland Springs water bottle across the table to her. She took a couple of big gulps and poured the rest over her head. Hamed handed the towel to her. She looked at it, wrinkled her nose, and then wiped her face and arms. Then she threw it hard at Hamed. "Get that disgusting thing away from me. Can I have some ice for this?" she said, pointing to her swelling eye.

"I'll get it," Swan said and slipped out the door.

Little ignored the drama and looked down at his phone to see her visa application and picture. "Ms. Hadar. We are holding you here on an urgent matter involving national security. I apologize for the rough handling and my partner's actions. It was important that we move quickly. I see you are here on a visa studying at MIT. Top of your class. Can you tell me what you were doing at the house on JFK Street?"

"I live there. I'd like to speak to an attorney or make a call."

"As Agent Hamed said, we only want to ask a few questions. Besides, we don't have time for an attorney."

"What do you mean no time for an attorney? This is the US I have rights."

Little drummed his fingers on the metal table. The sound reverberated in the room. "Ms. Hadar, I'd like to keep this friendly and have your cooperation. But let me remind you that you are not a citizen and you are not entitled to the rights of a US citizen. We can easily have you deported or even put you in a dark cell and lose the key. I don't want to do that. I just want your help, and I suspect you know why it's a matter of national security."

Hadar folded her arms and tightened her lips. She stared defiantly at Little. The stick was not working. No time for carrots. Maybe a bigger stick. "I see that you have family living just outside Mecca." Her eyes flickered. "Your father, mother, brother and sisters. We believe they may be in some danger. So we have dispatched a couple of our local undercover agents to meet with them." He let that sink in.

Silence. She dropped her arms by her side and slumped in the chair. "This is all too much. Just too much."

"What is? What are you talking about?"

"He threatens my family. Now you make a not so veiled threat. I just wanted to come here, get my degree and do something positive with my life. It's not easy being a Muslim woman in my culture, seeking an education to try to better yourself and your family."

"I understand. Who's the man threatening your family?"

"I don't think you understand. You couldn't possibly understand. You are a privileged man who is lucky enough to be a citizen of a privileged country. Being a white male, you enjoy the highest status. So don't tell me you understand."

"You're right. It's just something meaningless I say routinely. But as an adopted child who went from foster home to foster home, I would not say I was privileged. Like you, I had to overcome a lot of obstacles to get where I am and to be who I am today. Maybe not the same as your experience, but maybe not as different as you think."

Swan returned and handed Hadar the ice pack. She held it above her eye. Her expression softened a little. Some glint of recognition and a decision. "Look, I do have important information. I don't think you'll torture me. I don't believe you do that anymore. If you did, then all is lost anyway. You don't have the time to try to forcibly get it out of me."

"You're right. So what do you want?"

"I want my family not to continue to be a ping pong ball in your battles. You say you have agents on the way to my family. Get them safely out of the country and give them protection. Once I know they are safe, I'll give you what you want."

"I can do that and I'll do you one better. I'll make sure you are safe as well, but I need something to go on right now. We're running out of time."

"I understand," she said with a wry smile and let it sink in. "I can tell you that if I'm not back at the house before 11:00 PM tonight, he'll know something's up. I also know that if you raid the house, he has fail-safes in place that will execute his plan with or without us."

"You mean LaSalam, the Leopard, right?"

"I only know him as Rupert."

"That's not his real name. His real name is Ahmed LaSalam and he is a dangerous, a very dangerous, threat to our nation. So what's the plan?"

"I can only tell you that we are there to run computers and set off some kind of nuclear event at multiple locations sometime after midnight. If I don't return or you raid the house, it will probably happen anyway."

"Wow, so that's it," Swan exclaimed. She and Hamed had not been fully read in before.

Hamed turned ashen white. "Excuse me." He left the room, presumably to throw up.

Little banged his palm on the table, like a gavel calling the proceedings to order. "Let's focus. How do we know you're telling the truth?"

"You're getting my family. What choice do I have? Look, send me back to the house. Text me when my family is safe. Then I want to call and speak to my father to confirm they are OK. If you do that, I believe I can stop his plan at the 11th hour and then give you a chance to capture him."

"I might believe you. But as you say, what choice do I have? My agents say they can be to your family around midnight our time. Just know that if you fail, we will probably have your family and all bets are off."

"I understand. You keep your part of the bargain and I'll keep mine. Now let me go before he suspects something."

CHAPTER 99
WISE ASS

We entered a smaller building that overlooked a field of metal doors, loading devices, ladders and yellow nuclear radiation warning signs posted everywhere. This time, instead of descending, we rode an elevator up two floors to an office with floor-to-ceiling glass overlooking the nuclear, industrial garden out back.

I still had Frank on the phone and a decent cell signal. "Sam, plug in your earbud so I can monitor your conversation and keep in touch with you privately." I plugged in the earbud and slipped the phone into my breast pocket with the phone's camera lense facing out and above the lip of the pocket so Frank could see whatever I saw.

Tilson led us to a group of people gathered around someone's desk. "Hi guys, can I have a word with Ben?" The others moved away leaving a thirtyish male with black hair, a mustache and beard.

"Director Tilson, to what do I owe *this* pleasure?" Yolkum said with a smirk.

"Ben, these are Al, Gary and Sam from the NRC doing a routine inspection." Al again checked her clipboard. "What's that blinking on your screen. Is there a problem?"

"We've been having an intermittent problem with the cooling water in storage unit #5. Nothing to worry about. We're pumping more water in now."

Frank spoke in my ear. "Sound familiar? Ask him what's causing the problem and how many fuel rods they've got there."

Now I slipped off my glasses thoughtfully. If I had a pipe and smoking were allowed, I'd be smoking one now. "Mr. Yolkum, what seems to be the cause of the problem?"

"We're not sure. I have the maintenance team checking it out now."

"OK. Just for our records, how many rods do you have stored there?"

"We have 538, mostly used, but there are some new as well."

"And what's the capacity?"

"If you're from the NRC, you should know that the capacity is also 538."

Yolkum was getting a bit testy and I didn't want to raise suspicion. Sometimes the best defense was . . . "I knew it was 538. I wanted to see if you knew it."

"Hmm, am I being interrogated here?"

Frank in my ear. "He seems pretty defensive. This could be our boy and maybe our problem."

Al sensed the creeping tension and decided to play good cop. "I see here that you've been here six years and received two commendations and a promotion."

Ben smiled. "Yes, I received best all-around camper two years in a row. Now I'm a 'manager,' which means I work more hours and get no overtime pay. So, yes I've been a good boy."

Tilson interjected. "No need to get hostile, Ben. These people are doing their jobs just like us. And just like us, their priority is safety." Tilson gave Ben a conspiratorial look to try to calm him or to get him to cool it.

"Yes, Director. I apologize for my sarcasm. Staring at these screens all day, you have to keep a sense of humor or you'll have a meltdown. Ha, ha."

"Not funny," Al said and she meant it.

Tilson didn't like where this was headed. "Thanks, Ben. We'll be moving along now. Please update me on anything the maintenance team finds."

"Sure thing, *boss.*"

Tilson physically directed us outside into the hall. "Sorry about that. He's a bit of a wise-ass but a hard worker."

"In our business, we used to call that a toxic personality. It can infect and kill an organization. Of more concern is his cavalier and maybe dangerous attitude." My phone rang interrupting us with its Star Wars ringtone. The ringtone was my son Evan's idea of funny.

I kept it even though I had a new phone. "Sorry, I have to take this call."

Frank was shouting in my ear. "I don't like this guy. I did a quick search and apparently his parents are from Chechnya. Maybe a connection."

"But if he was going to sabotage the nuclear fuel storage, why would he telegraph it with this apparent problem."

Frank now went into his Einstein mode. "Two possibilities. One, there actually is a problem, which I doubt. And two, he's providing cover for what he actually plans to do."

"Wait, I don't get it. What do you mean?"

"If he is planning to sabotage the storage by draining the coolant, he could do it and claim it was just a recurrence of this mysterious intermittent problem. Before anyone could figure out that it was a terrorist act, he'd be buying time to make sure the plan was fully carried out and perhaps make a getaway. Like I said, he's got cover and guys like Tilson would buy it right up until the point of disaster."

"OK. Now I get it. So now what?"

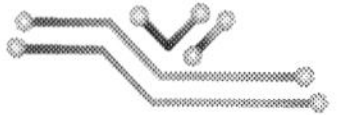

CHAPTER 100

MICHELLE RETURNS

Little gave Michelle some money so she could take the T from nearby Central Square to Harvard Square. She went up the escalator into Harvard Square and jogged back toward the house. She was only away for maybe a total of ninety minutes between being with the Feds, hopping the T and running back. She hoped it wasn't too much time to raise suspicion.

The only problem was that when she emerged from the T into Harvard Square, LaSalam was finishing his evening stroll at the same time. He saw her come up the escalator and jog down Mass Ave. Her face was bruised. *What could that mean*, he wondered. She did not look back and did not see him.

She jogged down Mass Ave to Plymouth Street and turned right. She could take Plymouth back to the bike path by the Charles and circle back to the house the way she originally ran, just in case someone was watching from the house.

By the time she got back, it was almost 9:00. She was covered in sweat, which may have been more from tension than from the run. They shared a bathroom down the hall that was thankfully empty. She looked at her bruised eye in the mirror. It was already swollen. By tomorrow, she'd need black and blue makeup to hide it. Not funny. She took a ten-minute, long for her, hot shower and then finished making the water as cold as it could get. The cold made her skin tingle and she felt more alert. Much of her tension drained, replaced by intense focus. She had to pull this off. A lot depended on it.

CHAPTER 101

INDIAN POINT

Al, Gary and I huddled in a corner. Frank was still on the phone and could see us through the cell phone camera.

Al started. "I think we need to lock this guy's ass in a room and interrogate him. Even if we don't get answers, isolating him may be enough to stop him at least here."

"I've had Frank on the phone this whole time. Here, I'll put him on speaker."

"Gentlemen and lady. We have a bigger problem than Mr. Yolkum here. If there are more like him out there, and we have every reason to believe there are, we need to act now in a way that might stop all or most of them."

"Even the idea of 'most' scares me. How do we get them all?" I said. "Gary, you've been quiet. Any ideas?"

"How about a virus?"

"What? What are you talking about?"

"I'm thinking about something like the Stuxnet virus that set back the Iranian nuclear program for a couple of years. If we had something like that and could deploy it to all the facilities to block any tampering with the cooling systems for long enough to round up these dudes, then we might stop this."

I put on my geek hat. "That's a big 'if.' First, something as sophisticated as Stuxnet probably took a team of world-class coders months to write. Then it needed an inside conspirator to plant it. I don't see how that's possible in days much less the few hours we have."

Frank crackled to life. "You don't realize the powerful resource you have, Sam."

"What's that?"

"Me! I can access the kernels of the Stuxnet class of viruses. I've also joined some of the best black ops, hacker groups in the last few days in preparation for something like this. Maybe with Gary and Bart's help, together with a few of my hacker friends, we can cobble together something workable in a couple of hours."

"Wait, how do you just join hacker groups and make friends in a few days?"

"Well I hacked my way in of course. When they saw what I could do and how fast I could do it, we became fast friends. I had to help them 'obtain' some classified docs and steal a few million dollars, but that seems like a small price to pay at this point. Time's a wastin'. What's the call?"

"OK. I should know better than to question you. Why don't you get started and then we'll need to figure out how to deploy."

"I already started about five minutes ago when Gary came up with this brilliant idea. Remember, I can multitask. Bart's on it and Gary, check your tablet for the login and check out a task. We have a checkout-checkin list for the thousand or so tasks that the coders will need to do."

"I think I already know the answer to how you're doing this. You've got hundreds of coders already working on it, plus you could probably work hundreds of the tasks yourself."

"You're catching on. But I have to ask you, Al and Little to work the deployment problem. We can get the code ready, but we can't get inside some of these air-gapped nuclear systems. You'd need authorization and maybe even physical intervention to get it done."

Al had been tapping her pen on her clipboard this whole time. "Air-gapped. What the hell is that?"

Frank was back in professor mode. "It means that to protect the systems from intrusion, they are not connected to the Internet or any outside network. Hence, to plant the Stuxnet virus, we had to have a confederate inside and plug a flash drive into their air-gapped system to plant it. After the Bowman Avenue Dam in New York was hacked by the Iranians, as a precaution, some essential infrastructure, like the nuke plants, were taken offline or air-gapped. The move was designed to prevent that same kind of intrusion that could take down the grid or worse."

"OK. I get it. So we may need to physically hand-carry and insert whatever Frank and his boys come up with. We'd need Little and his high-level connections to get that kind of access."

"Correction—Frank's boys and girls. Getting these plants to allow someone, even with DHS ID, to walk in the door and plug something into their systems is going to be at best tricky and at worst, a bureaucratic nightmare. Well, I wanted to see where Little was at anyway. Let's call him."

CHAPTER 102
UPDATE

"Madame President, we have Director Little on the line with an update," Hager said.

They were back to the Situation Room, looking at a dozen screens on the front wall, drone camera views of the Cambridge Surveillance, Indian Point and several other nuclear facilities. Hager pressed a button to put Little on speaker. "Director Little, tell me you have some good news."

His face appeared in the corner of one of the screens. "Madame President, gentlemen. As you can see, we have JFK Street under surveillance in Cambridge. We believe this is the current command center for the Leopard's next move. We have a cooperative collaborator inside. We're waiting for the Leopard to return so we can attempt a shutdown of their plan and seize the conspirators."

"When do you expect him to return and for this whole thing to go down?"

"We believe he will return in two to three hours. We have surveillance on him now at his hotel."

"I've been briefed on the general nuclear threat. Any progress there?"

"Yes. Our current theory, and I say 'theory' because we don't have hard evidence, is that their specific plan is to simultaneously drain the cooling water from the fuel rod storage facilities at some or all of our nuclear plants and perhaps, even ones in France."

"What happens if they do that?"

"Perhaps somebody in the room could better answer that, but I believe the fuel rods would overheat causing a kind of meltdown. I'm not sure if you would have explosions, but you could get uncontrollable fires in the storage areas spewing tons of toxic radiation into the air."

"How strong do you think this theory is?"

"Our analysts give it a seventy percent chance of being correct."

"I think my predecessor was only 50/50 when he launched the raid on Bin Laden. Doesn't look like we have much choice other than to go after it. If we're wrong, we haven't lost anything other than the opportunity to stop the actual threat. What's your plan to stop them?"

Little was glad she was using "we" in describing the situation. He felt like he had already stretched his neck out about is far as it could go and the rope holding up the guillotine above him was fraying rapidly. "We have a team of world-class coders writing a virus to stop the cooling system tampering–"

Hager interrupted. "Wait, have I got this right? You're going to infect our nuclear facilities with a virus? Are you nuts?"

Well as a friend of Little's once said, you're never really in the game until you feel the elephant standing on your chest. He was feeling it now. "Secretary Hager, this is a friendly virus meant to rig our systems in order to prevent tampering from inside the facilities."

"OK. So this is more like a 'vaccine.' I can understand that, but who's tampering inside our facilities? I thought by the president's executive order last year, we had taken these facilities offline to prevent tampering?"

"You're now getting to the heart of it General, I mean Secretary. The facilities are offline, so the only way to tamper is if someone at each facility at the controls manually drains the cooling systems. Based on Sunborn and his team's interviews at Indian Point, we believe the Leopard has recruited or coerced those individuals at each facility to manually do the deed."

"How the fuck, excuse my language, would he have been able to do that?"

"His pattern is to make both promises and threats to get what he wants. If they have family, those people are in danger unless the local operator cooperates. Just like 9/11 when Bin Laden used multiple trained pilots, LaSalam is using multiple trained nuclear operators on site."

"Shit."

"Exactly. So our task is to not only develop the vaccine as you call it, but to physically deploy it in the next few hours. That's where you come in. I need unfettered access to every nuclear facility within the next three hours. My agents are going to hopefully show up with the vaccine in hand. I need to get in—no bullshit, to get this done. I don't know how to cut through all the screenings and security checks that quickly. I need you to make it happen somehow."

Hager blew out a deep breath. "Madame President, do we have your permission to move on this?"

She didn't hesitate. "Do what you have to do."

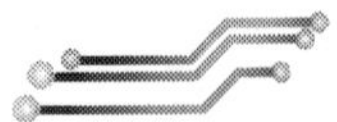

CHAPTER 103
BACK EARLY

At 9:30, Michelle Hadar went downstairs to the office, her hair still wet, combed back and smelling sweetly of rosemary and lemon shampoo. She didn't always wear it in the US, but felt she should put on her hijab. A few of her team were already back at their desks preparing for the big event. "Jack, you're back early."

Jack was a Harvard computer sci student who looked like he was too young to shave. "I just wanted to run a few simulations before we go live. I mean this is a big deal—the event we've been working toward, right?"

"That's right. I appreciate your dedication. No wonder you're top of your class. If, I should say 'when,' we're successful, this will look good on your resume too." Why was she still encouraging her team? She had to remind herself she was playing a role in a play where the ending was still to be written. She couldn't afford to deviate from her character until the last minute or all could be lost.

"I'm seeing some peculiar behavior at our Indian Point simulation. It looks like someone is already lowering and raising the coolant levels in the fuel storage units. What could that mean?"

"Probably one of the local personnel just doing a dry-run. Remember, this is all just a simulation for the DOD. None of it is real."

"You're right, but you said that to make this as effective as possible, we need to act as if it is real. I guess I really started to believe it, and I didn't want anything to go wrong."

"I did say that and still mean it. We just can't drive ourselves crazy when little anomalies appear. Part of the big event simulations is to see how different people and systems react here and at the local level. Real people at the nuclear power plants are participating in this drill. So just keep an eye on that activity. As long as it doesn't upset our schedule, don't worry about it."

Jack stroked his hairless chin. "OK. You're the boss." He swiveled his chair back around to focus on his screen. A little red dot was blinking on his map of Indian Point.

Michelle straightened her hijab, took a deep breath and walked into her office.

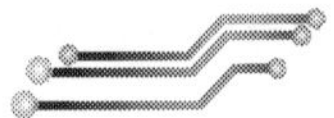

CHAPTER 104

THE VACCINE

Now I was getting really anxious. "How's the virus code coming? Oh, by the way, Little asked that we call it a 'vaccine' for political reasons."

Frank's image flickered on my phone's screen. "Vaccine, eh? I guess it's not politically correct to infect your own infrastructure with a virus, but a vaccine is OK. Politicians drive me nuts. It's just words."

"Well as somebody famous once said, 'Words matter.' But I don't think we have time for a political or philological discussion right now. Where are we?"

"I think we're close, but we need to do a little more testing."

There's that testing issue again, but this time the cost of getting it wrong was literally apocalyptic. "Can you use some of your superpowers to speed it up? I mean, can't you do hundreds if not thousands of test trials at once? I think we're running out of time."

"If I have nine women work on it, can a woman have her baby in one month instead of waiting nine months? Look Sam, the tricky part of this whole operation is security. Because we are using hackers and coders from your office to Russia to me. We can't do it offline. So we are creating a lot of maybe noticeable activity online. Even though we are using megabit encryption, we still create a ripple in the pond that would be noticeable if anyone, like the Leopard's team, is looking. So we have to limit our testing to a low enough frequency and bandwidth to avoid detection, if that makes sense. It's really more complicated than that, but I wanted to keep it simple for you." He winked.

"Yes, I know my small, limited, physical human brain can't handle nuclear terror and chew gum at the same time. How much more time?"

"You're an IT guy. You know how these things go. It's done when it's done. I mean we are doing something super-human here in a few hours that would take a much larger, normal team months. That's not an excuse or a dodge. Just don't get your panties in a twist. We'll get it done."

"I'm not sure if that last comment is vaguely sexist or a shot at my manhood or both. Just have one of your many *yous* keep me posted. Little has a chopper picking Al and me up here in a few minutes to fly us to Cambridge. I might lose cell signal on the way, so keep trying me if you're not getting through."

"What about Gary?"

"Well, he's going to stay and keep working on the vaccine with you. Also, Tilson is working on plugging Gary into their systems here. At least at Indian Point, he'll be ready to go once you have the bug, I mean vaccine, ready."

"Don't worry, I'll be in touch. Safe travels, son."

CHAPTER 105

SECURITY

The Leopard and Viktor strolled down JFK Street. It was 10:30 on a cool early summer night, but the chill in the air felt exhilarating. This would be the big night, the culmination of years of planning. LaSalam didn't really have any friends, but Viktor may have been the closest thing to one. When you fight a lot of battles together, you form a bond. Besides, Viktor had been loyal through it all. He might be the one person LaSalam trusted aside from his brother. Having Viktor at his side now made him feel calm and safe. He was still a bit troubled by seeing Hadar in the Square earlier, but wasn't yet prepared to jump to any conclusions.

They turned onto the walk alongside the house and down the back steps to the office entry. He gave his retinal and finger scan as before and the door buzzed open. He surveyed the room that was now only half full of staff. The glow from the computer monitors provided the only real light. The faint odor of onions from someone's dinner lingered in the air.

Hadar greeted him. "You're back early. I told the staff to rest, eat and be back at 11:00. Some came back early as you can see."

"Yes, I can smell them." He scrunched his nose and Hadar winced almost imperceptibly. "Very well. I like to get places early. Gives me a leg up on the enemy."

"I certainly hope you don't think of us as the enemy." She smiled.

"On the contrary. As I said before, I'd like to get to know you much better. How did you get that bruise on your eye?"

She knew she had to be careful here. She had learned growing up in a broken family and in a hostile country how to lie to protect herself. But she couldn't be sure how much he knew. The best lies were ninety percent truth and ten percent obfuscation. It was the ten percent that mattered and the ninety percent that sold the lie.

"While we had a break, I went for a run to visit my boyfriend in Central Square. Running helps clear my mind and keep my energy up for important things like tonight." She remembered that the other key thing about an effective lie is not to say too much. Otherwise, it sounds like you're making it up as you go. She got to the point. "We had an argument. It didn't go well. I was a bit shaken so I took the T back to Harvard Square and ran home from there."

Her story was consistent with what he had observed at the square earlier. "Maybe you should give me his name. I could pay him a visit when this is all over."

Now a little charm to complete the lie. She touched his shoulder gently, smiled and her cocoa brown eyes met his. "You are such a sweet man. You make me feel safe. Although I live an American lifestyle here, my boyfriend is more traditional. So sometimes he feels he needs to discipline his woman. I have to respect that. I can take care of it myself."

LaSalam grew aroused at her touch and her submissiveness. He wasn't sure he could wait until the plan went forward tonight to get to know her better. He had to control his urges. He took her hand in his, admiring the elaborate gold leaf tattoo on her forearm. "I understand. I just wouldn't want anything bad to happen to you. Promise to tell me if you ever need my help."

She could tell from his touch that she had sold the lie or he just wanted to get in her pants or both. She fluttered her eyelids coyly and looked down. "I will. Thank you."

"Michelle, I'm sorry. I have been rude. This is Viktor. He is my assistant and my friend." Viktor scanned Michelle like she was prey and showed a very faint, menacing smile. "I've asked Viktor to come along for security and as my advisor tonight. Hopefully, I'll just need him for advice and not security."

Viktor took a small black box from his jacket pocket, flipped a switch and a small red light began to blink. "Miss Hadar, this is just a precaution. It blocks all your cell phone communication in or out of this building—just in case one of your staff has other ideas, if you know what I mean."

"I understand. I suppose that makes sense." But how would she know that her parents were safe? How would she alert Little when to make his move? "What if one of our people inside the power plants needs to communicate?"

LaSalam held up a basic android smartphone for her to see. "Viktor said 'your' communications were blocked. Mine are not. If someone needs to get in touch with us, the agents have this burner cell number to call or text me."

Hadar did a hard swallow. This was a problem, a very big problem. "If you'll excuse me, I have some preparation still to do for tonight." She turned and walked to her office at the rear of the room.

CHAPTER 106
SPY STUFF

The view from the helicopter of the city lights below and the full moon above were spectacular. Part of me wanted the flight to just continue. It was serene, quiet and uncomplicated up here. I could think and even relax a little. However, I knew that danger and possible terror lay below and a tide of anxiety would wash over me when we landed. Deep breaths, I told myself.

Like Little, our transport landed on the JFK Park lawn. Al and I moved quickly away from the heavy wind created by the rotors and the chopper promptly rose again and banked sharply to the west. We were met by an unmarked black Dodge Charger out of which stepped Lea Swan. Despite the plain dark business suit and glasses, her looks were striking. She had the most attractive of Asian and European features—mysterious eyes, long dark hair, high cheekbones and pouty, full lips. I suspected the suit hid a very full figure as well.

"Welcome to Cambridge, Mr. Sunborn and Detective Favor. Nice to meet you."

I shook her outstretched hand. Her skin was warm and soft but her grip was firm like a vise. She definitely worked out. I tried not to wince. "Please, just call us Sam and Al. Thanks for picking us up. Please fill us in."

"Great. Just call me Lea. We have surveillance a couple of blocks away on what we believe to be the Leopard's current command center. He has recently returned there along with his sidekick, a guy who looks like Mr. Clean."

"I know that guy. We have a little score to settle. What about your inside woman? Please tell us about her."

"Her name is Michelle Hadar, a top ranked computer sci grad student at MIT. She had been coerced, by threats to her family, into cooperating with the Leopard and leading a team to carry out his plan. We think we may have turned her by guaranteeing her family's safety."

"When you say 'think,' what's the catch?"

"We have a team on their way to pick up and exfil the family. However, she says she will not act on our behalf until she hears directly from her father that they are safe."

"Why don't you and Little just raid the place and take them all down?"

"Whether it's true or not, Hadar has told us that there are certain fail-safe mechanisms in place that will carry out the plan even if the Leopard and company are taken out of the picture. She says that our only way to truly stop them is to work with her and thwart the execution of the plan at near zero hour."

Frank was back in my ear. "Sounds like real spy stuff, 'exfil,' 'failsafe,' 'zero hour.' I'd be entertained if I didn't know it was real. Sam, ask her what she knows about the nuclear plant inside saboteurs."

"What do you know about the inside operators at the nuclear plants that are cooperating in this plan?"

"Little finally read me and my partner in on what he knows. He thinks they are semi-autonomous, which is part of the failsafe, and why we aren't raiding the house that you see coming into view across the street. We think that the plant operators may have the authority and directives to go ahead on their own unless specifically told to stand down by the Leopard himself with some kind of coded communication. Unless we can get control of that, we have to wait."

"Well, we're still working on our end to inject our own code, for now we're calling it a 'vaccine,' into the local nuclear plant computer systems. That would block the actions of the saboteurs. But we haven't finished the code and we have to manually deliver and inject it. Two big 'ifs.' Frank, where are we on that code? Sorry Lea, I have one of our lead scientists on speaker here—Dr. Einstein."

"Any relation?"

"Just in spirit, intelligence and a bad sense of humor," I said and she smiled.

"We're code complete, but as I said before, we're still testing. It's going well. We fixed a few bugs and it feels like we're close, but you know how those things go. One little hiccup could blow the whole thing up at the last minute. Sorry, bad choice of words. It's just code after all, not a bomb."

"We knew what you meant."

CHAPTER 107

THE MOON

So now we sit and wait. Wait for the code. Wait for the Leopard to make a move. Wait for Hadar's parents to reach safety. Wait. Wait.

I sat in the car with Al and Lea, just staring at the house aka command center, watching the students stroll by, most with backpacks, some with obvious mates.

"Since nothing's happening, I'm going to make a call." I stepped out of the car.

Al slid her window down. "Don't go far, but for God's sake don't stand around like you're on a stake-out."

"10-4, Captain."

I walked a couple of blocks south toward the Charles River before I pulled out my cell. "Frank, I need to hang up for now. My battery is getting low and I want to call Monica."

"That's OK, son. I'm pretty busy at the moment."

I hung up and dialed home. Although I knew she was not physically at home, "Home" was wherever Monica was at the moment. It rang four times and went to her silly voicemail. "Hello, hello . . . "

I closed the phone and sat down in the moist grass on the bank alongside the river. Although I could feel the moisture seeping through my pants and the night was cool, I didn't care. Apparently, it didn't matter either for the young couple making out under blankets nearby. Young, in love and oblivious. At least I had one of those three. I looked at the full moon reflecting in the water. The moon seemed ever graceful, shining on both friend and foe alike. It's just there with no judgment, not caring. Maybe because it knows us humans can't screw with it, at least for the moment. So it was cool, very cool.

My phone rang. Thank God it was Monica. "Sam, hi. How are you? I was so worried."

"I'm fine. We're at a site where this whole thing may go down in the next couple of hours. Don't worry, I'm surrounded by DHS, FBI and probably a few other three letter and four letter people. Where are you?"

"We're tucked in at a motel in Fresno. That should be far enough away from any problem, hopefully. We're watching the TV news, and they've raised the terrorist alert level to orange."

"Hmm, I thought they stopped using those color code alerts after some politician used them to stoke fear and get re-elected. Well, anyway, everybody at the top levels on down are aware of what's going on. We're working several angles to stop it. By the time you wake up tomorrow, it should be over one way or another."

"If you think I can sleep tonight with this going on, you don't know me very well."

"I'd like to get to know you better, if you know what I mean."

"Sam Sunborn. Why can't you ever keep it in your pants? That's one of the many things or should I say, 'thing,' that I love about you. Save some of that playfulness for when I see you. You just need to get done with it and come home safe to us. Will you promise to call me at anytime during the night when it's over?"

"I promise. How is Evan?"

"He went out to explore a little. It's still early here, but he'll be back soon or I'll send Jerry after him."

"I'm not sure leaving him unguarded is a good idea."

"Don't worry. I really doubt anybody, good or bad, knows we're here. Besides I just can't keep a young boy like ours cooped up all the time. There's really only so many video games he can play."

"OK, but get him back soon. You don't want him outside when and if this all goes down."

"I will. Remember, call me. I love you."

"I love you too. More than you'll ever know."

CHAPTER 108

SIT ROOM

"Hager, get Little on the line again. I want an update," Longford said.

Hager whispered a command to a young marine sitting beside him in the Situation Room. The young marine typed a few commands into his console and Little appeared on the screen, "Madame President, gentlemen."

"What's happening? Please give us the latest."

"According to Sunborn, who's now here in Cambridge with us, they are doing final testing on the code for the vaccine. We have deployed agents to all sixty-one nuclear sites and have kept the French in the loop. Mr. Secretary, have you been able to clear a path for our people when they get to the plants, so they can get immediate system access?"

"We're still working on it. There's more protocols, thanks to the new law, that don't make it easy. Kinda like trying to squeeze a porcupine through a witch's c –. Sorry, just an old colorful Texas expression. It's hard, but we'll get 'er done. Let's just leave it at that. Probably, within the hour."

"Hadar said that anytime after midnight this could go down. So you better hurry."

"How long until you have the vaccine?"

"I can't get a straight answer on that either, but we're pushing as hard as we can. Hopefully, we'll have it by the time you get us clearance."

"This is all a little too tight or what we used to call 'close to the limit.' That's when mistakes happen and things go wrong. What else have you got going?" Longford said.

"We're working on identifying who the likely saboteurs might be at each location. We'll have our DHS teams ready to move on them when the time is right."

"Why not move on them now?"

"Madame President, pardon my frustration, but this question keeps coming up. You have to trust that you've got the right people on this. But to repeat, and this applies to the Leopard and his command center as well, we're concerned there is some kind of failsafe in place that will push the plan forward, no matter who we apprehend. In fact, making a move now might tip them off and cause them to accelerate the attack. Again, I apologize. We're just feeling the heat out here."

"Director Little, I appreciate all that you and your people are doing. Stay calm. Stay focused and let us know whatever you need from us to get the job done."

"If you can just cut the red tape at the power plants so we can get right in when the vaccine is ready, that would be huge."

"Hager here. We're all over it. We're all behind you."

"I appreciate that. It's what's in front of us that scares me."

CHAPTER 109

NO BUTS

LaSalam, Viktor and Hadar were now standing in a corner looking over the office as midnight approached. All the cubicles were full now. The Leopard looked at his watch. "Miss Hadar, we're pushing up the Go time to 1:00."

"What? I thought we agreed on 2:00?"

"Another security measure. If we are being tracked, this will throw them off. If we're not being tracked, well, sooner is always better."

"I'm not sure we'll be ready. I have everyone tuned and coordinated for 2:00."

His demeanor took on a kind of dark menace that she had never seen before in anyone. It was the look of pure evil and it was frightening. "Change it and change it now."

She knew instinctively not to cross the devil. She stepped forward toward the middle of the room. "Listen up everybody. Stop what you are doing and look at me." It was always hard to pull people away from their keyboards and monitors. It was like they were in a trance. "Stop *now*. Look at me so I know you are paying attention." She waited for everyone to look up. "We're pushing up the zero hour to 1:00 instead of 2:00."

There was a low, but audible grumble coming from the team in the room. "But . . . "

"No buts. When we said we wanted to make this simulation realistic, these things sometimes happen. We want to see how successfully you can react to things like this schedule change. So get on it. You have an hour." Sometimes she scared herself at how easily she could slip into a convincing lie. *Was there any limit on it? Would there ever be a time when she didn't need to lie?* she wondered.

LaSalam stepped toward Hadar and slid his hand around her waist. "Very good, my dear. Sounds like we'll be ready. Maybe while we have a little time, you could show me your room upstairs." He was already getting aroused.

She knew this was coming. She just didn't know when and she didn't know if she could stall him any longer. Funny, it made her think of a story her father used to tell. Of course, he told it with a thick, almost comical Farsi accent. A poor but clever man was about to face a firing squad for some unspecified crime. The king asked if the man had any final words. The man said, "If you give me a year, I can teach your horse to talk."

The king said, "That's absurd. Nobody can teach a horse to talk."

The man said, "I have done this before and can you imagine having a talking horse. Think about all the acclaim you will get for such a miraculous horse. Besides, what have you got to lose? If I fail, you can still kill me a year from now. But if I succeed . . . "

The king thought about this and finally agreed. When the man was returned to his cell, his cellmate asked what happened. The man told him the story. The cellmate marveled, "Can you really do this?"

The man replied with a smile, "I doubt it, but three things could happen in a year. I may die, the horse may die or the king may die. I like my chances."

"Well?" LaSalam snapped Hadar out of her daydream. She missed her father very much.

"Sorry, I'd like that very much," she lied. "I just need ten or fifteen minutes to finish the preparation here. Once I feel we're ready to make the new time work, we can go upstairs."

"That's cutting it a little close, but I suppose business has to come first." It was what his mind said, but other parts of his body disagreed.

"It'll be worth it," she said, running her tongue lightly over her lips.

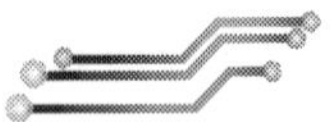

CHAPTER 110

BREAKING NEWS

Michelle returned to her terminal and started rapidly typing commands. She peeked over the partition to make sure LaSalam and Viktor were not looking. She brought up a program she had written herself. An image of a cellphone appeared on her screen. She typed in a few more commands and the image blinked red and then green. She had successfully cloned LaSalam's burner phone. Now she typed a few more lines and the image of the phone was replaced by lines of code. A list of contacts came up. There were just phone numbers, no names or other information. She clicked away. There wasn't much at all on the phone, but there were two text messages queued up, but unsent.

In the "Recipient:" line at the top of each message was one word, "List." The body of the first message just said, "Confirmed." The body of the second message said, "Clear." She also saw only one SENT message to List that said, "1ET." Obviously, the recipients would know what he meant, but she could only guess. She hoped she was right. As she peered over the partition again, she saw the Leopard approaching her. She quickly closed the program and replaced it with a map of their targets.

He looked over her shoulder. He was so close, she could feel his warm breath on her ear and smell what seemed like the residue of beer. "Is everything ready? I really would like to have a few moments with you, alone upstairs."

She reflexively raised her shoulders to put some distance between them. "I think we're all set." She wondered about her parents and her siblings. With Viktor jamming their cells, she could not receive a call or a text. She'd have no way of knowing. Time was running out, and she'd have to act one way or another. "Sure, let's go upstairs now." She smiled, backing away from her desk.

On the front wall of the office were several screens. Most showed maps or Chinese satellite images of their targets. China was very helpful with this kind of intelligence. However, on one screen they had CNN running. Cable news would be a key to confirm the success of their plan.

As LaSalam and Hadar passed the CNN screen on their way out, "Breaking News" flashed on the screen. "Nuclear Accident in India."

LaSalam's face flushed. "Can we get this in the conference room?"

"Yes, but –"

He hit the OFF button on the screen. Nobody in the room seemed to notice. They were too busy staring at their own screens. He grabbed Hadar's upper arm and squeezed hard. "Let's go."

They went into the small conference room at the end of the office. He closed the door and released her arm. There was only one screen and a whiteboard in this windowless room. Hadar didn't need to be told what to do. She picked up the remote, pressed a couple of buttons and CNN came up on the screen.

Anderson Cooper appeared against a backdrop of a nuclear power plant. The crawl under the picture said, "Nuclear Accident—Narora Atomic Power Station, Pradesh, India."

"Turn up the sound," he commanded.

She did. "We have word from a few moments ago that there has been some kind of meltdown at the Narora Atomic Power Station located in Narora, Bulandshahr District in Uttar Pradesh, India. We're getting more details as we speak . . . "

The Leopard exploded. "What! That moron." He looked at his watch. "I know just what happened. So stupid."

"What?" she said. "I don't understand."

"The field agents were supposed to drain coolant so the meltdowns would occur at 1:00 AM our time here. Uttar Pradesh is nine and a half hours ahead of us. So instead of figuring in the half hour, he used 10:00 AM their time instead of 10:30. So he went off a half hour early at 12:30 our time. These time zones are nuts. Do you know just across the border from him in Nepal, there is a fifteen-minute difference? So it's actually 10:15 there. This is just nuts."

Hadar was in shock. She could hardly speak. She whispered, "What does this mean?"

The Leopard took a deep breath and calmed himself. "It means, my dear, that we have proof of concept, as you scientists would call it. Our man has overheated their fuel storage area. Radiation should be leaking and it will be fatal for thousands, if not tens of thousands of people. Uttar Pradesh has over 200 million people in it. But Narora, the local area most affected, has 20,000. We should get most of them." He smirked.

She didn't know what to say or do. He continued. "Just imagine when this happens all over the US, India and France. It will be millions." She actually saw some drool come from the corner of his mouth and run down his chin. He wiped it away with the back of his hand.

"So what do we do now?" she said.

"We go forward with the plan. I now have more confidence in it than ever despite, or maybe because of, this little glitch." He looked down again at his watch. "We still have about twenty minutes. Let's go upstairs."

CHAPTER 111

EXFIL

Little's cellphone rang. It was Rhonda Hanes from DOD. "A Ranger team has picked up the Hadar family near Aleppo. They are driving them to a secluded exfil point nearby, where they'll be met by a Super-Huey Helicopter to take them out of country."

"That's good news. Give me a percentage likelihood of success."

"I'd put it at ninety-five percent at this point."

"That's plenty good. Thank you, Captain. Please let me know when they're out."

He clicked off. Now to tell Michelle the good news and hopefully lockdown her cooperation. He rang her cell and it didn't even ring. He just got a clicking sound. He tried again, same result. He knew what that meant. LaSalam had jammed cell phones in the building. It's what he'd do. But how could he let her know? He was stuck. If he moved on the house, the plan might still go forward and they'd have no way to stop it. He couldn't count on Frank and the geeks. So it might be down to Michelle. Little had spent five years as a profiler with the FBI way back when. So what did he make of Hadar and her willingness to do the right thing, even not knowing if her family was safe? He'd spent less than an hour with her, but he could see something in her eyes that told him maybe, just maybe, she would come through.

All he could do now was wait and think. Maybe she would send a signal. What choice did she have?

CHAPTER 112

CODE COMPLETE

"OK Bart, the vaccine code looks good to go," Frank said.

"I don't know how much time we have. I mean do you have any idea when these guys plan to pull the trigger on this?"

"We have intelligence that we hacked that indicates 2:00 AM. But I only give that a thirty percent chance of being accurate. We've all seen how clever the Leopard is. That time marker could be a diversion. We have to act as if this could happen any minute."

"Got it. I'm downloading the final vaccine code to the DHS agents' laptops on scene at all the nuclear power plants now. They'll copy it to flash drives and plug it into the air-gapped computer-controlled cooling systems."

"Push a copy right away to Claudette Clouseau at the direction générale de la sécurité intérieure and Rami Patel at India's defense intelligence agency. They've been waiting for it and will know what to do. Same protocol as we're following."

"India, why India?"

"Guess you've been too busy to see the latest news. A nuclear site in India blew and we're pretty sure it's related. We had advance intelligence about France, but nothing on India. We just missed it, but maybe now we can help them to minimize any further disaster."

"OK, done."

"Now we wait," Frank said. "Our work is done for now. Since I've gotten used to moving at digital speed, waiting for physical things to happen is not my strong suit. By the way, according to my inventory of what DHS agents carry as standard issue, I see the laptops but not flash drives. Where'd they get the flash drives?"

"Walmart, of course."

"Ah, I see the receipts now. Want to play some chess while we wait, take your mind off of this?"

"Sure, black or white?"

"You choose."

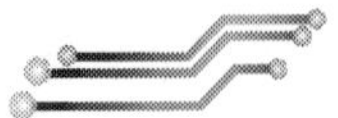

CHAPTER 113

NOT FUNNY

I checked my watch. It was 12:40. My new cell phone rang. It was Monica. "Sam, how are you? I saw the report on CNN about the accident in India. Is that this? Was it sabotage?"

I stepped out of the car to take the call. "Honey, we're not sure. But all indications are that the 'accident' was not accidental. It seems to follow the scenario we're working with here. How are you? Are you OK?"

"We're fine, just really worried. I'm sitting here with Jerry watching CNN. Evan is in the next room."

"Don't get any ideas with Jerry there."

"I don't know. He's pretty hot. He's so strong and good looking."

"Not funny. You better cool your jets until I get back."

"You better hurry. I don't know how long I can hold out. But seriously, where are you now? What's happening?"

"I'm not supposed to give out that information, but to hell with it. My priority is you, us and Evan. We're still outside what we think is the Leopard's command center. He's inside. We have a plan, albeit a shaky one, to stop him and the nuclear threat."

"When will you know?"

"Frank picked up some chatter that it may go down at 2:00 AM Eastern Time, but we don't have high confidence in it. I think that's probably the latest it could happen. I've dealt with this animal, and I'd bet it will happen sooner. We have two possible ways to stop it and him. Hopefully one or both will work."

"OK. I won't press you for more detail. Thanks for sharing what you did. I know I said it before but promise to call me as soon as you know. I mean when it's over."

"I promise. Listen, Little's getting out of his car. I think we're going in."

"Going in? Are you crazy? You're not going to put yourself in the line of fire. Just when I was feeling a little less anxious, you tell me this. Uhh, I can't believe it."

"I love you. Gotta go." I clicked off.

CHAPTER 114

TATTOO

Hadar didn't know if she could do this. How could she stop this madman, much less hold herself together. And her family? What would happen to them? She had to make a decision. They walked out of the conference room and Viktor approached. "Boss, is everything OK?"

"It's actually better than I expected. We had a little unplanned test run and it seems to have gone off perfectly. So I think we're all set. It's everything we planned and worked for, Viktor. It's all going to happen and the fun starts in twenty minutes. Miss Hadar is going to show me the upstairs here. I know we don't have much time, but we'll be back before 1:00." He winked at Viktor. Viktor smiled back with his wolf's grin.

LaSalam and Hadar climbed the steps of the old brownstone to the second floor. She led the way, unlocked the door to her room and led him inside. The full moon shone through the window and her pink curtains. She turned on a table lamp.

"This is very nice," he said. He was already starting to get aroused. He removed his jacket and threw it on the bed. "We don't have much time and as I said, I'd really like to get to know you better."

A thousand things were going through her head. Fight, flight, scream, yell. What good would any of it do for her, for her family or all those innocent people? This was truly a nightmare. But she had to hold it together. Think. If she only had more time. "We have so little time and I would like to get to know you better too. Maybe we should wait until this is all over. I should really be downstairs to make sure everything goes well." She backed away toward the door.

LaSalam was having none of it. "Take off your clothes," he commanded. Then more gently, "You're right, we don't have much time. So please undress for me." He smiled.

She hesitated but then removed her hijab, blouse and jeans, revealing her beautiful curves and tanned skin. "Oh, very nice," he said. "Now the rest please."

She removed her bra and dropped it to the floor. Her round breasts and taut nipples looked like candy to him. "That's all you get unless you take off your clothes," she said playfully, tilting her head and pursing her lips.

Now he was fully aroused and could feel the tightness in his pants. He slowly removed his shoes and unbuttoned his shirt. She gave a little chuckle. "C'mon, c'mon," she said. "We don't have much time. Hurry it up."

He removed his pants and threw them on the floor. His thin aging frame made him look much less imposing and maybe a little sad. He felt embarrassed by the protrusion in his boxer shorts. He was both excited and tentative at the same time. "Now you."

All she had left on were her beige silk panties trimmed with lace that narrowed almost to a thong in back. "Let's do it at the same time." She put her thumbs under the waistband then hesitated. "No cheating." They both lowered their bottoms at the same time. "Now come here." Somehow she had taken charge and he was letting her. It was rare that he was not in total control and the pleasurable sense of abandon consumed him.

He wrapped his arms around her naked waist and she put her arms around his shoulders, pressing her full breasts against him. He shivered at her touch, the softness of her skin, the lemon scent of her hair.

Behind his back, her right hand stroked the gold leaf "DuoSkin" tattoo on her left wrist. This tattoo was the ultimate "wearable" as they said in the tech world. The gold leaf was a perfect conductor that she worked on at MIT with the help of Microsoft. She stroked the tattoo and it sent a signal via bluetooth to her computer downstairs that sent the text through the Leopard's cloned phone. It went to the List and said the one word, "Clear." She hoped it was the right choice.

He pulled her roughly down on the bed, forcing her onto her stomach. He grabbed her rear cheeks in both hands and lowered his lips to kiss them. "So beautiful. I'm going to enjoy cuming between those cheeks." He raised up and slapped her bottom hard, raising an immediate red welt.

"Ouch," she cried. Then more composed, she said, "Not so rough, we're running out of time." If she was more traditional, she would never have said anything. She'd just take the abuse and bear it, but she was not traditional. Her hands were crossed over her head on the pillow. She stroked her tattooed wrist once more, which sent another signal. This one went to Little and just said, "Now."

He looked down at her. He wished he had more time. There were so many things he'd like to do to her, but he needed her downstairs just in case. He paused. "I've been admiring that tattoo of yours, what is it? It almost looks like a circuit board." He spread her cheeks ready to make his move. Then it dawned on him, but he couldn't help himself. He plunged ahead.

The door came crashing down as Little and two others, in full riot gear, charged into the room. LaSalam hardly had time to turn over, before Little grabbed him, lifted and slammed him against the wall. He fell down on the floor beside his shoes and pants. The Leopard raised both hands in defense.

Little looked down at the frail man. He thought, *how could he be so dangerous*? "Stay right there. You seemed to have shriveled up a bit, Buddy." Little turned to Hadar. "Are you alright?" He reached for the blanket on the bed and handed it to her.

She wrapped the blanket over her shoulders and around her torso, shivering and sweating at the same time. "I will be. He's a monster."

The men with Little turned their heads to look at Hadar. Their guns were still trained on LaSalam, but they couldn't help looking. She was beautiful.

LaSalam cowered in the corner, but he noticed his assailants' momentary distraction with Hadar. He quietly reached into the pocket of his pants lying on the floor beside him. Little shouted, "Stop right there." The Leopard pulled out his Sig Sauer P290, pointing it toward them. He fired. One of Little's men took it in the neck just above the bullet-proof vest and bright red blood sprayed all over the wall behind him. The man dropped to the floor. One more victim of the Leopard. Little and his remaining man fired simultaneously. LaSalam made a choking sound. Blood oozed from his forehead, but he grabbed his chest and then toppled sideways to the floor. The room was silent as everyone froze in place. Smoke seemed to rise to the ceiling. Little kicked LaSalam's weapon under the bed and rolled him over. His eyes were blank.

Michelle rolled over and pulled the blanket tighter around her on the bed. The scent of cordite and death hung in the air. "Is it over?"

"Not yet, but your family is safe," Little replied.

"Thank you, Allah."

"And thanks to a Ranger team that risked their lives to rescue them." Little looked down at his fallen comrade. Tears welled in his eyes. He felt an indescribable pain in his chest. "I'm afraid my man, Alex here, was not so lucky."

CHAPTER 115
MR. CLEAN

Al and I were out of the Charger as Little emerged from his car up the street. I had just finished my call with Monica. Little went to the trunk of his vehicle and held up a vest for us as a signal. Swan popped the trunk of our car and we put on the vests. Two other DHS guys came out of nowhere behind us. One said, "Director Little told us to go with you to the office in the basement. I'm Ed and this is Larry. Entry is in the rear. He's going with those other two agents upstairs. He has tracking on Hadar and knows she's up there. He suspects that Target One is up there with her."

OK, was I really walking into a gunfight? At times like this, thinking too much was not helpful. You just had to act and let instinct take over. Plus I was with three trained professionals. What could go wrong? I didn't want to think about that either. I could feel my heart thumping in my chest. I wondered if it was possible to OD on adrenaline. If so, I was a prime candidate.

We walked as quietly as possible along the side of the brownstone and down the back steps. We saw the scanners on the door. Remembering I had my cellphone still sticking up in my breast pocket with the camera facing forward, I whispered into my pocket, "Frank, are you still with me? Can you do anything about these scanners?"

"Yes, I'm here. Did you think I fell asleep? You know I don't sleep now. Pretty cool, eh? Anyway, give me a minute on the scanners." We waited. Shallow breathing. Sweat beaded up on my forehead despite the cool air. The pungent odor of my own moist armpits even wafted into the air. "OK. Bart disabled the scanners. I disabled the buzzer that comes with them. Just push in the door and you're in."

Al stepped in front of me followed by the two agents. "I'll take the lead." And just like in the movies she pointed to her eyes and then to the door. She held up three fingers and then bent them over one at a time. 3 . . . 2 . . .1. She burst through the door with us behind

I didn't know what to expect. There was an array of cubicles in front of us. I swiveled my head to the left and there he was. Viktor, Mr. Clean, was pointing a gun right at us. Before I could blink, he fired. Al groaned and fell to the floor. Oh no. There was a collective scream from the cubicles. The two agents fired their MP5s on full auto into Mr. Clean. He wriggled and twitched like he was doing a Steve Martin dance. Blood stains dotted his shirt. He hit the rear wall and slid down.

The room smelled of cordite and gunpowder with a haze hanging in the air. My ears were ringing from the gunshots. But now, there was silence. I ran to Al who was lying face down on the floor. I rolled her over. Her eyes were closed. I felt for a pulse. I couldn't feel anything. I lowered my head to her chest to see if I could hear anything.

"Umm, that feels good," she said. I lifted my head up to look at her. Her eyes fluttered open. "You're not going to get rid of me that easily. Thank God these vests really work." She lifted herself up forty-five degrees onto her elbows. Ouch, that hurts like a son-of-a-bitch." I could see the bottom of two slugs collapsed in the vest over her heart."

"You were really lucky," I said. The two agents helped Al to her feet. They held her, one under each arm, to steady her. Heads slowly and tentatively began to appear above the cubicle partitions. We heard more gunshots from upstairs.

CHAPTER 116

PLAN B

We went back outside. I helped Al limp up the steps. Lights were flashing everywhere. It was 12:58 AM. I could smell the exhaust from all the emergency vehicles whose engines were still running. Several uniformed officers led the office team out in handcuffs. Had to be close to a dozen of them with their heads hung low. Cameras were clicking and flashing nearby. They had no idea what just happened to them. The officers started loading them into an actual school bus. How ironic.

As they were loading the handcuffed group on the bus, a black Crown Vic pulled up in front of the bus blocking its path. Two men in matching black suits, white shirts, black ties and fedoras stepped out. One had blond hair and the other brown. Otherwise, both were indistinguishable with their pale skin and dark-rimmed glasses. They approached the officers loading the bus. Blond flashed his credentials. "DHS. Please stop loading the prisoners." The officers hesitated. Then both Blond and Brown held up their credentials for the officers to see.

About a third of the group were already inside the school bus. The remainders were in a line ready to board. The two men examined the lineup. Brown spoke pointing at one of the detainees. "We need to take that one with us. You can take the rest downtown as planned."

The two junior officers guarding the group looked at each other and shrugged. "OK, sir."

Blond stepped forward and grabbed one of the young men out of the line and led him to the back of the Crown Vic. The young man looked Middle Eastern and had a slight mustache. Standing by the rear door of the car, he surveyed the chaotic scene of emergency vehicles, reporters, bystanders and helicopters hovering overhead. He made the slightest of grins before Blond opened the back door, pushed his head down and shoved him roughly into the rear seat of the car.

The officers resumed loading the bus. Brown took the wheel of the Crown Vic and backed out of the swarm of traffic. He opened his window and put a turret flasher on the roof to help cut through some of the congestion. Once he turned onto Storrow Drive, he pulled the flasher back inside.

Blond, who was in the backseat with the young man, cut off the flex cuffs. "Where to?"

The young man rubbed his sore wrists. "Take me to the safe house, then ditch the car. We need to regroup."

Brown picked up speed. "Will do. We thought you were dead."

The young man smiled. "That was the idea. The exploding sub was a diversion. As far as anybody including you knows, I'm long gone."

"We're sorry about your brother. He was a great leader for the cause."

"Yes, my brother was a great man. He will be missed, but he taught me an important lesson. When performing a mission, always have a Plan B. I guess you could say that I'm the Plan B," the Cub said.

They drove on in silence.

We met up on the street with Little and Hadar, who was now dressed, but pretty disheveled. "I gather from my guys that Viktor went down hard," Little said.

"You could say that. No more Mr. Clean. What happened upstairs?"

"LaSalam met his maker as well. Michelle got off a message to the saboteurs a few minutes ago. Hopefully, it was the right message."

I looked at Michelle. "How'd you do that?"

She lifted her wrist up to expose the gold leaf tattoo. She then silently ran her finger across the design. "We should know any minute if it worked. The team of saboteurs were supposed to execute at 1:00 AM."

"Holy shit, Frank. Frank, what's your status?" I said.

I pulled out my earplug and put Frank on speaker. "We only got the code working about ten minutes ago. We uploaded it to the agents who were on standby at the power plants with laptops and flash drives. The bad guys were already draining coolant so they could achieve meltdown at 1:00. It's close. We were only able to stop the coolant drain and reverse the process in about half the sites. We sent the code to India and France as well, but we don't know yet how they're doing."

Little looked pale and worried. All the self-confidence I'd seen in him drained away. "Looks like Michelle's signal better have worked or we're toast or at least half-toast."

I glanced over Little's shoulder to see Al being treated on the tailgate of an ambulance. What a night. How could this be real? I looked down at my watch. It was an old Pebble Smartwatch, but it displayed traditional minute and second hands and was perfectly synched to atomic time. I watched as the second hand crossed the 12 and the minute hand struck 1:00. We all held our breaths.

Little picked up his phone. "I guess I'll call it in."

Frank spoke up on speaker. "No need. I'm monitoring all news outlets and other feeds. I should be able to tell you the instant anything occurs, if it happens."

I couldn't help myself. "So what do we do, just wait?"

Little was more composed now, but no less anxious. "Yes we wait. Waiting is what we do." A little weird and redundant, but I understand how stressed he was. We all were.

Seconds later, Frank came on again. "Shit. Fessenheim, France has blown. They have two of France's fifty-eight reactors. The local population is small, only a couple of thousand. It's virtually on the border with Germany. The radiation cloud will blow east over West Germany. It's raining there now so, with any luck, it will wash the radiation out of the sky onto the ground before it can do much more serious damage."

"What about the others? Any others?" Little said. Michelle was starting to shiver either from the cold evening or the shock. Ed and Larry were still nearby. "Ed, could you take Ms. Hadar over to one of the paramedics and get her checked out."

"I'm not going anywhere until I know what happens." Little put his arm around Hadar in a weak attempt to warm her up. She still shook like a leaf in the autumn wind.

So we stood there and waited. Police lights were flashing and the media was shouting questions from behind the police cordon. Two TV station helicopters hovered overhead, the din of their rotors making it hard to hear. I spotted Nancy Lu in the front of the throng of reporters. After twenty minutes, I shouted over the noise to Frank for the tenth time, "Anything?"

"Yes, I've had the guys pull data from all sites. There are no more incidents. It appears that the incident in France happened because our vaccine did not get there in time and the saboteur either didn't get or ignored Michelle's text."

Little had been on his cell and he clicked off. "We have successfully installed the vaccine on all our reactors. I don't know about France or India yet. But our guys have been rounding up the saboteurs at each site. It appears they got Michelle's text and were recooling the nuclear storage anyway."

"So we're clear?" I said.

"It appears that way. Frank, do you have anything different?"

"No, what you just reported is consistent with the data I have."

We all started breathing again.

Nancy Lu appeared at the ambulance where Al was being treated. "How you doin' girl?"

"Oh, you know me. I took one for the team. Can't say I'm in the mood for an interview at the moment," Al said.

"That's not what I had in mind." Lu took Al's hand, leaned forward and gently kissed her on the lips. She sat down beside Al on the bumper of the ambulance and wrapped her arm over Al's shoulder. "You're a real hero, my love."

"I don't feel like a hero. Medic says I probably have a couple of broken ribs. They hurt like hell."

"So I guess the love-making will have to wait a little while."

"Yeah, I guess you'll just have to keep it in your pants a little longer." They both laughed. "Ouch, fuck it hurts to laugh."

"I'm just glad you're OK. Now about that interview . . . "

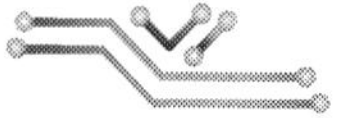

CHAPTER 117

DAMAGE REPORT

"Madame President, it appears we dodged a bullet or a catastrophe I should say. All our nuclear sites are secure. The saboteurs have been rounded up and the Leopard has been neutralized. Unfortunately, we have the two incidents in France and one in India. The good news, if you can call it that, is that both were in low population areas and we expect the number of casualties to be low. It may be days before we have an exact count. At least we could help both countries secure their other reactors," Hager said.

"Please extend my condolences. I will call both Prime Ministers when we're done here. How are Little and his team?"

"Detective Favor took two bullets, but her vest stopped them. Otherwise, they are all OK. A remarkable young woman, Michelle Hadar, helped them foil the plot. Also, Sunborn and his geek squad may have saved lives as well with their vaccine."

"Get Director Little on the phone. I want to congratulate him, Sunborn and the others and extend the thanks of a grateful nation. We should also look at what we can do to reward their efforts. A promotion for Little at the very least.

"OK, so what's next?"

"We have a situation in the DMZ between North and South Korea that we should brief you on . . . "

"Great. I love this job."

CHAPTER 118

AND THEN IT HIT ME

I called out, "Frank . . . Frank!" I let out a final breath, and I could swear I saw butterflies rising with it. Blue butterflies. My eyes closed. Silence. Then my eyes opened again and I saw Frank standing in front of me—his full body this time, not just a head on a screen.

"Frank, what happened? I don't understand," I said.

Frank looked at me with a faint smile. His gray hair was disheveled as I remembered. "Well, do you want the good news or the bad news?"

I snapped, "I thought I told you that I hated that game. Cut the crap and give it to me straight. Wait. I'm sorry. That doesn't sound like me. Deja-vu or somebody else's voice. Sorry, Frank—I'm confused."

"That's all right. It's a bit of an adjustment. I *know*. The good news is that we were able to save you digitally, just like you did with me. The bad news is that you no longer have a physical presence."

I gulped and took a deep breath. At least I thought I did. This was the whole point of our big idea to digitally preserve ourselves, even when our physical selves were gone. I just didn't know if I was ready for it for myself. "When did this happen? I mean, what or how did this happen?"

"Do you remember the shoot out at the office in the lab?"

"Sure, that's when you got killed, I mean physically, and we brought your digital self online," I said.

Frank hesitated and looked even more serious now. "Well, you got killed then too."

"Wait, that's impossible! I got up from under your body. I met Al and Little. I helped fight the Leopard and stop the terrorists. I felt the pain of being shot and the freezing cold water after being thrown overboard of the *Take Down*. It just doesn't make any sense. How could I be dead and feel those things?"

Now Frank took a deep breath. "You had a different setting. You look puzzled. I understand. Let me explain. We had a choice of settings when we uploaded our digital selves back in the lab. I chose 'Pure Digital.' This gave me the freedom to move at incredible speeds around the Net without any physical-like encumbrances. You chose 'Physical Simulation,' so you could feel hot and cold and move about as if you were physically alive. You were even able to enjoy sex. We did it. It worked. Just what you and I imagined could be done. We did it! The only downside for you, from my perspective, is that the Physical Simulation meant that you could only move and process thoughts at normal human speed. I chose to give that up for my digital freedom. Besides my physical body was getting old. Pains were everywhere—back, knees, neck, especially in the morning. I was happy to give that part up. No pain now."

This was a lot to process, even for a pure digital self. "So, all these things, Al, Little, the Leopard, the *Take Down*, Cambridge—were they real or not?"

Frank had a bigger smile now and put his arm around me, digitally at least, "Some of it was real physically and some of it just happened digitally. Some of it could have been your imagination or come from other people's experiences. I can see how you could be confused. It's complicated. But now that you are completely digital and no longer physical, you can go back and retrace what happened and where. Everything is saved in the Cloud."

The Cloud seemed like an ironic term to me. The traditional portrayal of heaven was in the clouds and now I was somewhere or everywhere in the Cloud. "But why am I now Pure Digital? What happened to my Physical Simulation setting?"

Frank held both my shoulders and looked me in the eye. "The last sequence of events was or had to be fatal for your physical self. The simulation had played out or maybe your system metaphorically ran out of storage space. I'm not sure. So like with me, we kept backups of you. However, when we did the 'Restore,' we could only bring you back digitally. Maybe in version 2.0 we can do better. I'm working on it."

"Wow, I can't believe it. This will take some getting used to," I said.

"Oh, you'll get used to it. You may even enjoy it. The freedom to go anywhere you want instantly, the speed and the infinite knowledge is invigorating. No more depression either."

I tried to absorb what he was saying. It was just gonna take awhile, maybe a very long time even digitally. "OK, so now what?"

Frank put his finger to his chin like Rodin's famous sculpture. "Hmm, wouldn't it be something if we could download ourselves back into real physical bodies again? I wonder."

Some time has passed and I suppose I'm adapting to my new form. Although "adapting" may be an overstatement. I still spend some quality time with Monica, but I miss the warmth and softness of her touch or the feel of her warm breath in my ear. At least I can watch my son grow up. All is not darkness.

Frank treated me to his anti-depressant script, which helps me break out of my funk. The other remedy Frank prescribed is getting back to work. Focusing on helping others is always the best cure for what ails you, both in life and in this digital world.

Meanwhile, Frank continues working on reversing the mind to digital process with the goal of reinstating a digital mind into a physical body. This will be a long, hard, if not impossible task. As of this writing, he is still not there.

While Frank works on his Sisyphean task, I've chosen a different project. As the world nears the Singularity, where machines and Artificial Intelligence (AI) become smarter than people, we need to be prepared. Our species will be at a distinct disadvantage and maybe in peril if machines can both replace and dominate us. I am ever more convinced that day is coming soon.

When Big Blue, the IBM supercomputer, beat the world's best chess player, I thought that was a milestone. However, chess is a game of logical rules, you have complete information on the board and hence, a certain combination of moves will always win. So to me, it just seemed like it was a "solvable" game like Tic-Tac-Toe but much more complex. I took comfort in the notion that machines were a long way from inventing solutions to games or situations where the information was incomplete, the opponent irrational or where some intuition might be required.

My comfort was short lived as games that require more than logic, and where information is incomplete, were solved. The very complex and highly intuitive Japanese game of Go was solved by Google DeepMind's AlphaGo AI in 2015. A game of incomplete information and bluffing, No Limit Holdem Poker, was solved by the Carnegie Melon's Liberatus AI in 2016. AI then started learning Quantum Physics and solving complex problems on its own that humans couldn't solve. Something had to be done.

So I took up the challenge, that Elon Musk and many others expressed, to find a way to directly link a physical human brain to computers and the Internet. Our limitation as a species is bandwidth. Our physical brains were and are the most awesome computers ever invented with the ability to do billions of computations and, more importantly, analysis at high speed. However our output and connection to the world is slow. You can only speak or type up to a hundred or so words per minute. That limits us. So if I and my team could figure out a way to provide a high-speed connection, the human-digital combo could not only survive the Singularity, but thrive in the world of Artificial Intelligence. I hesitate to use the word, "Cyborg," because it sounds too science-fictional, but the merger of human and digital intelligence is no less real or important.

Steve Jobs once said, "The computer is the bicycle of the mind." We are out to make that literally true. Bart, Killer and I are making some steady progress. We've gotten beyond the simple manipulation of a mouse using your thoughts. We have developed a feedback mechanism that allows a human brain to read directly from a computer via an implant connected to Wifi. Our first subjects were a bit overwhelmed by the fire hose of information coming at them. So we had to dial it down while the subjects' brains adapted and learned to sort it all out. That's another advantage of the human brain, the ability to adapt to complex changes. I guess I was the "living" proof of that.

While I'm encouraged and excited by our progress, I still feel there is a long way to go. It seems kind of like a lot of complex journeys. You slog away, overcoming obstacles, for a long time and then one day you are there. No fanfare. You just arrive and say, "What's next?"

EPILOGUE

The morning after the raid and the real death of the Leopard, Little and Hadar sat down in a corner table at the Crema Cafe off Church Street near Harvard Square. It was one of Michelle's favorite spots and she needed a strong cup of coffee. They both did. The aroma of coffee brewing was better than her favorite perfume.

They were silent for some time, but it wasn't awkward. It was as if they were forever attached to each other by the previous night's events. Little finally broke the silence. "I checked this morning and your family is fine. They are settling in at an undisclosed location. I don't even know where it is. But once we have security set up, you'll be able to visit them probably sometime next week."

"I appreciate all that you've done for me and my family. I was happy to at least have a phone call with them earlier. My father sounded better and more relaxed than I can remember. It's a great relief for me. Meanwhile, what's going to happen with my staff?"

"We're still verifying what they told us, that they had no idea this was real and not a DOD simulation. Based on what you've told us, I'm inclined to believe them. We just want to make sure there weren't one or two real co-conspirators mixed in that even you didn't know about. The innocent ones should be released in the next couple of days. By the way, didn't you say there were twelve in your team of engineers?"

"That's correct, and they all had reported in last night."

"Hmm. Well the local PD only put eleven on the bus. I'll have to look into that."

"What happens with the house and the office? I still have all my stuff there."

"Right now it's a crime scene. That's the official designation. No need to panic the public. We're in the process of legally confiscating the computers and any other items related to the conspiracy. Once we clear it in a few days, you can move back and stay as long as you like. The US government owns the house now and for the foreseeable future."

"I'll have to think about that. I really liked the house. But with all that happened there, I'm just not sure. Maybe I'll move back to campus, if they have space and I can afford it. Good luck with that," she said, talking mostly to herself. "This whole thing has really been unreal."

"'Unreal' is the perfect word for it. It's over for now, but who knows what new menace will rear its head tomorrow. Speaking of which, how would you like to come work for me at DHS? With your technical, personal and natural undercover skills, you would be a real asset. Plus I like you, which really helps for what I have in mind. We could arrange for you to finish up your degree at the same time. We might even be able to pay for your housing. I'd just have to get that one approved."

"Whoa, that's a surprise." She glanced down at her hands and remained silent for a few moments. She was trembling. "But it's not an unwelcome offer. What would I be doing, if I were to accept? I just have to warn you that that is a big 'if.'"

"You would be my assistant, which would involve both technical analysis and some field work. Kind of like last night but hopefully not as scary. You'd even get to keep your clothes on. You also made a big decision last night to help us, even though you didn't know for sure your family was safe. I value people who do the right thing despite the risks."

"What did you mean by 'personal skills?'" She smiled.

He smiled back and choked awkwardly on his mouth full of coffee. "I hope you didn't take that the wrong way."

"What if I did?"

"You did look pretty good there up in the bedroom."

She threw her half-eaten blueberry muffin at him, hitting him directly in the forehead.

"Good aim too," he said. They both laughed.

"How could you make a comment like that considering what went on last night?"

"One of the first things you'll learn in this kind of work is you're going to see and encounter some pretty terrible things. If you don't keep your sense of humor, you'll go crazy. I promise to stop short of harassment. So, will you consider my offer? Besides, there is already talk of me getting a major promotion. We could move up the ladder together."

Her grin was even more playful now. "Well if you really get a promotion, I'll consider it."

AUTHOR'S NOTES

All the science and technology in this book is currently available and being deployed. The one exception is the digitizing of personalities, which is 'in development' and may arrive in the near future. If you're curious, as I was, about some of this amazing stuff, here are some links to further information and insights on the topics mentioned in the order in which they appear in the book.

Computer control with your mind:
technologyreview.com/s/534206/a-brain-computer-interface-that-works-wirelessly

Trachtenberg System for doing complex math in your head:
Trachtenbergsystem.org

Schrödinger's Cat and quantum superpositions:
en.wikipedia.org/wiki/Schr%C3%B6dinger%27s_cat

NSA's Bullrun program bypasses https and encryption protocols:
securityaffairs.co/wordpress/17577/intelligence/nsa-bullrun-program-false-perception-security.html

Nano sized computer processors:
bbc.com/news/technology-29066210

Colin Powell's 40/70 Rule:
https://digitalkickstart.com/the-4070-rule-and-how-it-applies-to-you/

The world's first Webcam - the Trojan room coffee pot:
http://www.bbc.com/news/technology-20439301

Backscatter detection systems:
https://en.wikipedia.org/wiki/Backscatter_X-ray

How do they lay transoceanic internet cables?
http://www.itworld.com/article/2947934/networking/heres-what-to-takes-to-lay-googles-9000km-undersea-cable.html

How good are Facial Recognition Systems?
http://www.theatlantic.com/technology/archive/2015/07/how-good-facial-recognition-technology-government-regulation/397289/

Persistent Surveillance watches a whole city:
https://www.bloomberg.com/features/2016-baltimore-secret-surveillance/

Bowman Avenue Dam Iranian Hacking Incident:
http://www.nytimes.com/2016/03/26/nyregion/rye-brook-dam-caught-in-computer-hacking-case.html?_r=0

DuoSkin Digital Tattoo Interface:
https://techcrunch.com/2016/08/12/duoskin/

Merging Human and Digital Intelligence:
http://www.cnbc.com/2017/02/13/elon-musk-humans-merge-machines-cyborg-artificial-intelligence-robots.html

The Artificial Intelligence That Solved Go
https://psmag.com/environment/alphago-go#.fvc9b8jl8

A.I. machines are learning quantum physics and solving complex problems
https://fossbytes.com/ai-learning-quantum-physics-solving-problem/

You can learn more about this book and the author at charleslevin.com

Contact or follow the author at facebook.com/Charles.Levin.Author
and twitter.com/charlielevin

ACKNOWLEDGEMENTS

I'd like to give my utmost thanks to Steve, Kristine, Jess, Judy, Ken, Audrey, Luis and the team at Authorbytes for helping turn my manuscript into a finished novel. I can just hope it matches up to the cool graphics they produced for the cover and website.

Thanks to my early readers, Amy and Dan, for their constructive feedback. Finally, a big hug to my family who supported and put up with this crazy endeavor for three years.

ABOUT THE AUTHOR

Charlie is an emerging author who has written the novel *Not So Dead*, based on his 20 years of experience in the high-tech world and his degree in philosophy. He is the founder of Pathfinder Consulting Group, which builds, maintains, and markets multi-million dollar websites together with providing Strategic Planning and Business Development services. He lives in Tewksbury, NJ with his wife, Amy, and has two sons, too far away in California.

Made in the USA
Middletown, DE
24 August 2022

71578410R00187